THE LAST SOULS

ANYA OF ARK II

KRISTIAN JOSEPH

For Ronnie.

1

THE ARK

Together they soared before breaking the water's surface and diving back down into the dark blue abyss. Violent waves crashed as the killer whale's tail cut the ocean, and the girl, the green girl, moved with her. In and out, up and down, Anya and Oracle were as one. Every day and every evening they swam for hours. Anya was older now, more agile and athletic than ever, wiser, and still strong of heart. She moved with graceful balance as she surfed on the orca's back. When Oracle leapt up and out, Anya followed; she launched herself and balanced on only a fingertip on the edge of the whale's tail.

Suspended in the air, all of Anya's worries seemed to melt away; with Oracle's touch she felt alive, and when they separated, she flipped through the air and dived under the surface. The sudden rush of ice-cold water brought peace to her mind, and the temptation to venture forth and scour the whole ocean with Oracle took hold. The idea of soaring, of hunting and roaming in the great beyond—but that was just a dream. It was easy to swim, to lose track of time and forget her troubles, but soon enough Anya had to surface, and she had to go back. She was no longer the girl who dreamed of being a Hunter, but the Ark's protector, its saviour and its leader.

The whale thrust her back towards the Ark and up into the air. Anya flew up high and landed upon the Ark's edge. There she stood, her long brown hair falling over her fish-leather crop-top, bottoms and forearm braces, with her emerite necklace tucked away.

Anya opened her eyes and soon a crowd of children came forward as their timid mothers looked on. The children cheered; they had waited to watch her jump, and they celebrated as Oracle flew out of the water, over the corner of the Ark and close enough for Anya to touch the grand black and white tail with her fingertip. Oracle crashed back down with a tremendous splash, covering everyone in view, especially the scolding mothers. The children exploded into screams of laughter, the elders ducked for cover, and many more looked on, still finding it hard to believe.

The children huddled up to Anya, giggling and smiling. "Again, again," they said, but as many times as she would do it, they would still ask for one more demonstration.

"That's it for today," she said as she ruffled their hair and smiled.

Tomas stood closely as he waited for her, spear in hand. He had become quite the hunter over the past few months, but despite that, he never appeared to smile. Anya noticed that he had grown bigger over the past few months, heavier-set every day; his thick brown hair was long, tied back, and a thick beard was forming.

"Tomas, what news do you bring?" Anya asked.

"No news."

"Any movement?"

"No one moves. Not the tanker, not the dwellers, and not us."

Tomas was right: the oil tanker had not moved since its arrival, and it remained northeast. The Ark's council had waited and had drawn-out discussions over many days and nights. Anya had wanted to investigate the tanker, but the Arkers dismissed such a notion. Some of them said it was haunted, that there were ghosts on board, but Anya knew it was because her people were afraid of such a remnant of the past. Days had turned to weeks, and weeks to months, and neither the tanker nor the Ark moved.

Anya knew that the elders were putting it off for as long as possible. They dreaded what might be found, whereas the young longed for new discoveries. She wanted to go there and had argued with her uncle for many nights over her intentions. She had wanted to explore much further than that, too, far into the sea, but she could not leave her people.

The water dwellers had not investigated the tanker either, and though Anya listened out for them every day, they had never tried to communicate with her since she had left. She thought about making the journey south to the shallows, visiting them, and sometimes her mind would wander back to her time at the bottom of the sea, to all the colours, the smells and the taste of fish. Down there were newfound friendships and adventure, but the thought of rejection also played on her mind. She was sad to leave such a life behind; she missed them all, but Hali, Pearl and Kai most of all.

Anya shook off such thoughts and tried to stay strong. She had to think of the Ark, of keeping everyone afloat, and so she marched along the deck as Tomas ran to keep up with her. She took a loose rag and tied back her long brown hair.

"Where's my uncle?" Anya asked.

"He's on the South side."

"What about Jake?"

"Probably with Wilson."

At that moment Anya heard a commotion across the Ark. She ran in the direction from which it came, jumping and diving from rope to floor and back again, the whole time imagining some grand struggle, that a war was breaking out, or something even worse. She stopped upon the roof of a shack and there she saw a small crowd below. Within the crowd was a man called Owen, he was in his late twenties; he had red hair and the passion that came with it. His skin was pink from years in the sun and sea, and his leathers were dark and dry. In truth Anya had barely known him, but she knew enough when she saw that he had his hands on Elder Frederick and was shaking him back and forth.

"How much longer can you let this go on, old man? Our people are dying, our Ark is cursed! We have to do something," Owen said.

Anya jumped down from the rooftop and split the

crowd of ten or so Arkers. "Put him down," Anya said. Rather startled by her sudden appearance, Owen let go of Elder Frederick.

"What's going on here?" Anya asked. Owen turned toward her sharply as the crowd looked on.

"Everything's fine Anya," Elder Frederick said. "Owen was just … just raising his concerns, isn't that right?" he replied whilst trying to catch his breath.

"Yes, yes, that's all." Owen took a moment to calm himself; he was sweating, and Anya noticed that he wouldn't look directly at her. She knew many of the men aboard were intimidated by her strength, and though he wouldn't say it, he was less than fond of her scales.

"It isn't, though, is it?" Anya asked. "You take me for some sort of monster. I see it. But I'm a friend, Owen, I lived with Riley, your cousin. I mean you no harm."

"It isn't that," Elder Frederick butted in. "Riley's brother is seven years old, and his condition worsens every day, Simone is due any day now, too, but she and many are suffering on the Ark," Elder Frederick said whilst trying to catch his breath.

The fact that Elder Frederick was defending Owen surprised Anya, given the likelihood of him doing something rather rash if she hadn't appeared.

"My nephew grows worse with each passing day. There's nothing I can do," Owen replied. "I wanted you to see if you could search for medicine down below."

Anya remembered the world she had left behind, and right now, it seemed only a dream. Neptune, Hali,

Kai, Polka, Grey and Fin. That wonderful society of freedom, free from illness, weakness, cold and struggle. But there was no medicine down there: everything in the pharmacy had been looted before the flood. Besides, the dwellers had moved past medicine; Hali and Guillermo could treat dwellers, but not humans.

"I'm afraid there's no cure down there, no medicine," Anya had to say, no matter how much she wished it wasn't so.

"What about the oil tanker?" Cayden asked, as he slurred his words. The well-built Master Hunter had a blond Viking mohawk and a tin tankard in his hand, and it surpassed Anya that he has snook up on her in such a drunken state.

He pushed his way through the rabble, his presence alone making everyone around him quiet and still. When Anya looked at him, she saw someone who had once joined Tyson in revolt, but much time had passed and she had to see beyond his mistakes. Cayden had paid his dues, yet his loyalty hadn't been truly tested.

What about the tanker? Anya thought. She had asked herself that question every day for six months.

"They must have medicine," Owen said.

"They can ease our pain! A place of warmth, free from rain!" a woman shouted from the crowd. Anya could barely hear them, and for a moment she had the strangest feeling, a feeling that she hadn't felt since being down below. The air was cold, and as everyone began to shout over each other she couldn't breathe, as she had when she'd heard the Ark calling her back from the water dwellers.

If only my uncle was here, he would know what to say, he would know what to do ... but instead everyone looked at her, and she had to choose her own words.

"If neither the dwellers nor the tanker have medicine, then this is no life for my nephew," Owen said. "I beg you, do to him what was done to you," he continued.

Anya didn't know what to say; she wouldn't wish that upon anyone, for she remembered the pain, the feeling in her chest and the reality of being left alone in the cold dark ocean to drown. But then she remembered the dwellers swimming free, living a different life, a life she craved but feared all the same. She winced and clutched her chest before rubbing her hand back and forth on the emerite stone of her mother's necklace.

"Owen," she said before going towards him. She rested her hand on the back of his neck and went forehead to forehead. "I wish it were that simple. No one should go through what I did: to drown, to fight the fever and burn, just to die again." Her words were wise but deep down she wished they could all be dwellers. Only a handful, however, would face the pain, fewer would survive the fever, and even less the burn. She knew that if it was easy, every water dweller would come above, and every human go down below.

"If the boy is strong, let him show his strength," Anya muttered. It was a phrase she hated, a phrase of the Ark. It had excused the deaths of old and young for cold and weakness on the Ark; but they were her people's words, and a phrase they often needed to hear in times of sickness. Owen gave a reluctant nod, as the words of the Ark's way, were repeated by those around them. The crowd soon dispersed, and Anya walked off.

"You can save him, Anya, you can save my nephew, I know you can, you can save them all," Owen said.

For a moment Anya wanted to say something back, but then Riley came, and she put herself between them before guiding her uncle away.

Anya remembered a time when Riley and the other girls had teased her, where now they had nothing but respect for her. They had all grown up and gained so much since the days of Tyson, but their reliance on her leadership was affecting her, and the burden growing by the day.

How can I, on my own, save everyone? If I could, I would. Anya kept walking, she had to get away from it all and clear her mind. Her council position was causing her strain, everything was. She wished she could go away, leave this place, go far and free. She had wondered whether coming back was the right thing, whether the Ark would have sorted itself out anyway, whether anything she had done had made a difference. Sometimes, it felt like it did; other times it didn't.

Anya stopped. Her trail of thought ended when she saw someone, or at least she thought she had. It was Miles, son of Tyson—but when Anya blinked, he was gone. Despite the Ark only being a mile or two around, there were many places to hide, and in the time gone by since Tyson's death, Anya had never found him. She only ever saw his face in crowds, and she considered that it might just be the guilt and the trauma from what had happened. Anya looked around for him, but then she felt Tomas's large hand come down on her shoulder.

"Anya, are you sure you want to?"

"If not now, then when?" she asked before chasing after Miles. Every turn she made, he was just out of reach: through crowds, over rooftops, back alleys, and rope swings. Miles was fast, and no matter who she asked, she just missed him. Ever since his father's death, Miles had remained alone. Anya knew he would feel like an outcast, just like her.

She wondered where on earth he could be. She stood still, closed her eyes and cleared her mind. When she opened them, she saw the soft pink and blue sky, and then she saw the first crow's nest, her mother and father's—somewhere she hadn't been since her return from the water dwellers. Now Anya climbed it, and sure enough, there was Miles, son of Tyson. He was taller now and was inheriting his father's strength. His long, wild hair contrasted the mellow sky.

"You shouldn't be here," Miles said. His once bright smile was gone, hidden behind dark eyes, but Anya still saw the boy she used to know.

"I'm sorry, Miles, I'm sorry I haven't found the courage to say it sooner, so much has happened. I—"

"What are you sorry for?"

Anya remembered the day Tyson put her in the net, when he kicked the pulley and let her drown. When he sawed down the crow's nest and grabbed her by the throat in front of the whole tribe. It was Miles who had said Tyson was a monster; it was Miles who was the real hero, but he was a walking reminder of the tyranny, the starvation. She remembered the way Tyson had stumbled back, the way he lost his footing, his sea legs, and how the ocean took him in the storm. She thought it over and realised that even though Tyson was his father, she wasn't sorry—she was guilty, yes, but never sorry.

"You didn't do a damned thing," he said without any emotion, and Anya felt that was worse. She wanted him to cry, to scream, to show her something, but just like the other men he stayed quiet.

"Miles, you lost your ..." Anya reached for his hand, but Miles brushed it away. There was a cold blank void inside of him; he was numb and angry, having obsessed over events long since passed. "It took a lot of courage to do what you did," she continued.

Mile chuckled. "Courage? I remember the day I turned and ran from the rooftop in the shallows. How you mocked me, how you called me a coward. But you didn't know. You didn't know how terrified I was, how weak. The thrill of adventure wasn't in my mind, only the fear of my father's shouting, his mighty fists and the bruises they left behind. Behind closed doors no one—not your uncle, nor your precious elders—helped me, they all turned a blind eye, but they heard, they all heard."

Anya's lip quivered. She wanted to say something, anything.

"Since I was a little boy, since we lost my mother, I've wished so many times that I could've had some superpower to make him stop, to teach him a lesson. I prayed every single day that I could catch his mighty fists in my hands and crush them. Make him feel the pain I felt, just once—but they gave *you* that power. I wanted to run away, to swim far away from here, but again, they gave *you* that power. Now I see you, the girl who can go anywhere, who can do anything, moping around like it was you who had lost everything; but you didn't, did you?"

"Miles, I drowned, twice. I lived for months in an underwater world. I went through hell to get back, and I take nothing, *nothing* for granted. I'm sorry I—"

"I don't need your sympathy. I don't need anything from you or from this place anymore."

Anya tried to take his hand, but he moved it away. She hugged him; he couldn't fight that. His head made its way down into her hands as he held back tears.

"It's going to be okay, Miles, everything's going to be okay."

2

MENTORS

High above the Ark upon the Sorth Crow's Nest, a heavy sandbag swung back and forth from the rope. The wind was violent, the sway of the South tower endless, but the old man in the navy sail coat and white captain's hat didn't falter. "Again!" he shouted. "One, two! One, two! One, two!" The heavy bag swung up and down after each blast as Anya struck it with thunderous blows—light on her feet, she put her whole body into it. Her breathing was heavy after hours of training, but her sweat was lost to the cold salty winds. "Break," the old man said, and Anya hunched over her stool and tried to breathe. Her hands wrapped up tight in old rags, she took a drink of filtered water, but he snatched it from her hand.

"Wilson, that's mine!" Anya glared at the man; he was getting older, his skin paler than pink and his beard white as snow.

"True power comes from your hips , Anya. You can have water when you deserve it, when you move like you need it, and when I damn well say so." Wilson finished off the liquid in the wooden container, every last drop, and then he tied it onto his pulley system before sending it back to the ground.

"What the hell do I need power for? I'm the strongest—"

"On the Ark, no doubt, but stronger than any water dweller? I think not. There may come a time when your so-called *friends* aren't your friends anymore, and if that day comes, all we have is you."

"The dwellers are good people."

"Well, you would be surprised what one bad egg can do—why don't you ask old Greg? Oh, wait … old Greg had his heart torn out of his chest."

Anya wanted to say that it wasn't one of her friends but Neptune's brother, Enki. He was the monster who had committed such a heinous crime, and his actions proved that Wilson was right. The old man was often right, but he was never nice about it and that made it all the more satisfying to get under his skin. He trained her every day, any way that he could, if his patience could stand it.

"One of these days I'll be gone, you will remember my words and think, by god, that old fool was right!"

"Yeah, when the world dries up and seals can fly."

Anya spent most of her time disagreeing with him, just to pass the time. When he taught her how to navigate by the stars, she would argue that there was nowhere to go. When they spoke of politics, she argued that there was no government. When he spoke of wars and strategy, she said there were no guns. When he tried to teach her new words, she insisted that the Arkers were rude and the dwellers no better. When he taught her how to stand with good posture, she said there was no one worth standing properly for. When it came to the art of defending herself, Anya always said that no one would ever be brave enough to fight her.

Despite her backchat and Wilson's rather vocal impatience, they went to work each day, and she had learned much from the old man. They had come to know each other very well, and today Wilson couldn't help but notice that Anya was distant: she was spending more and more of her time in her head. At first, he worried that it was some boy, but the way Anya had reacted told him all he needed to know. He often caught her gazing at the oil tanker from up here, and also in the direction of the water dwellers.

"I can tell your heart's not in it, we're done for today," Wilson said, and he was right. It was easy for him to see that Anya's mind was elsewhere.

"Wait, I'm not done."

"You're too easy to read, Anya, far too easy."

"We were just getting started." She stood to face him, confused by his dismissal.

"Your mind's on other things, you're not giving your all, and until you do, we're all in danger."

"If I give you my all, that sandbag will fly off into the ocean."

"Then on that day, if it ever comes, I'll carry it up on my back."

Anya approached the sandbag, pulled back her fist, and hit it with all her might. The old weathered rope snapped before flying over the side and descending into the sea. They both stood in silence for a moment a huge splash echoed below.

"Go on then, go and get it," Wilson said as he folded his arms.

"But you said—"

"I said *you* would have to carry it back up. You never listen. Now, stop wasting my time and bring me that bag first thing tomorrow."

Anya blocked him out; she kept looking down at the oil tanker, and then at the shallows.

"Did you hear what I said? What are you thinking about?"

"I'm thinking about the same thing I do every day," she said as she unwrapped the leather from her hands. She took to the edge of the nest and looked down as it swayed from side to side. She saw the entire Ark, the sea stretching for miles beyond, and she saw the oil tanker, shrouded in shadow.

Wilson approached her. "Three different worlds, one below swallowed by pride, one on a raft drifting on by, and one still a mystery."

"Do you think there's anyone on there? Maybe they're all dead."

"Something tells me that they're waiting—watching and waiting. That they study us from afar and that they want something. My worry is what they'll do to get it, or what might happen if they don't."

"What do you think they want?"

"That's the most dangerous bit: we might not know until it's too late."

Anya let the old man's wise words sink in as she enjoyed a moment silence. That was what she most enjoyed on Wilson's tower: that the world was quiet, but it wasn't quiet for long. She heard a voice on the wind, calling up to her, and she looked down to see her brother Jake. He was but a speck below, but she could still see his wavy long blond hair. Anya and Wilson looked at each other once more, shared a nod and saluted one another before Anya ran and leapt from the side.

She soared, free-falling before breaking the water feet first and descended into the abyss. She found release in her green-scaled form, and took a moment to feel the peaceful movement of the ocean. Then she forced herself back into her human form and pulled herself up onto the Ark's side. Jake was waiting for her; his poorly grown moustache had aged no better. He was taller and had filled out slightly, as most men do at twenty. His genuine smile appeared to shine—he truly was kind-hearted soul, and although some were jealous of Anya's newfound powers, he wasn't—he was just glad to have his sister back. Jake offered her a hand, and though she could easily propel herself up and over the side, she took it.

They embraced. "Brother, what's wrong?" Anya asked.

"It's Aunt Lyn, she won't leave her bedside, she's rather pale." Anya knew about the illness: she hadn't left her bed for days and Tomas had been taking care of her. They walked at pace over the Ark's uneven floor, past the children in the company of Carers, and the Makers carrying out their daily repairs. Some of them smiled, and some of them avoided eye contact.

"Can she walk?"

"No."

"Is it her diet, or sleep, or—"

"It doesn't matter what she eats, even the underwater fruit you bring doesn't do her any good."

Anya knew Aunt Lyn was in great pain, and that she was up late at night and having strange nightmares. What Anya had said to Owen took over her mind. There was no miracle cure; every now and then, she thought about how, if they transformed, Hali could end their suffering, but there was no guarantee that anyone could survive the sickness. There didn't seem to be an answer, but everyone always turned to her to find one anyway.

Anya opened Aunt Lyn's shack door and walked right in. She found her aunt sitting in darkness with only a crack of light from the door. She was sitting in her rocking chair, which had long been moved inside. Aunt Lyn was pale, and her hair was dry and grey. It was a sad sight to see a such a master Maker so devoid of energy.

Anya perched on the makeshift stool opposite; she didn't know what to say.

"Anya," Aunt Lyn whispered.

"Yes, Auntie?"

"You look more like your mother every day," she said, so faintly it was almost a whisper. Anya did look like her mother more every day; she had her eyes, whereas Jake had her hair. Anya looked at Aunt Lyn and knew that no matter her own strength, she could not make her better. It made her want to cry, to share her pain, but here she was with all the power in the world and no way to help her.

"Your uncle and I are very proud."

"I love you, Auntie."

"I love you too."

"Has everyone been taking care of you?" Anya asked.

"That friend of yours, the big one, doesn't say too much—he helps me every day."

"Tomas?"

"Yes, he's nice, he might make a good husband someday. It would be nice to see a wedding. It's about time you had a boyfriend, isn't it, or a girlfriend?"

"Erm, no, Aunty."

Anya thought for a moment about her feelings, feelings that she had buried deep, with her drowning twice and burning alive. The whole Ark and everyone upon it were on her shoulders. There wasn't time to feel anything else, for all those relying on her. "Is there anything I can do for you?" she asked, attempting to change the subject.

"I just wish I could go outside these days, I just get so cold."

"I'm going to get you better, Auntie, I'm going to get you making the finest sculptures, just you wait, you'll see …"

"Oh, Anya, I'm quite happy here. Now, enough about me, tell me what's on your mind, I always know when something's wrong, you do wear your worries on your sleeve, just like your mother."

"Nothing …"

"Nothing?"

Anya sighed. "I want to unite the Ark with the water dwellers, but I don't know if they will ever forgive me."

"I wanted to know what was wrong with *you*, not the Ark, not the water dwellers." Aunt Lyn paused and thought for a moment, then extended her hand with great difficulty, and from a shelf withdrew a small carving with a shaking hand before passing it to Anya. Anya took it and opened her hand to see the jagged wooden sculpture of a dolphin; she immediately thought of Kai and fought back tears. "If Neptune, Kai and Pearl, these *water dwellers*, have half the heart that you do, then they will come around. All it will take is time, but you must be careful."

"What about the tanker? We have to do something; I've waited long enough. What if they have guns? Or what if there's someone worse than Tyson?"

"When that day comes, you will look them in the eye, and you will know whether to trust them. Trust your instincts, Anya; you aren't my little girl anymore, you're a woman. And who knows, maybe they have someone just like you."

Anya laughed; she was no leader, and she found it impossible to tell whether she was feared or respected by her own people. Everyone looked to her—the elders and her council—and all she wanted was to be with Oracle.

"You have to believe in yourself."

"I do."

"You don't. What you did, standing up to Tyson, you freed us all. You faced monsters and death and …" Aunt Lyn began to hyperventilate. Anya didn't know what to do except to move forward and hold her. She could feel the bone, the lack of muscle; Aunt Lyn felt so much smaller now. "Our Ark will follow you to the ends of the earth," Aunt Lyn whispered.

Though Anya could not see it, she had captured the hearts and minds of her people. The young, all those little girls who could now be whatever they wanted to be, and every woman who wanted to be treated equal. They all knew what Anya had given, and though her journey had been mostly told in whispers, they all knew that she had died for them.

It was at that moment that an icy wind whistled through the shack and Aunt Lyn's hand became cold. She began to tremble before raising her head. Her eyes turned grey and then she stared past Anya.

"The way the cold wind blows," she muttered as she began to take slow and heavy breaths. "The way the cold wind blows."

Anya came forward, grabbed Lyn by the shoulders and shook her. "It's okay, Auntie, it's okay, it's just me, I'm here."

"The way the cold wind blows," she said once more, and then Aunt Lyn fell fast asleep. Anya retreated to the door; she felt a strange shiver down her spine—she was afraid, but there was nothing she could do. She turned and left the shack to wander alone for a while as she tried to put her mind at rest. She made her way to the South docks; she wanted to be alone, so she sat on the wooden edge. She looked out at the moon and the stars, as she had done many nights before, and then in the direction of the water dwellers. There she caught a glimpse of the endless infinity she yearned for.

It was impossible to have all the answers. She knew that Neptune or Hali might know, but she had let them down, all of them. She had thought of swimming down there to apologise many times, but never did, for she could never find the words to say, and she feared their rejection. Anya could picture the dwellers in the town hall as they held meetings about the surface dweller who had stolen all their secrets, who had bonded with the orca and left them behind as if they were nothing.

The stars and the moon were at their brightest as Anya watched the water. She hoped for some sort of signal, a dolphin or something else. She waited and waited but nothing happened, and so she burst into tears. Despite all those around her, she felt so lost. The dwellers had given her purpose and friendship, a friendship she had never had before, and now she felt alone, as if the weight of the entire Ark was on her shoulders. She could picture Pearl and Kai in her mind, and sometimes she would imagine they were human. She wanted to dance with them, to sing with them, to hunt and explore and to play waterwheel.

"I miss you; I really miss you." Most nights, Anya found herself speaking to the ocean as if they were listening, but they were miles away.

She thought about the day she had left them, the

celebrations, and the day she took her sea name. How she had heard the Ark and left them all at the feast. She wished she could take their advice, feel the warmth of their company, and she wished it was easy to swim back to them. But Anya knew it would never be that simple. The dwellers were a proud people, and she would never expect them to find it in their hearts to forgive her, for the reality was that she could not forgive herself.

"I miss you, Pearl, Kai, Hali and Neptune. You too, little Guillermo, Polka, and everyone else."

It was at that moment that Anya saw a silhouette coming towards her. *It's them, it's one of them*, she thought. She smiled and then she tried to hide it, to act normal. When the figure got closer, Anya saw that it was a man sat down on the back of a great sea turtle. "Do I disappoint you?" he asked.

"No, Lord Turtle-Head."

"It's just Terrance now, unless you want to provide me with a knighthood, milady; then I would accept the name 'Lord of the Turtles,' if you don't mind." Then he stepped onto the Ark and the great sea turtle swam away.

"When are you going to stop calling me those names?"

"What? Milady? Anya of—"

"All of them. I'm not royalty, I'm no queen. Ugh, I'm not special in any way."

"I beg to differ. You gave yourself the name Anahita down there, the name of the Persian goddess of water. You saved us from the wrath of Tyson, from starvation, and, most importantly, you saved me from my own mind. You helped me to understand my power, and I'm eternally grateful. You are our queen, if not a goddess, but seeing as you're so against that idea, I thought 'milady' might do."

"You speak big words, Terrance. Sometimes I prefer your barrel and your turtle-shell helmet."

"Simpler times, eh. I didn't take well to the flood; I lost myself for a long time and burrowed inside myself. I still miss it."

"The old world?"

"No, being mentally unwell. There was safety in that barrel, but there was also fear, and now it feels as if there's still a piece of me missing. You may not want to take credit for saving us from Tyson and starvation, but you helped me come to understand that I wasn't mad, and that I can actually hear the turtles …"

Anya flicked back her long curly hair and glanced at Terrance before looking back to the ocean and folding her arms.

"I still don't understand my power," Terrance went on. "One day you will have to take me down there, so I can find my missing piece."

"I hope that one day I can … but you do know you're the exception: no human has ever been able to hear and speak to sea creatures like you."

"I don't know—the young, the weak, and the old hear something."

"What do you mean?"

"There's an illness spreading and a curse upon the Ark."

"I know," Anya admitted, as much as she didn't want to.

"It started when you first left."

"What do you mean?"

"First the famine, the lack of fish and now the illness. There's an eerie feeling in the water Anya, and I can't quite explain it. What's wrong, Anya? You look rather deflated."

Anya looked down as if to blame herself. "I'm afraid that I can't solve everyone's problems and I'm even afraid of being afraid."

Terrance placed a hand on her shoulder. "We're all afraid of something, Anya. We're fighting for survival on a floating piece of driftwood which is decomposing under our very feet. It could fall apart any minute and the sea swallow us whole. Oh, and the world is a blue ball floating through space at a million miles an hour, flying around a huge ball of fire. There's a lot to be afraid of."

Anya let go a tear.

"Come on, I'm not that bad at giving advice, am I?"

"No, I'm just afraid of feeling, of letting go, of letting anyone in. I have to protect everyone, I have to make sure everyone respects me, because they look to me for guidance."

"Many leaders who came before you never had that quality, maybe if they did the world might've been a better place."

"I just miss the water dwellers. God, I miss them, but no one understands. The way they swam, the way they used to feast, the warmth, the love …"

"We'll see them soon, Anya, of that I'm sure."

The Ark was quiet and peaceful for a moment, and Anya was about to say goodbye to Terrance, but then the sound of the South nest bell rang out. Something was wrong, Wilson had only ever rung it once before, and that was for the storm. Anya looked at Terrance as if she had so much more to say, but she had to move. She looked up at the South tower and Wilson was pointing in the direction of the oil tanker—she knew he was pointing for her. She ran fast, jumped over shacks, and swung through the air on ropes and pulleys. She moved at such speed and velocity whilst thinking through the worst possible outcomes, over and over again.

Maybe we're sinking, maybe we're at war, Anya thought. Then she saw the crowd. She pushed through and saw a large man with frizzy grey hair looking out to sea, it was Uncle Isaac.

3

THE LAST SOULS

The North dock was quiet. Anya couldn't move; her eyes were fixed upon a shadow upon the open ocean. It was a boat, a rowing boat, and upon it were three hooded figures dressed in black. There was silence except for the oars of the large rower cutting through the waves as the setting sun shrouded the boat in mystery. At the back of the vessel, a black flag was blowing in the cold wind, and upon it was a bright white skull which could only mean one thing …

"Death … Death and his henchmen," whispered Elder Frederick.

The three hooded figures were getting closer, and Anya could see their clothes now. Where the old saw raincoats, the young saw the unknown. The Ark was split: the young were in awe, shaking for thoughts of mythical tales of pirates and ghosts, but the old saw the past, a remnant of a world lost more than thirty years past. And just like that, the trauma of all those years ago came back.

In moonlit shadow, the large rower lifted his oars from the water as the boat glided toward the Ark. The nearest shadow rested its foot on the bow, and then they pulled off its hood. The crowd of Arkers gasped. To Anya's surprise, it was a woman, with bright red hair. She had a scar daround her left eye, her lips were black with lipstick, her ears and nose were pierced, and she was armed with a makeshift hatchet at her side.

"People of the raft, I mean you no harm," the woman's voice echoed, but no one on the Ark said anything in return. "English—do you speak English?"

English? thought Anya, for the Ark called it "the common tongue."

"I wish to speak to your leader."

The crowd split around Anya as everyone turned to stare. Anya and Uncle Isaac exchanged a short glance before he too stepped back. "This is our leader," he said, "her name is Anya."

The red-haired woman smiled as the rower stopped the boat just short of the Ark's edge; now she was close enough for Anya to see her age. She was older, in her late-thirties, and they locked eyes. To Anya's surprise, the red-headed stranger took a small bow, as a sign of respect. Anya looked past her to see the other two figures pull down their hoods and take to standing. The one on the left was a good-looking, heavy-set giant of a man with a thick beard and long black hair. Alongside him was another man, not so tall or heavy: he was lean, and bald, and his eyes were cold and quiet.

"My name is Rosita, and I come from the tanker," the woman said as she pointed to the mysterious ship on the horizon. "My people call ourselves the 'last souls,' and we thought we were all that was left, until we found you. Forgive us for not coming sooner, we had to take our time, to examine you from afar."

"This place is our Ark, our home," Anya said with pride.

"How biblical … It's a pleasure to meet you, Anya of Ark," Rosita said as she bowed her head.

Anya saw the strange look in Rosita's eyes; she was being polite, but only as polite as one can be whilst staring into another world, one of fish and seal leather, of rotted wood and hardship. Anya looked around her, the Arkers didn't show any signs of welcome. The young —who hadn't seen land—looked at her as if she were an alien; it was hard for them to decide whether she was an image of the future, or some forgotten vestige of the past.

The feelings of the young, though, were nothing compared to the feelings of the old. The old struggled to take their eyes off the boots and the rain jackets, strange remnants of the past which sent them back to trudging through the end of the world, a time they had tried hard to forget. The black waterproof ponchos were something no Arker had come across since the flood— in such conditions they had never lasted long enough, and nor had the jeans and worn black boots which Rosita was wearing, as opposed to the Arkers' bare feet.

"Do you rule alone?" Rosita asked.

"With my council," Anya replied.

Rosita nodded. "This is Barnaby, my second mate." She ushered the gentleman to her right. The long-haired giant took off his raincoat to reveal a tank-top, jeans and boots, all in black. Barnaby seemed rather good-looking, until he gave a smile full of missing teeth.

"And this is Nameless," Rosita said, pointing to the silent man, "he has no tongue, so you won't hear much from him." Anya found him to be peculiar; his gaunt cheeks and pale complexion made him look rather ill. He kept his raincoat on; he was also wearing black trousers, but like the Arkers, he wore no footwear. Anya fought the temptation to stare at him for too long and forced herself to turn back to Rosita.

"Why are you here?" Anya asked.

"We want to form an alliance; we want peace, and we waited because we had to be sure that we could trust you. We have been watching you for some time, we've seen you hunt and feast. We know you now, and now I wish for you to know us. May we come aboard?"

Anya could feel Wilson watching in the South nest, but none of the Arkers said a word, for they were all so weary, and the air was tense. "I permit you to come aboard," Anya said. She signalled for a rope to anchor the boat, and when the rope came Barnaby caught it mid-air. He pulled it to the dock and tied a tight sailor's knot to secure the vessel.

Most of the Arkers dispersed and only a few remained: Anya's brother Jake, Tomas, Uncle Isaac, the elders and Terrance. Anya extended a hand and Rosita took hold; Isaac did the same for Barnaby, and Nameless climbed aboard himself. Anya escorted the last souls, who followed close behind. The Arkers' eyes were on the strangers, watching them closely whilst keeping a safe distance. No one said a word as Anya and Uncle Isaac escorted them to the most secure building on the Ark, a reinforced holding cell where they would wait until the council had spoken.

Anya and the council went on to their storm shack a short walk away to debate the arrival of their guests. The storm shack was the council's meeting place in rough weather, but right now they needed it to ensure their privacy.

Inside the storm shack, forever flame candles lit the round wooden table in its centre. To Anya's right was Uncle Isaac, Elder Frederick, Elder Vanya, and Tiff the Master Carer. To her left was the big round Head Chef known as Ezekiel, Wilson the Master at Arms, and Cayden the Master Hunter—the same Cayden with his blonde mohawk and braided beard who, Anya often remembered, had been forgiven for being a Tyson loyalist and had pledged his allegiance to Anya. As of late, Cayden had looked rather tired; he wasn't sleeping, and all knew it was because his wife was due to give birth any day now.

The council hunched over the table and shared worried looks with each other. They knew the danger that strangers could bring, and they knew that this day had been coming.

"Do you trust them?" Elder Vanya asked, her stooped frame barely reaching above the tabletop. She was the oldest person on the Ark but remained quick-witted all the same.

"They're bad news, I don't trust them, especially her with that red hair. Cursed, they are, cursed," Wilson said. He was always one to speak his mind, and he would only ever made his way down from the nest for something special.

"No one trusts them," Elder Frederick confirmed, his eyes barely visible under his walrus cloak. "How can we, when they live with such comforts?"

"For once we agree on that much. Do we know whether they have guns?"

The word brought a shudder to those old enough to remember such things, but Anya didn't fully understand, and didn't ask.

"We don't know," Uncle Isaac said as he shook his head.

"The c-collision of our c-communities brings great danger," Elder Frederick continued.

"If they try anything, if they put anyone in danger, I'll shove the blunt end of my spear down their throats," said Cayden, and he wasn't joking.

Usually, Anya would have laughed about such a remark, but right now she stared into the old wooden table, the cracks and rotten wood. It was difficult to speak, or take anything in, for she too was tired and barely sleeping.

"A spear can't fix this," mumbled Elder Frederick. "The dangers of the old world have returned. You all remember those first days in the flood, how violent it was. It reminds me of what I had, what I—what we—lost. It could undo everything—*they* could undo everything."

Wilson put his fists on the table. "Never mind that, do we know what they want?" Wilson's question was fair, but nobody knew the answer and he looked at each of them with a short cold glare, and then at Anya. "What do you think?"

Anya took a moment to consider the options. "They don't belong here, but we can't turn them away. We need to know what they want."

"Then I suggest we find out."

The last souls were soon brought into the storm shack. Wilson signalled them in, and Rosita led the way. She approached the table tall and proud, with a slow gait, and her second mate, Barnaby, stayed close behind. Nameless stayed back in the corner of the shack, forever scowling, with his arms folded.

"It's quite the raft you have; how did it come about?" Rosita asked in an attempt to make polite conversation, but her question was met with silence.

Anya looked to Uncle Isaac, as did everyone else: he was the only one who was there at the beginning. He thought about the flood, of trudging through the water and fighting to put together the makings of a pitiful raft with his brother.

Isaac didn't know he would find it this hard to speak, but everyone could see how hard it was for him to answer as they awaited his words. "My brother and I built this raft from nothing. Richard was an engineer … but that was more than thirty years ago."

He found no comfort in reliving such memories, and he folded his arms and stroked his beard as he attempted to bring his focus back onto the strangers. Anya noticed that her uncle looked tired and much older than she remembered. She saw fear, but only in his eyes: fear of the past, perhaps, as he stared at their clothes, their coats, their leather belts and boots.

"Quite the engineer he was … Our tanker went through many different hands in the beginning; it's seen much change, but we've worked hard to keep it running. Has your raft seen many changes of hands?"

"Only one,," Wilson butted in. "We don't take kindly to new leaders, or strangers."

"Well, sometimes strangers bring great gifts. We have beds and heating, and many more things that you may have missed."

The elders' eyes flickered at the mention of beds and heating, those long-lost memories of comfort, and Anya knew she would have to intervene. "With all due respect, Rosita, our people are hardened, we have moved past the need for such things."

"My apologies, I shouldn't have said that …"

Anya didn't know what to think of this mysterious stranger, this odd-looking character with piercings and bright red hair. Part of her wanted to say it was all just an act, but another part of her romanticised the idea of their life onboard the tanker. Rosita looked fresh and free, where her own people were cold and tired.

"Have you met any other people?" Anya asked.

"You're the first. What about you?"

"None," Anya said, but it was a lie. She wondered whether Rosita was lying too, but that didn't matter, Anya's primary concern was keeping the water dwellers safe.

"Tell us Rosita, in all honesty, why are you here?" Uncle Isaac asked.

Rosita's smile flickered in the candlelight as she glanced between Isaac and Anya. "Our tanker has run for thirty years. We may not be as hardened as you Arkers, but we're survivors all the same. We have survived this long because we refine oil. It has kept us warm and kept us moving to good fishing grounds, but our supplies will soon be at an end and we will have to go without it." Rosita took a breath. "There's an offshore rig not too far from here, with oil that can give us warmth and light for a hundred years, but the pump which extracts the oil from the seabed is broken. We wanted to fix the rig, but we can't, and so, in order to prepare ourselves, we want to learn your ways so we can survive without our comforts."

"How is the pump broken?" Anya asked.

"It's disconnected, and as for how far down, it's out of human reach, that's for sure. There's nothing we, or anyone else can do to fix it."

Anya knew that she and she alone could resolve Rosita's problem, but she had to be careful. It could be a trick, they could be lying, and even if they were not, she didn't want to pollute the ocean. She knew that if the dwellers found out, they would despise her even more, and she knew that they would never agree to help those who sought oil.

"If you teach us your ways, we will give you medicine, forge you tools, give you beds or anything else you desire."

Anya thought about that for a moment. "We would be open to forming a truce. I would like for you to feast with us tonight, to celebrate our worlds coming together and learn more about you. You can return to your ship tomorrow."

"A feast? We would be delighted. All I ask is that you, Anya of Ark, sit with me, and by tomorrow I promise that we will have formed an alliance."

Drums bellowed as dancers swung from rope to canopy, and the Ark sang loud and proud as they roasted endless fish for all to enjoy. Rosita found the bellowing of makeshift drums overwhelming at first, but it didn't take long for the rhythm to take over and for the forever-flame firepits to erupt.

The fishermen's fire burned bright, the choir's melody took hold, and the Ark felt the weight of its rhythms upon the grand stage. The twinkle in Rosita's eyes told Anya that she saw the Ark's beauty, its wonder. It wasn't a world of grey metal, but wooden and real, its people and its culture so easy to fall in love with.

Anya sat next to Rosita and felt rather timid at first. She had never had a dinner guest like this one, and she felt such pressure to assess her. All the while Rosita smiled and laughed, and Anya ended up feeling a fool for trying to read her. In the end, Anya had to lighten up and laugh too.

"This place is a thing of wonder," Rosita said. "It is magical. When I first saw you all standing there so moody and cold, I thought about turning around, but now I know the truth!" She expected Anya to say something, but she said nothing. "It's strange to see a girl so young in charge—is it ever too much for you?"

"All the time."

"I'll tell you a secret, Anya: no one is born to be a leader. But if we don't do it, some other idiot will, and they'll mess the whole thing up."

"I think you might be right."

"You know I was your age when I took the tanker."

"Really?"

"Maybe a year or so older. How did you get the Ark?"

"It's a long story," Anya replied, as she realised she had never told the tale.

"Let me share my story first. Thirty years ago, my father knew the flood was coming. He was a weather-man." Rosita laughed and looked at Anya before realising that she had no idea what a weatherman was. "A man who predicted the weather."

"Really? I never knew that such a man existed. We could do with one of those on the Ark."

"Never mind … anyway, so he took me to the docks; he was a sailor and boarded the tanker with a few others. He was a remarkable man, smart, kind, and caring, but it was his trust in others that let him down. We allowed people onboard, too many people, but as the water level rose, we had little choice, for otherwise they would drown. Some got sick, but we had medicine, and this was before we had fishing sorted. But there was too many of us, and the younger men rose against my father. They executed some, threw more overboard, and my father, well, my father was stabbed in the back. I watched him die while I was hiding in a vent. I stayed quiet and escaped. I knew the ship well, every nook and cranny. For a while I survived by eating rats and sneaking into the fish stores, only ever moving in darkness; and revenge kept me going. One by one, I took my vengeance with this knife."

Rosita withdrew a beautiful golden blade. It reminded Anya of her mother's necklace, so she tucked it further into her leather brace to keep it hidden.

"Some said the ship was cursed, but it wasn't a curse, it was justice. I cleansed the ship; I took command, and I led my people through years of storms and salvage. We are fortunate to have survived so long."

"It must have been hard," Anya said.

"It was. Most men don't like women who know what they're doing … Don't get me wrong, some don't mind, but most men don't think with their brains." Rosita pointed to the other end of the table, where Anya caught sight of Barnaby chugging fish broth with Pierce and Cayden. From the noises that came next, it was clear that they were having a belching contest; they had been on the seaweed wine and had drunk a whole barrel. The council members around them showed no signs of amusement, though, and that made Anya snigger.

"There it is, I was starting to think you couldn't smile."

Anya corrected herself. "I do sometimes. How did you get your scar, if you don't mind me asking?"

All of a sudden Rosita stopped smiling. "One of the men tried to take my eye, and so I took both of his."

A swordfish was slapped down on the table and Anya went to cut it. "No, allow me," Rosita insisted. Then she cut a generous piece for Anya with her gold knife. A tin of seaweed wine was placed by their sides, a stern beverage that seemed alien to Rosita. After smelling it, she didn't seem too keen.

"What's this?" she asked whilst making a strange face at the fermented liquid.

"Seaweed wine, it's an acquired taste."

Rosita nodded, then smiled, and began to take a big swig before almost spitting it out. It was an odd, silky yet burning taste, but it got better with every sip.

"So, are there any dashing men on this Ark? Any you recommend?" Rosita asked, and Anya blushed.

"No, sorry, no. I've never …"

"You've never? Oh, sweetie," Rosita took her by the hand, "in truth you're not missing much: there's not much choice in the new world—plus, the Ark and tanker aren't big enough to ensure that you never see them again! They must bother you all the time, with eyes like that, and that smile."

"I don't have time for relationships," Anya said. "I'm too busy sorting out quarrels or hunting with …" She had to remind herself not to mention Oracle.

"Well, men were never my thing either. The odd one, yes, but they always bored me in the morning. I have a partner, and she's my world. We watch a show called *Baywatch*; I've watched it a million times. Oh, I've just remembered: you probably don't know what television is."

"I do: a picture box," Anya said; she had seen one sunk below the surface.

"So, have you ever left the Ark?"

Anya considered her time in the Oasis, and swimming thousands of miles with Oracle. If it was up to her, she would go now and never come back. "Never," she said.

"Do you have a proper name then, Anya? A title? 'Chancellor,' how about 'queen,' or something like that? They call me captain."

Anya laughed; she didn't know what to say, and then Rosita leant back in her chair as it creaked. She put her boots up on the table and played with the knife in her hand. "We're the most powerful people in the world, Anya, you and me, but you need to learn to relax. I can see it, you're all tense."

Anya smiled to hide her nerves; Rosita reminded her of how she had been when she had wanted to do the trials, fierce and unafraid of anything, and she realised she had lost that part of herself over the past few months.

"You have to speak more," Rosita said. "You're in your own head a lot, I can tell."

"Well, when you let me get a word in, maybe I will!"

"Jeez, there we go. So, where do your people sleep, Anya?"

"In shacks."

"But where? Beds, or bunks, or hammocks?"

"Hammocks and in seal leathers."

"How do you stay warm?"

"We're strong, we move to keep warm, we're not soft like you," Anya replied, and Rosita laughed.

"I suppose we are soft, I'm not afraid to admit that I like the softness of our sheets and the warmth of our heaters. You should see some of the things we have on the tanker: aged whiskeys, fine wines. Early on we ran into a drifting merchant ship and took everything! Back when we were real pirates," she confessed. "We have wind-proof cabins with mattresses, and duvets clean and white. Have you ever seen anything white, like truly white?"

Anya thought for a moment; it was hard to understand what "true white" was. Then she remembered seeing pearls under water, and then she thought of Pearl, of dancing, and playing waterwheel, and of Kai, Polka and Hali and …

"We're too strong to need such comforts."

"Well, I don't believe you … You'll have to see— you'll have to see our sheets and stay the night on our tanker while the electricity is still running. You can't agree to help us without seeing who we really are."

"I don't think that's a good idea, our cultures are so different. Most of my people are afraid of you, I can see it in their eyes. We're years past beds and mattresses, maybe it's best if we stay on the Ark."

"I'm sorry, I didn't mean to overstep—"

"We will make our decision after the feast."

"We? It's you they all look to," Rosita said.

The singing started and the night went on. There were cheers, and talks of alliance, of sharing stories of the old world, and much more dancing. The Arkers treated it like any other feast and the guests seemed most respectful. The party ventured on through the night as Arkers sang, banged their drums, and swung from ropes in various acrobatic displays with purple forever-flame torches. Both Rosita and Barnaby were good company, but Nameless—well, one had to remind oneself that he was even there. He was more of a shadow than a man and blended into the background as the more boisterous took centre stage.

The night was long, and Anya listened to Rosita talk of scavenger missions, and of her many woes with men and women. Eventually, they well and truly broke the ice, and Anya opened up about the woes of leadership. "Sometimes they want too much, and I just want to cover my ears and dive under the water."

"You need them to respect you, you need to be strong, you can't show any weakness. If you do, they will take everything from you, take more and more until you have nothing left to give. I can tell how much you care; I can see it in in your eyes."

Anya felt better than she had in a long time, and knew she had made the right decision to let them onto the Ark. Soon she decided that the last souls could stay in the holding shack, and their journey home would be made tomorrow. The shack would be windy and cold, and constantly creaking, but she hoped the wine would send them off to sleep.

At the end of the night, Rosita took Anya' hand. "It's been quite an evening," she said.

"It has," Anya replied, and so she escorted them to their shack. Barnaby and Nameless made their way inside first and Rosita hung back; she appeared anxious as she crouched down to Anya's level and secretly forced something into her hand, wrapped up in cloth.

"What is it?" Anya asked as she started to unwrap it.

"A gift," Rosita replied as looked around.

Anya revealed the gold knife. Anya was confused and she looked up at Rosita unsure of what to say. "I can't take this," she said as she tried to give it back.

"Nonsense, It's a gift … I used it to take back the tanker for my father, and I would have given it to my sister if she had made it this far. Maybe one day we can be sisters." Anya tried to give it back, but Rosita closed her hand and smiled again before leaning in to whisper, "It's sharp, sharper than anything on your Ark. It might just be the sharpest thing you'll ever see; you have to take it, and never go anywhere without it."

Rosita touched Anya's cheek and then she turned and headed inside. Anya wondered whether Rosita knew about the water dwellers, and whether she was trying to send some sort of message, but she was too tired to try to work it out. She wanted to sleep, to be alone, and then she remembered she had to attend the council.

4

SEEKING COUNCIL

W hen Anya entered the storm shack, she was smiling after her refreshing conversation with Rosita, but her smile was soon washed away by the sound of bickering. The sea had turned rather restless too as the deck creaked, and the candles fluttered.

"It isn't right, I tell you; something isn't right," Wilson said, with a rather red face.

"They need to set sail at sunrise and never return," Elder Vanya added, "I don't want to see beds and heating and … We can't go back, we just can't."

"No, but they could have medicine, they could answer our prayers," Tiff the Master Carer said, as her primary concern was always the care of her people. "They could help us with the weak and the sick. Every day more and more fall ill."

"They've done nothing but bring their stuck-up boots to our Ark. They need to go, and never come back," Wilson said. "Something's off about this, something big, I'm telling you; I know liars when I see them, and that Nameless, he'll be the death of us all I g—"

"Wilson, get a hold of yourself, I can barely hear myself think." When Anya interrupted him, there was quiet for a moment, and then Uncle Isaac came forward.

"Did you tell them what you can do?" he asked.

"No, I told Rosita nothing."

"Good, the best thing we can do is let them go back to their tanker; we don't need this right now."

"Rosita isn't as bad as you all think, we could help them."

"I know what you're thinking Anya, teaching them our ways is one thing, but if you think I'll let you risk your life to give them oil …"

"I don't need your permission Uncle. Rosita seems kind, and they want oil to keep their people warm. They will give us medicine and trade in return, things that we need—they could help us with the sickness. We, I have to give them a chance."

"You're making a mistake."

"Am I? Or are all of you afraid?"

"You don't know what they're capable of! What they've been through, and what they've done."

"I won't turn my back on them. They're human beings, just like us. I'll give them a chance, one chance."

"How will you explain that you've fixed a pipe that's out of human reach? When they see your scales, do you think they will be kind? They will hurt you, and gut you like some sort of trophy." Uncle Isaac banged his fist on the table and fled the shack. The council stayed quiet, and they exchanged uncertain glances, as they had done many times before.

"Well, we side with you, Anya, as always" Elder Vanya said.

"No, I'm sick of everyone simply siding with me, of treading on shells. We vote." Anya walked into the open space and turned to address them again. "Stand with me if you wish to help the last souls and stand with Wilson if you don't." At first no one moved, and then Tiff the Master Carer came to her side and Ezekiel the Chef soon followed.

Anya looked back to see Elder Vanya and Elder Frederick at Wilson's side. "It's a draw," she said.

"What about Cayden and Isaac?" Tiff asked.

"If they aren't here then they don't get to vote," Anya said in frustration. Then she left the shack and ventured to the Ark's edge. There, she looked up at the huge white moon which was bright and at its zenith. She didn't wish to ask her aunt or uncle for advice—no, not tonight. Instead, she wanted to turn to someone else, and beneath the moon Anya dived into the dark and stormy sea, where, upon breaking its surface, she turned green and scaled. Finally, she could breathe again. It was tranquil and beautiful beneath the surface, free of the constant creaking, the cries of children and the splash of water. She swam down, way down below the Ark, to the bottom, and forced herself to stand on the seabed as Neptune had taught her. Closing her eyes, she concentrated and called out, searching for one mind and one mind only. She had tried every few days since returning to the surface, but not one had returned her call.

"Hali, I *need* you. Please, come to me."

Anya waited but there was no reply. She watched the schools of fish move around her and she sent them in a gentle figure of eight motion. She watched the octopi and stingrays hover above the ocean floor, but where she was once moved by their beauty, now she felt a numb sense of normality. This dissatisfaction also permeated the Ark, for despite having fought so hard to get back there, the water felt more like home. Anya cursed herself for having taken it all for granted: being torn between two worlds was harder than being forced from one to the other. She felt so low, so over-relied upon to help keep order above. Ever since Tyson had passed, she had felt such a weight upon her shoulders to please everyone: the hunters, cooks, makers, carers, women, families, and children. Petty fights were rife and arguments about fish were far too common. There was so much tension and anger, and all she wanted to do was leave it behind, and to go far away with Oracle.

Amidst her reflections, she let her guard down. A creeping feeling of imminent danger came to her; from behind her something was swimming at her fast. The sand in front of her exploded, causing a storm and blocking her view. Anya looked around, and mere seconds from calling Oracle she saw a figure, and she knew that it was Hali. She stared back at Anya with those all-knowing eyes, and for a moment Anya didn't think she was real. Then she embraced her without want to let go.

"Anya," Hali said, and her voice had the same tender kindness as when she had healed her.

"Hali, it's really you? I've missed you. I've called for you many times."

"And I haven't heard you, not until now; I would have come sooner if I did."

"Why do you think you haven't heard me, and why have you heard me tonight?" Anya asked.

"I don't know … but it doesn't matter, I'm here now. So many things have changed since you left. Kai and Pearl miss you; all of the young fins miss you, everyone misses you!"

That broke Anya's heart, for she missed them too. Life wasn't the same without them, as if part of her was missing. "I called out for you, for all of you many times."

"We didn't hear anything, and I was listening, I promise you."

"Why didn't you come for me?"

"We thought it best to leave you until you were ready."

"Can I come back?" Anya asked with hopeful eyes, but Hali looked rather defeated.

"Someday, but not today. The people, Neptune, have spoken. You know how they feel about those above, and you abandoned your sea name on the day it was given to you. I wish it wasn't so. It might not have been this way, but some tried to face the light as you did and couldn't stand the fire, the burns. Even some of the young fins tried it, Pearl and Kai, and now they are forbidden to visit you."

"It isn't fair," Anya said as she pushed past their private mind-speak conversation out of frustration.

Hali put a finger to her lips. "Sometimes it feels as though someone is still listening, Anya, we must be careful."

Anya remembered Serus, the ancient one who had once told her about those who had disappeared, and then she remembered Cray's illness and watching him go. She realised that she had suppressed those memories until now, and then she thought of what Terrance had said and what was happening to those who were getting sick. "Maybe someone blocked my attempts to reach you …"

"No one has such power. You know I can sense the good and bad in others—I haven't sensed anything since Cray's death."

"I know, but I get this feeling. When I returned to the Ark the people were starving, and they hadn't caught any fish since we disturbed your people."

"And?"

"I think someone tried to starve the Ark; they might've succeeded had I not returned."

Hali didn't want to believe it. "That isn't possible. How can someone keep the Ark in famine? It must be the currents, the way of the ocean. I sense your worries, Anya, there's great conflict in you, maybe this is all in your head?" Hali placed a webbed hand on her cheek and Anya felt a little better.

"You could be right; I wish you were on my council."

Hali laughed and gave a fang-toothed smile. "No

thank you, politics is much simpler down below where we have infinite resources …" she said in jest.

"It really is. Tell me, how are Kai and Pearl, how are the others? I miss Guillermo, I really do."

"Kai has had a growth spurt; he's much taller, he's turning into a little man, and Neptune has taken him under his wing in your absence. But you know how different they are: Kai is anything but serious, and Neptune is nothing but. Kai has never known such loss as losing you, and he spends most of his time with Polka."

Anya felt beyond guilty for leaving him behind. "What about Neptune?"

"He spends most of his time alone except for his time with Kai. I think he lost a part of himself, too, the day you left. If he could see you again, it might lift his spirits."

"What about Pearl?" Anya asked as she thought of dancing …

"Pearl is okay, but she hasn't danced since …" Hali looked at Anya and saw her heart break as she tapped the shining silver headband, they had foraged for her just to make sure it was still on her head.

"I'll come soon," Anya said with a smile and a nod. "I'll come and see them all, I'll bring Oracle and make everything right and we will hunt and fish and … and one day you can come to the Ark, to meet my family."

Hali chuckled. She wanted to, she really wanted to. "I don't know if that will ever happen, but I did bring someone special to see you." Hali reached behind her and brought forth the happy little yellow axolotl known as Guillermo.

"Guillermo!" Hali passed him forward and he began to crawl up Anya's arm, over her shoulder and around her neck. "Oh, I've missed you." Anya took her time playing with him before eventually handing him back.

"Anya, there's something else I need to tell you. Something I'm ashamed of …."

"What is it?"

"I too tried to surface. I tried to withstand the burn … but … but it was too much, it wouldn't work. Maybe I'm too old, or maybe I've just been a dweller for too long—we may never know, but I do know that it cannot be. To tell you the truth, I was ashamed of trying, but to my shame I would do anything just to breathe, to taste, to feel the wind and the cold again— to be human."

"There's no shame in being human."

"I know that, but some of the other dwellers don't seem to think so."

"I know, I'm sorry."

"Don't be. If I didn't come back, if I lost Guillermo, then who else could heal our injuries?" Hali was right: she kept many members of the tribe alive, especially the older ones. "I only wish I could share my gift with those above, those who need it most."

"I've missed you, Hali."

"I've missed you too, Anya. I'm proud of you and deep down I know everyone else is, too. I imagine that you're running things up there since you're return."

Anya smiled; somehow Hali had a way of making

everything better. She remembered how Aunt Lyn used to do the same, and then she looked up toward the bottom of the Ark and knew that she could not stay.

"I don't want to keep you waiting. You should get back to your family, they'll be missing you."

"You *are* family to me, Hali, I think of you every day." They embraced once more and rubbed each other's noses.

"And I think of you, too; let's not leave it so long next time."

"Let's not."

Hali swam back towards the dwellers, and only when she was far out of sight Anya surfaced at the South dock. She pulled herself up to sit on the ledge and look out to sea. She became human once more and let go a tear.

Anya wiped her eyes; she knew she had to be strong for them all. She lay back, looked up at the stars and wondered what her mother and father would do. Anya fell asleep, but then she felt the strangest feeling, a sudden rush of cold, as if someone was watching. Back on her feet, she turned to the Ark's structures, and saw a shadow looking down at her from one of the old crow's nests. At first, she thought she was imagining things, but the shadow remained, so she ran toward it. Anya jumped from roof to roof and launched herself into the air; she scaled the post at speed and swung herself over the side. To her disbelief, there was no one there. She looked over each side, all around the Ark, but still saw no such shadow. It was time to get some sleep.

5

NIGHTFALL

The night was growing dark, most of the Ark was asleep, and only the motion of gentle waves and the creaking of wood could be heard. Anya was tired, but she couldn't sleep, so she walked three laps around the Ark deep in thought, worrying about her guests and her people.

She ventured past Uncle Isaac's shack and found him sitting on the step of his porch, looking down in quiet contemplation. He was so deep in thought that he didn't even notice her. He was older now; it seemed that Tyson had taken the last of his strength, and there was no longer a need for him to mask his true emotions. Now stooped rather than stood, he was his most natural, his most vulnerable, and seeing him this way made Anya feel awful for what had happened in the council meeting. When Isaac saw her, he sat more upright, his look of vulnerability disappeared, and he tried to play the role of a father who was afraid of his child seeing any weakness.

"Anya, what are you doing up at this time?" he asked, though he meant to say he was sorry.

"I should be asking you the same question," she replied, knowing that she should apologise too. "You're usually tucked up by sundown gramps. You look tired."

"That's because I'm tired, tired and old. Come, sit with me."

Anya smiled; she crossed the uneven wood to sit alongside him and Isaac wrapped a huge arm around her. They both looked out upon their Ark: the run of uneven shacks; the way it breathed with every wave, and the same strange feeling that something, somewhere was watching went away.

"I'm sorry about before," Uncle Isaac confessed.

"Sorry for what?"

"For not respecting you." Uncle Isaac sighed. "Everyone asks a lot of you, be it your strength, your intelligence or your composure. You cope well, but it's too much for someone your age. This isn't the life that I wanted to give you, that your parents wanted to give you. We wanted you to laugh and play, to draw with crayons and go to school. Richard wanted you to study whatever you wanted and go wherever you wanted. And I want you to find someone you love, to build a family of your own—but not here, not like this."

Anya took a moment to let him vent. "You and Aunt Lyn gave me everything I ever wanted."

"But we couldn't give you what you needed."

"It doesn't matter now, all that matters is the here and now, Uncle, and right now we have three strangers aboard our Ark."

"We're keeping an eye on them, every move."

"What do you really think of Rosita, Uncle?"

"She has made it this far, and anyone who has made it this far has seen struggle, and danger. They have lost, and they have done everything to keep going. We can never trust her, Anya, but we have to be diplomatic. My only fear is what she reminds me of, the old ways, of beds and boots, of the ways before the water. Our people may become angry and afraid: we may long for the ship as we long for warmth and shelter. There's only one way to know her for sure: we must see the ship, for only her people can show us who she really is."

Anya had not thought of that. Being born on the Ark made her take such thoughts for granted, and she admired her uncle's opinion. "You never speak of the old ways," she said. Uncle Isaac laughed, and he stroked her cheek.

"We had jobs, hot water and electricity. Children went to school, and, well, we all had it easy. Our clothes were new, as were our cars. Our houses were warm and dry, and when you heard the rain on the windows, it helped you get to sleep. Your mother and father's house was built of brick. It had a green door, white window-panes and green hedges."

Anya didn't know what to say, for his words surprised her. Uncle Isaac never opened up in such a way about the old world, or about himself.

"I wish you had not been robbed of school, of church, of high-school dances, proms and college."

"I don't need any of those things, Uncle, as long as I have you."

Isaac faced her. "I'm proud of you, Anya, so very grateful that you saved us, and so sorry for what you went through. I'll always be here for you; I need you to know that."

Anya wrapped her small arms around his, and leant in. "I love you Uncle."

"And I love you too. What was it really like down there?" Isaac asked.

"It's heaven, magic, everything comes to life, you can't feel the cold, and everything is warm, but …"

"But?"

"I could not live without you and without our home."

Isaac smiled; he messed up her hair and they continued to embrace and let the world go by.

"Why can't you sleep uncle?"

Isaac was afraid, for he had not spoken aloud. He sighed, repeating the words in his head, and wondered what they meant.

"The words that the children and Aunt Lyn whisper. Line after line, they haunt me."

"I don't understand—"

"*The way the cold wind blows, water echoes and flows,
When you're alone I'll find you.
What you've done, you know, you reap what you sow,
For this, be sure I'll drown you.*"

Anya froze, and she felt that cold, watchful stare again.

"Do you know what it means?" Isaac asked, after taking time to summon the courage.

Anya thought about Cray's death, it had to have

something to do with him. "I don't know for sure, but I know it's meant for me."

"Then you must be careful."

"I will be."

Anya closed her eyes. She was beyond tired and wanted nothing more than to forget those words and go back to Oracle, to swim far away and never be seen again, but that was impossible. Instead, she buried herself in Uncle Isaac's side and drifted off not long after. Exhausted, she was carried inside and laid down alongside Lyn. Uncle Isaac stepped back and looked at the two of them together, then he took to his own hammock and tried to get some rest.

Anya awoke to the flash of lightning. She found herself alone in a shack, so she ran outside as fast as she could into the eye of a storm. The Ark was split in two, her people were running and screaming, and the sea was ablaze. The Ark was dying, and no matter how hard she tried to move, and to call for Oracle, nothing happened. She looked around to see people flailing in the waves. Every Arker floated away and Anya couldn't save them, for her arms were too heavy. Even the last souls were there; Rosita and Barnaby were begging for help, but there was no way for her to save them. She tried to summon the water dwellers, but no one came, and all she heard were the words:

The way the cold wind blows,
Water echoes and flows,
When you're alone
I'll find you.

What you've done, you know
You reap what you sow
For this, be sure
I'll drown you.

Anya shot up in bed. Lyn was asleep in her chair, but Uncle Isaac was nowhere to be seen. She ran outside into the early morning, where the sun was only just teasing the horizon. To her relief, the Ark was whole, but still she ran at speed, stopping for nothing, past endless shacks as she pondered the harrowing poem. She had the feeling that something bad was happening, something awful. She ran to the hut where the last souls were staying, but when she got there it was empty. Then she heard a loud scream, and she feared that someone was being hurt, that a war was starting. She saw a crowd and so she leapt from rope to rooftop and rooftop to rope before jumping back down again and rejoining her uncle.

Anya worried about what she might find—whether someone had been murdered, whether there had been an altercation with their guests; and then she saw Simone, the young fair-haired wife of Cayden the Master Hunter. Simone was pale and sweating, barely conscious, and her huge belly foretold that she was ready to give birth at any moment, despite being a month early.

"I can't see, I can't see," she mumbled, her forehead red and dripping with sweat as she squeezed Cayden's hand. She looked weak, and even Tiff the master Carer, who had helped with every birth on the Ark, was worried.

"Come on, you can do this," Cayden said, and then he appeared to be in great pain as Simone squeezed his hand. A moment later, she passed out from the pain.

"Is everything okay?" Anya asked.

"She's too early," Tiff said.

"What do you mean 'too early'?" Cayden asked as he massaged his hurt hand with the other.

At that moment, Barnaby pushed through the crowd to let Rosita through and check Simone's pulse. "How old is she?" she asked.

"Thirty-seven," Tiff replied.

"Do you have a medical room?" Rosita asked, but Anya shook her head. "She needs a doctor."

"We don't have a doctor."

"Well, I do, and we also have hospital beds and heating; we can help any woman who needs to give birth."

"That isn't our way," Elder Vanya said from the edge of the crowd.

"*Your* way? I wonder how many women have died giving birth on the Ark because of your way. How many more will you allow Anya?"

Anya couldn't answer. Simone had already lost two

children, and she had almost died for the second. As the pressure mounted all around Anya knew that her choice was already made.

"I can't lose her," Cayden said.

"There's no time to lose, get her into the boat," Anya replied, and so the hunters stepped forward and assisted Cayden in placing her inside. Anya took a deep breath before stepping inside as well.

"What are you doing?" Uncle Isaac asked.

"I have to go, she's my responsibility."

Uncle Isaac said no more, and then someone else pushed through the crowd. It was Wilson, and without hesitation he came forth and hopped into the boat. "If you think you're going anywhere without me, you have another thing coming," he said.

Cayden held Simone's hand and kept applying a cold wet rag to her forehead as Barnaby and Nameless readied the boat for departure.

"Very well," Rosita said, and she kicked the side of the Ark to launch the boat toward the tanker.

Anya looked at her Ark, her people, one last time as they all stood in silence, hoping that Simone would be okay. She picked up the rope at the front of the vessel. She knew how long it would take them to row. She was prepared to go green, to dive in and swim or use Oracle to pull them along, but just before she turned, she heard the strangest rumble as the boat came to life.

The smell of burning fuel took over as Rosita whipped a cover from the back of the boat to reveal an outboard motor. "It's for emergencies," she shouted as the boat roared into motion. Anya held on for dear life.

Her long dark curly hair flew behind her as she finally sat up. The waves chopped underneath the boat as they flew toward the horizon and the black silhouette of the ship. Anya looked up at their destination, the strange metal beast in the distance, and prepared herself for what the future would bring.

6

THE OLD WAY

The speedboat soared towards the tanker. Anya smelt the toxic scent of fuel for the first time, as it whirled into smoke behind them. The huge ship became bigger and bigger against a sky of dark clouds. When they were close, what had been just a shape on the horizon became a massive, rusted metal wall nearly forty feet high. When they were an arm's length away, Anya placed her hand against the rust-red paintwork and felt the cold reality of steel. Her fingertips became cold as ice as the boat absorbed her heat.

Two ropes came down, which Rosita and Barnaby secured to either side of the speedboat, and it was hoisted into the air. The tanker creaked; it was a giant metal creature, so different to the Ark. It wasn't natural, it wasn't wooden, but it was alive.

Anya neglected to notice that beside her Cayden and even Wilson had turned rather pale. Every Arker aboard had failed to fully consider what they were getting themselves into, and though the process was slow as the pulley squeaked and the boat swayed in the wind, their destination was certain.

The sky was dark and it began to rain; Anya could smell the fumes from the tanker's mighty funnel. She turned to see Cayden holding Simone's hand, and wondered whether it was for her safety or for his. When Anya turned to see the Ark; it was far away, so small and insignificant now despite its mighty size.

A few more heaves and the small boat was finally level with the deck of the gargantuan oil tanker. Anya saw a whole new world open up to her, but it wasn't one of beauty. It was rusted, cold and dark. Black shadows in raincoats ushered Anya across. One by one they crossed the small gap that separated the boat from the tanker, and when Anya's foot reached the icy chill of the metal deck, she felt disconnected from the water, as though upon stepping onto the steel there was no turning back.

The floodlights lit up around the outside of the ship, brighter than anything Anya had ever seen, and she brought up a hand to shield her eyes. She wanted to change back to her green form and hiss, to screech and jump back into the water, to swim as far away as possible.

The sound of screeching metal echoed across the colossal structure, and when Anya's eyes adjusted a little more, she stumbled forward to take it all in. The tanker stretched far and wide. Railings surrounded the sides and the outer platform upon which Anya stood; the middle of the vessel was flat and all on one level; and she looked up and to the right to see the funnel and the vessel's mighty bridge. She looked around to see many more last souls; they were all the way around the tanker and busy at work.

Anya saw a group of last souls in grey overalls run toward her from the bridge; it was strange to see so many people wearing real clothes rather than sea leathers. The men in grey were pushing a metal bed on wheels toward her. Behind these men was a short dark brown-haired gentleman in a long white coat. Anya watched as Barnaby and Nameless lifted Simone onto the bed, unconscious, as the man in the gleaming white lab coat approached.

Anya tried to run forward, feeling the urge to protect them, but she couldn't move. Cayden and Wilson also appeared to have frozen due to the brightness of the lights, but when Caleb saw what was going on, he panicked. "Get away from her!" he shouted.

"She'll be safe with me; my name is Doctor Phillips. You remember doctors, don't you?"

Caleb was hunched over, his breathing heavy; he looked like a wild animal amidst this company. He was ready to fight, but then a child-like look appeared on his face for a moment. "A doctor?"

"Yes, that's it. Remember?" Doctor Phillips said. "I'm going to help her," he continued with a nod as the trolley came past.

"No!" Cayden shouted, and he ran at them. Four of the last souls tried to apprehend him, but he was much stronger than they, and he threw the first one to the side with ease, and then another. Barnaby ran toward him, but he too was knocked away with two punches.

Nameless stopped pushing the bed and turned to see what was happening. He ran, jumped, and kneed Cayden in the face in one fell swoop. Cayden was out, and so Wilson ran to his side.

"What the hell are you doing?" Wilson asked, but Nameless ignored him and continued to follow the trolley. Four more last souls surrounded Wilson, tand then they carried Cayden in the direction in which they had wheeled Simone.

Anya wanted to help, but Rosita placed a hand on her shoulder. "He's dangerous, Anya—as I would be, if I was in his situation; we have to give him the help he needs."

"Where are you taking them?" Anya demanded as she watched Cayden and Wilson being escorted to the doors.

"Somewhere where they can get the help they need. Simone's going to our medical bay; we have enough rooms here for all of you."

Anya watched Wilson give a cold glare before he passed beyond the doors and the last souls closed them behind the group. Only Anya was left. She didn't like this place; she didn't like it at all. It made her feel small and helpless, compared to the Ark and the beautiful world below it.

"You don't want to overcrowd her during the birth; here, come with me," Rosita said before walking away, towards the staircase to the bridge. Anya followed close behind, her feet echoing on the ice-cold metal. The stairs ahead looked better kept than any she had seen under water.

She admired the looming structure as she held on to the handrail and followed Rosita. Anya focused on her black hooded raincoat and red hair to distract her from the stairs. Up and up they went until they stopped at a large metal door that opened with a loud creak. Rosita went inside and Anya waited for a moment before finally following her in. The room smelt strange—of metal. It was cold and dark, but a little brighter than those Anya had seen below, although without algae, coral, or fish. Everything was dry. Bone dry.

Rosita closed the door behind her, turned on a light, and Anya flinched. The room seemed to hum above her in a strange way. She noticed the lack of wind, of movement: the room was a box, closed to the elements, and therefore it felt dead. Anya had never known such quiet, or such stillness, above the surface.

There were a large number of screens dotted around, and many buttons. Anya saw the ship's wheel, which was much smaller than she had imagined from the pirate tales of old.

"This is the bridge from which I command the ship, and that's the wheel I use to steer."

Anya placed a hand upon it to feel the smooth leather texture, and as she stood at the wheel, she felt like a sea captain, like Wilson; then she dismissed such immature thoughts. She moved toward a cylinder on three legs, an alien thing.

"That's a telescope; you put your eye to it," Rosita said, before walking to an old red couch at the back of the room and sitting down. She flicked her boots off and sank back as if all was well, whilst Anya approached the telescope with caution.

Anya smelt it at first, and then she looked into it, and everything came into focus. She saw the Ark in the distance, her home. Even from here, she could see everyone and everything: the hunters, the makers, the chefs salting fish to keep it fresh, and the children at play. Then she saw Uncle Isaac on the dock; he was staring at the tanker, and Anya waved. She waited for him to wave back and then she stepped back from the telescope and realised that her uncle couldn't see her. Anya wondered how long the last souls had been watching her people for, and whether they already knew whether she was the green girl.

"It's beautiful, isn't it?" Rosita asked.

"It is."

Anya backed away until her legs bumped into a large desk wooden desk. She had seen a desk like it before, but only under water. The wood on the Ark and down below was so rotten, so worn, but this was smooth and varnished. She ran a hand along the surface before noticing the map.

"Those are nautical charts, for sea captains to calculate distance and plot journeys—at least they did before the flood. Now everywhere we go is the same."

Anya didn't respond, for she had seen something else. It was a globe, the entire earth as it was before the flood, blue and green. "Wilson told me about these," she said.

"That's the world, Anya, the whole world," Rosita

replied. "Or at least it was. What I wouldn't give to have it back. I would give everything, wouldn't you?"

Anya thought for a moment. She would give everything for the Ark, but then she thought about the water dwellers and how perfect their way of life was. "I would do anything to help my people, to give them freedom from the cold and rain."

"As would I."

"There was so much green."

"A third of the earth used to be land."

"Why is some of it green and some brown?"

"Some is grass and some desert. I guess you've never seen sand?"

Anya had to think for a moment, for she had seen sand many times at the bottom—but she would never say how. "No, I haven't, but I've been told what it is. What are the white bits?"

"Those are mountains, ice and snow-covered rocks high above the earth."

"Do you think they were flooded?"

"I don't know, we've sailed to many places and are yet to see anything above the water, except for the rig of course."

Anya imagined travelling the whole world. Even if it was under water, she could see it all with Oracle.

"The earth was beautiful: every continent and every country had a different language, a different way of life. It was incredible, but like everything, it had to end. We took too much from it."

"What do you mean?" Anya asked.

"We took every resource the old world had to offer, we bled it dry, and so it took everything from us. It was hard enough to keep this ship; I have one hundred and fifty people here who fight to survive every day. My people, *our* people, are the last people on this earth, Anya, but my people are not as strong as yours, they can't survive hardship like yours can and I fear for them. We need warmth, we need sheets and showers and heat."

Anya knew what Rosita was hinting at: she would soon be speaking of how Anya might help, how Anya could save them by fixing the oil platform. "I think it's time I went to see Simone," she said.

"No, Simone will be fine … she needs a doctor, and you need to rest. Come, sit with me."

Rosita sat on her old red couch; she looked quite relaxed and had taken off her black raincoat, her boots and long-sleeved shirt; now she was wearing a grey vest and black jeans, where Anya remained in her sea leathers. Anya sat down and sank into the strange soft couch; she tried many different positions—lying back, staying up on the edge—but none of them seemed right; she had never sunk into anything like this before.

Rosita came forward and pushed Anya's curly dark hair out of her eyes. "Relax, you're safe here, I promise. Close your eyes." Anya hesitated for a moment before doing so. "What do you hear?" Rosita asked.

"I don't hear anything."

"What do you smell?"

"Rusty worn metal."

"Well, thanks, I didn't say anything about the smell of your Ark!"

Anya couldn't help but laugh, and she opened her eyes to look at Rosita once more, and then she looked past her to a bookshelf. "Are those what I think they are?" she asked as she picked one out and held it upside down.

"They are the last books on earth. I saved as many as I could."

Anya couldn't read, but she knew by the way the elders reminisced just how important they were.

"We could only save a few hundred, but we do have a library."

"I can't read very well," Anya said.

"Books are an incredible thing, maybe I can teach you some day?"

"Maybe," Anya said, before placing the book back on the shelf. "What are these?" she asked.

"Those are magazines," Rosita replied.

Anya withdrew a magazine from the cascading pile; it was pink and had a girl with sunglasses and beautiful hair on the front.

"You will like that one, it's full of pictures."

Anya picked up the magazine and looked at the woman on the front: her straight blonde hair, her sunglasses, handbag and jewellery.

"She looks like you."

Rosita couldn't help but laugh. "Her? I have more style than her!"

Anya flicked through the pages. The colours were a little faded, but you could tell that they were once bright pinks and oranges. Pictures of people laughing and embracing gave her a view of another world. Their shining white teeth and make-up made them look alien. Each page brought another glimpse of what was lost.

"What are they doing?" Anya asked as she stared at a girl sitting at a dressing table whilst her friend gave her a makeover.

"They're making each other look nice."

"Why?"

"For confidence, for boys."

"Oh."

Rosita took a moment to think of the right thing to say. "Many things were different back then. We had everything, and when you have everything, people needed more and more to be entertained. They took things for granted; those who survived lost their vanity and our world is a better place without it."

Anya flicked another page to see two swimsuit models. The girls had orange skin, bleach-blonde hair, and large curves. Her eyes widened, and she felt a little embarrassed. "Is this how you used to look?"

"Ah, no. Not me, I was too rock-and-roll."

On the opposite page was a muscular male model with long hair, and Anya's eyes widened again. "Jeez, what are these?"

"Those are abs, Anya, rock-hard abs."

"Why does no one on the Ark look like these people?"

Rosita laughed again. "If they did, I probably would have stayed aboard!" The two of them burst into laughter until Anya turned a page and saw a holiday advertisement with sandy beaches. The sight of such a thing put her brain into overload. She had a sudden phantom pain on her leg from where the kraken had touched her, and then she remembered how Neptune had saved her.

"You look tired," Rosita said, and Anya was indeed running on empty; she had barely slept, and it was sunrise. "Why don't I show you to your cabin?"

"Cabin?"

"It's a little like your sleeping shacks."

"I don't know, I really need to see the others …"

"Nonsense, your friends will be fine and will do better if they see you well-rested."

Rosita led Anya down a narrow corridor and down another staircase, this one indoors. She could hear all the metal clink as she moved, and every corridor looked the same, rust-red, as they passed through the labyrinth. They went through many doors until Rosita stopped at one.

"You're going to like this," she said before lifting the latch and forcing it open to reveal a beautiful room. Anya stepped in and for the first time ever her feet touched fresh fluffy carpet. The gentle warmth between her toes brought a sweet feeling of release as she stepped forward into the dimly lit space.

"Just wait until you try the sheets," Rosita said, pointing to the crisp white bedding; but Anya stayed still. She had been told of such comforts a thousand times and had considered them to be folklore, having never seen any above the surface. She looked at Rosita with a puzzled face. She felt dirty; everyone on the Ark was filthy compared to this place, and she didn't feel fit in her fish leathers to touch such a perfect thing.

"I'm sorry, I can't; look at me, I'm filthy."

"Well, through there is the shower."

"A shower?"

Rosita opened another door and there was a bright white and blue tiled bathroom. Anya had never seen anything so clean as she looked around at the walls and then the ceiling. She watched Rosita over at the sink as she turned a dial, and Anya flinched in disbelief. Then Rosita went over to the shower and pressed a button. It was like rain, and Anya was in awe.

"When I leave, you can have a shower; there's soap and shampoo, dry yourself with a towel before you lie down on the bed. Soap is for—"

"I know what soap is, duh."

"Well, you Arkers don't smell like you do."

"How rude!" Anya shouted in jest, and Rosita laughed. Though Anya knew Rosita had a hard outer shell, she couldn't help but see her as a big sister, no matter how many times Wilson had told her to keep her guard up.

"Sorry, Anya, I have to go," Rosita said, in a sudden rush as she turned to leave. "Have a shower and I'll bring you some food as soon as I can, okay?"

"Okay."

The door closed behind her and Anya was left alone. Everything was silent without the hustle and bustle of the other Arkers or the sound of the ocean. Everything was white, blinding white, and the electric light above her hummed ever so slightly. Anya made her way to the bathroom and stared at her reflection, her worn sea leathers and her long curly brown hair. She had grown taller since the last time she had seen her reflection; she was far wiser, too, and carried far more scars than before her journey down below. She remembered the day in the office block when she had stared at herself in the mirror, when it had all been taken away; little did she know that it would be returned with many other gifts.

She took off her top and bottoms. She didn't judge: she just was, and she accepted herself as such. Her hair went over her shoulders and down her back, and then, in the blink of an eye, she turned to her green scaled form. Her yellow eyes were glowing, her scales shining, her fangs long and sharp. Anya looked at her claws and the way her green body glimmered blue in the light. She smiled, and within the blink of an eye, she turned back to her human form and headed for the shower.

Anya pressed the button and jumped back to watch the rain come down once more. She examined the strange device and tried to imagine where the water came from, and then she placed a very hesitant hand under the water. It was warm. Soon her whole body followed, and she let out a huge sigh as all the tension of every struggling day seemed to wash away. The warmth of the water was unlike anything she had ever experienced; it was heaven. Anya had heard elders talk of shampoo, so she took the bottle and squirted some into her hand before rubbing it into her hair. Next, she washed her body with soap, and then she let it all drain away.

Anya knew now more than ever what the old world was like: it was warm, and it was quiet. She wondered how something so simple as taking a shower could be such bliss. There was something about this room, this place, that made her feel safe; she was free from the woes of the Ark and the judgements of the water dwellers. She sank down, held her knees to her chest and shielded herself from the world as the water ran all around her. She sat there and let all the dirt of the Ark wash away, and she knew peace for the first time.

When she was done, she took the white towel and dried herself and half-dried her hair. There was a robe by her side, and she felt its softness before slipping it on. It was one more thing to amaze her, one more thing to teach her of the old world—the softness of cotton.

There was a knock at the door and Anya opened it slightly to peer out. Rosita was carrying a tray of strange things, foods long since lost: biscuits, fresh fruit, and some sort of broth. "How was the shower?" she asked.

"Amazing, I've never—"

"Just wait until you try the bed. Now, come over to the dressing table, let's dry your hair and get you some moisturiser."

Anya sat down awkwardly at the dressing table and once again beheld her reflection. Around her was a clean wooden surface, and the furniture was so immaculate compared to anything she had seen before. She sat down on the edge of the stool, and when Rosita turned on the hairdryer, the loud roaring noise made her jump.

"What's that!" she shouted.

"Don't worry, it's perfectly safe," Rosita said, so Anya slowly made her way back onto the stool whilst covering her ears.

Rosita began brushing her hair and blow drying.

Anya remained perfectly still, wary of making any wrong move. It was only when she looked at herself properly and the volume of her curls that she understood. Her hair was bouncing, fresh and beautiful.

Rosita knelt down and took something from a drawer. "Close your eyes," she said, and at first Anya didn't know whether to trust her—but still, she had come this far.

Rosita applied a cream to Anya's face and let it settle before applying eyeliner around her eyes. "Open them."

Anya looked in the mirror. She had never considered herself to be a thing of beauty, and the memory of her reflection in the water was overshadowed by the office block. Now she looked back at herself with confidence.

Rosita put an arm over her shoulder and held her; she knew it was an emotional moment for her; it would be for anyone.

"I'm sorry, I just—I didn't know that this, that this could be—"

"I know, Anya, I know. It must be tough for you girls—but you can come here any time you need to, and so can anyone else who needs our help. Anyway, let's not talk about that now, you need a good meal."

Rosita picked up the food tray and placed it on the dressing table in front of Anya. Then she passed Anya a spoon for her soup before sitting down on the edge of the bed.

Anya took her first spoonful; it was hot and strange, unlike anything she had ever tasted, unlike any fish broth. "What's in this?" she asked.

"Potato and leek … We have a hydroponic farming system, row after row of fresh vegetables. We make wheat and flower, even sugar cane. The biscuits are for special occasions."

Anya had a sip of soup before drinking it all from the bowl and moving on to the biscuits. It was the first time in her life that she had tasted sugar, and she could not describe how sickly sweet it was. Every bit was delicious, and she swallowed it down with a glass of cold water.

"I didn't know it was possible to still live like this."

"Anything's possible here, but the haven we've created didn't come without struggle. I've fought for this, bled for this, as I'm sure you've bled for yours."

Anya knew at that moment that Rosita was just like her.

"You look beautiful, by the way; I want you to know that. Here, I want to take a photograph of you."

Rosita took a small device out of her pocket and Anya her gave a stern, uncertain look. "This is a camera; all you have to do is smile."

Anya tried her best to force one.

"Great … I'll show you the print later."

Anya nodded, as if she knew what Rosita was talking about, and Rosita checked her watch. "You still look tired. Once you've rested, I'll take you to see Simone; she's doing well, by the way. We have a state-of-the-art medical bay. There's a fresh set of pyjamas on the pillow that should be really comfy. Have a good sleep."

"Goodnight," Anya replied. Rosita shut the door

behind her, and she was left alone once more. It was quiet, so quiet, and everything was white and spotless. She changed from the dressing gown into the pyjamas that were laid out on the bed.

Alone again, she listened for the wind, but it was gone, along with the rain and the constant rush of water. She stared at the bedding for a long time, rather unsure of what to make of it until she peeled back the covers. Anya sniffed them, and rubbed her hands across the soft cotton over and over, to check that all was safe; then she jumped into the bed. On all fours she crawled around, before bouncing up and down. The bed was as soft as a cloud, and she lay looking up at the ceiling with a huge smile on her face before pulling the duvet over her. She remained still, and then she pressed the nightlight, as Rosa had done. She closed her eyes and within a heartbeat she fell fast asleep.

7

COMFORT

Anya awoke from the deepest sleep she had ever had. The bed was so comfortable, so warm and fresh, that she had slept right through. Then she remembered Simone. She got up and made for the door in her pyjamas. She caught a glimpse of her sea leathers on a coat peg, but instead of putting them on, she left in her pyjamas. Anya ran along endless cold metal corridors with identical numbers of doors. She searched for a way out, as the corridor closed in around her. She ran so fast around a corner that she crashed into Barnaby before falling to the floor.

"Woah! You need to watch where you're going little one," he said, exposing his crooked teeth in a smile.

"I'm sorry, I'm lost. Can you take me to Simone, has she had the baby?"

"Rosita was just coming to get you, follow me."

Together they made their way down a few more corridors and flights of stairs to a door with a red cross painted on it. Barnaby opened it up and led Anya inside; the room was a dull cream colour, and within were a number of hospital beds, all perfectly made. One had a drawn curtain. Behind the curtain Anya saw Simone, who was resting with her child in her arms. Doctor Phillips sat on a chair close by, writing an entry in his journal.

"Anya," Simone said with a worn but welcome smile.

"Hi, how ... how did it go?"

"The little devil nearly tore me in two, but I feel pretty good after the gas. We did well, didn't we, Doctor Phillips?"

"I don't think I'd ever heard so much profanity, but yes, very well. To be completely honest, I don't know how any of you would give birth on that, *thing*."

"That *thing* is our home," Anya warned.

"Oh, sorry, I meant nothing by it. It's just that anyone in my profession would want you to be as comfortable as possible, and to have the right level of care. It makes me sad that in less than a year, our lights will go out for good."

Anya could see the doctor much better than on her arrival. His short brown hair was perfect, and he had no muscle, unlike the people on the Ark. His skin was smooth and not red and rough like most with his pale complexion.

"Doctor Phillips has been asking me lots of questions."

"What sort of questions?" Anya asked.

"Oh, just about how many of you there are, how long you live for, how many young and old. Everything, really," Doctor Phillips said, but Anya was distracted by the tiny child in Simone's arms. "I've called her Fiona; that was your mother's name too, wasn't it?" she asked.

"It was," Anya replied.

"Do you want to hold her? Come on, sit down and hold her."

"Go on Anya, hold her, she won't bite," Doctor Phillips echoed.

Anya sat down on the chair next to Simone's bed. She readied her hands for the child, having never held one herself. "Okay, here you go," Simone said as she passed Fiona over.

The child was tiny in her arms; she had dark eyes and in them Anya saw the future. She was the first child born since Anya had made her great underwater venture, and the first Arker to be born outside the Ark.

"She's very healthy, and I'm sure she'll be as strong as you," Anya said.

"Or as strong as you," Simone replied with a smile.

"You must be strong to have been raised in such conditions Anya," Doctor Phillips said. "You, must have spent your entire life on that thing," he continued.

"I have, and I wouldn't have changed it for the world—or for your tanker. And that thing has a name, it's called the Ark."

"I understand, and again, I don't mean to offend. I just want to understand you. Now, Simone was telling me that there's a very strange illness afoot."

"Yes, yes there is," Anya replied as she finally looked up from Fiona.

"We have lots of medication, and I would very

much like to examine some of the ill. Perhaps you could arrange this with Rosita?"

Anya didn't know what to say, and she wondered what else Simone may have said. She politely returned Fiona to her and watched the pair of them; there was something so special about a mother and child cuddling in clean blankets in the warmest and safest place she had ever seen.

"Rosita and I will talk," Anya said, in belated reply.

"Also, Simone told me about another illness that affects the old and the young."

"Where are Wilson and Cayden?" Anya asked in hopes of changing the subject.

"Cayden had to be locked up after his outburst; he was a danger to us all. We couldn't have him running around like a wild man."

"And Wilson?"

"The bitter old grump is just down the corridor."

Anya got to her feet and wandered down in his direction. She found Wilson in one chair and his old wrinkled feet resting on another. His old worn captain's hat and large navy jacket appeared even more out of place here than they did on the Ark, as they contrasted with the dull yellow room around them.

"Nice of you to join us," Wilson said as he stroked his beard. "How was rubbing shoulders with the enemy?"

"No, actually I was—"

"Well, whatever you've got to say, your gleaming white pyjamas say otherwise. You're playing right into their hands—have I not taught you anything?"

Anya made sure no one was listening and then she crouched down. "What would you have me do? Let Simone and the baby die on the Ark? Have more women go through what too many have already been through?"

"I've a bad feeling about this, Anya, this place is full of ghosts." Wilson pointed down the corridor, where one of the last souls was lingering at the corner. "Notice how they keep checking up on us, they don't want to leave us alone."

"They left me all night."

"Oh, I bet they did, behind closed doors all safe and sound."

At that moment, Barnaby came thumping down the corridor with Doctor Phillips. "Ah, Anya, Mister Wilson," Doctor Phillips said.

"It's just Wilson."

"Okay, well—*Just Wilson*, we need a favour: we need you to calm Cayden down. He hasn't stopped banging on his door all morning and it must be hurting his hands."

"Well, it might be because you locked him away after kidnapping his pregnant wife."

Doctor Phillips held his polite nervous smile, as if he was unable to deal with confrontation. "Oh, yes, I suppose … Follow me."

The pair followed Doctor Phillips toward Cayden's makeshift cell. Another long corridor and two sets of stairs later, they could hear banging on a metal door ahead. Four last souls were standing guard, their eyes fixed upon Anya and Wilson as they arrived.

"Cayden, if we let you out, will you promise to behave?" shouted one of the guards, and there was silence for a brief moment before Cayden banged against the door from the other side.

"Let me out, let me out. You took her from me, she needs me!"

"Cayden, It's Wilson! You have a baby girl waiting for you on this side of the door, but these raincoat-wearing softies won't let you out unless you promise to behave."

There was silence for a moment. "It's a trick!" he shouted, before booting the door again.

"Can we go in?" Anya asked.

"I'd let you in, but that guy would overpower an old man and someone of your stature in a heartbeat, miss," said one of the guards. "We can't allow it."

Anya shoved them back with ease as Wilson stayed close behind her. She unbolted the door and pushed her way inside before closing the door behind them. With the last souls outside, Cayden ran at the door full pelt, but Anya grabbed hold of him and launched him to the other end of the room so hard that he toppled over the couch and landed on the floor.

"What the hell do you think you're you doing?" she asked. "Simone's had the baby without you because you couldn't keep control of yourself."

Cayden crawled out from behind the sofa. He looked at them both for a moment, his head in his hands, and then he began to cry. It was something Anya had never expected of the blonde-mohawked fighter who, for a moment, seemed more like a child.

"They have electricity, rooms free of water, boots, clothes—they have everything. We've been living on that thing for so long, and there are places like this! It's alright for you, you can escape whenever you want, take your whale and go, but not me, not my family. Do you think I want to raise my child on the Ark?"

Anya didn't know what to say. She took a seat on the small kitchen counter nearby rather than the chairs around her as Wilson approached Cayden, offered him a hand, and after a moment Cayden went to accept it. At that moment, Wilson slapped him across the face as hard as he could.

"Look, Cayden," Wilson said. "Being a father is the hardest thing in the world, trust me. You have to make it up as you go along. Forget the Ark, forget the tanker, because right now, you have something much more important to fight for. Part of you may want to run or hide, but you have to go out of that door, you have to face them, whatever the future brings."

"Thanks, I needed that," Cayden said as he began marching toward the door.

"Wait," Wilson insisted. "This might be our *only* moment alone together; we need to talk about this place."

"Well, what do you think of it?" Anya asked.

"They seem genuine, but I still don't trust them," Wilson continued. "Rosita, Barnaby and the doctor are the only ones who'll talk to us. Everyone else looks sheepish and afraid, and that Nameless fellow hasn't showed his face since we got here; there's something not right about all this. What did you do when you arrived, Anya?"

"Rosita showed me the bridge, the controls, some books and magazines—that was it really."

"Did you see anything out of place, anything at all?"

"No."

"Something's not right …"

"Something doesn't always have to be wrong Wilson. I like her, and come to think of it, I like this place."

There was a knock on the door and Anya unlocked it. Barnaby entered first, followed by Doctor Phillips and a few more of the last souls.

"So, Cayden, are you ready to see your little girl?" Doctor Phillips asked, and Cayden nodded.

The Arkers were led down the corridor and up the many stairs to the medical bay. At the top, Cayden pushed past them all and ran towards Simone. When he reached her side, he stopped upon seeing the new life in his wife's arms for the first time. At that moment, the boisterous sea-weed wine drinking master hunter façade melted away, and he became a father.

"You big dumb idiot," Simone said before he leant down and tried to kiss her. He took her hand and sat beside her in the chair, which bowed below his mighty weight.

"I'm sorry, I was afraid. I'll never leave your side again," he replied as he hung his head in shame.

Anya and Wilson looked on. Anya knew that they had to give them the privacy they required as a family, so she stayed back, but behind her and Wilson were four raincoats and the overgrown lump that was Barnaby. She wondered whether Wilson was right, and that, wherever they were, the last souls weren't far behind. Moments later, Rosita and Doctor Phillips came in by another door. They were both smiling, and Rosita had a basket covered with a cloth.

"Hello there Arkers, did we all have nice morning snooze?" Rosita asked, but Anya didn't answer for Wilson's look of disdain. "What about you grandpa?"

"I'm nobody's grandpa, and no, I didn't sleep because this ship is too loud."

"Aww well, you must be tired, and hungry. We brought you some lunch from our hydroponic garden. Why don't we eat outside and leave the new family to get acquainted?"

"Why don't you—" Wilson tried to say.

"We would like that," Anya replied having interrupted him.

They walked through the endless metal labyrinth, up some stairs, and then they were outside. Anya could breathe again, and this time Rosita walked them to the front of the ship. There was a picnic table on the deck. Anya and Wilson sat down, and Rosita put down the basket to reveal bananas, apples, and tomatoes. Even Wilson found it hard to hide his surprise at such foreign luxuries.

"How did you do it?" Wilson asked as he examined one of the apples.

"We managed to get our hands on all sorts of seeds, and now we have quite a garden, but really it's all thanks to the oil …"

Wilson took a suspicious bite of his apple, and his face seemed to shrivel for the sourness before he had had to hide his smile for the taste. Anya watched him before picking one up too and taking her first bite. It was sour but sweet, and crisp, but it fell to nothing in her mouth. It didn't taste like fish, and she really wasn't sure how her stomach would take to it. She tried to eat the whole thing, stalk and core, but Rosita snatched it from her.

"Don't eat the middle," she said.

Anya gave a suspicious scowl and then she tried the banana by biting straight into the skin.

"Don't eat the skin!" Rosita said.

"Eat the skin, don't eat the skin, eat the middle, don't eat the middle … which one is it?"

Rosita laughed. "You peel the skin of a banana." She peeled it for Anya, and when Anya tasted it, she found it much sweeter than the apple; softer, too. Next came something else, something that took even Wilson by surprise.

"You have wheat?" he asked.

"We do."

Wilson took a piece of the bread. It was hard and crusty, but he took a bite and swallowed it down nonetheless. Anya took a bite too, but she was less than pleased: it was hard to chew and heavy compared to the fresh fish they were used to.

"We have luxuries here, as you've seen, and we see no reason to hide them from you. If your Ark wishes to share them, then I welcome it. I don't want anyone to go hungry."

"Neither do I," Anya said, but Wilson sighed and folded his arms.

"Anyone but stubborn old men whose rotten old ways should have drowned with the flood at least," Rosita said with a smug smile.

No one was surprised, for Wilson had poked and pushed her and all her people whenever he could since his arrival. "What'd you say to me?" he asked.

"I save a child's life, I let you in to our world to make peace, and still, you sit there like a miserable old man missing his right to tell kids to keep off the lawn."

"Finally, the shell cracks," Wilson said as he pointed at her with his mouth wide open.

"Stop it, both of you," Anya said, but she knew too well that Rosita had just earned Wilson's respect more than anything.

Rosita took a moment to calm herself. "I'm sorry, Anya, I've said what I wanted to say. Now, do you want to see our garden, our supplies?"

"We do," Anya replied.

Rosita led them back down endless flights of stairs and into darkness. Down they went and then, through a set of double doors, they were in a storeroom as wide as the tanker. Stretching as far as the eye could see were shelves filled with endless supplies and boxes piled high.

"This was all for oil, but we converted it into storage. Now it contains our spoils from the early days. We worked non-stop to fish whatever we could out of the water and dry it off. We maintain rigorous stock checks and keep certain supplies for only the most special occasions."

Side by side they walked between the rows of shelves; bright lights lit the place in long strips all the way down, and Anya saw members of the last souls hard at work.

"Are you ready for the real surprise?" Rosita asked.

"A surprise?" Anya responded—and then she saw it. At the end of the shelves the cold rusted metal opened up into a forest garden. There was soil and grass, and tall trees holding big red apples. There were green pears, oranges, and bananas. Even palm trees with coconuts and bushes of berries. There was wheat and barley, potatoes, and carrot tops sticking out of the ground ready to pick. It was a world of colour, of life, the like of which Anya had never seen before. Even Wilson wasn't frowning any more.

"How did you do this?" he asked.

"With great difficulty ... We use hydroponics, the roof opens up too and we use the sun where we can." Rosita had a small box in hand; she pressed a button and Anya watched the ceiling split in two above her. The metal doors above let the blue sky flood down through the garden. Anya said no words; she walked ahead of the others and her feet met the soft green grass as she wandered in. It smelt wonderful, fresher than anything she had ever smelt, and she couldn't help but take to her knees to look at the flowers.

"It's beautiful," she said as Rosita approached her.

"This is what I missed most about being on land, Anya: the gardens, the living breathing flow of nature, so I thought why not bring it back to life."

"I feel privileged to see it."

"I wish there was more. Before the flood there were forests, fields, and great big gardens. Without oil, the plants are hard to germinate in cloudy weather. The hydroponic equipment we use requires energy."

"If you had enough oil, would you have enough food for the Ark as well?"

"I don't see why not. Now, follow me this way, I can show you our other storeroom."

Anya and Wilson followed close behind and they soon entered another large room, with crates of goods piled high to the ceiling.

"During the flood, this ship was a trade vessel. It was used to transfer goods and my father managed to catch it just at the right time. We used the crane on the east side to fish for other goods, and he found a few large warehouses whilst the water levels weren't too high and lifted many things out. We make sure we ration everything and keep an accurate log of all stock."

Anya had never seen anything like it. The room was full of tins of vegetables, and there were many small plain white boxes. "What are those?" she asked.

"That's our pharmacy. And those drums over there, they contain oil—everything from our showers to our appliances and food growth is reliant on oil. Without it, this place will be a cold heap of metal, and our people will be without hope. That is why I asked you for help."

Anya looked at the barrels, most of which were turned on their side and empty. She knew that that the subject would arise sooner or later. Teaching them to survive would be one thing, and she didn't know where to begin, but Anya knew she had the power to keep the lights on for hundreds of years to come. She wondered what Uncle Isaac would do and whether he would reconsider. She thought long and hard about it, and then Doctor Phillips approached.

"I'm delighted to say that Simone is doing incredibly well. I insisted that they both stay for a few days to ensure that little Fiona is fit and healthy. That is with your permission, of course …."

"They're most welcome," replied Rosita.

"I think it would be best, too," Anya agreed. "I'll make for the Ark and tell them the good news."

"Anya, wait. I want you to stay, too."

Anya looked at Wilson, who folded his arms with a frown, and then she looked back to her host. "We would be delighted."

8

THE DECISION

The next two days were a blur. Anya didn't grow to like the cold metal walls, but she did enjoy the tanker's hot showers and fresh fruit. She found peace; this was a place of relaxation, and she had again taken to the meditation that Neptune had once tried to teach her. The constant stress of the Ark melted away with clean white sheets and other comforts. Anya was more relaxed than she had ever been, yet this simpler life was having an effect on her in other ways. She felt a little less sharp, and she was losing touch with the ocean.

Anya craved to dive, to swim with Oracle, but she knew that if she did, Rosita would know that she was the green girl, and then she would have no choice but to help her. She remembered her uncle's reservations but despite their want for her to distrust these people, she felt a connection to the last souls and their old ways.

She tried her best to analyse them, but she was conscious of their constant wish to appease her, and it was growing harder to notice anything amiss. The last souls were all polite, well dressed and well fed; everyone she saw was happy—though she had noticed that only Rosita's lieutenants spoke to her, while most of the workers stayed quiet. The only person who appeared out of place was Wilson. He kept to himself, but at every opportunity he berated the last souls; he was awkward, rude, and downright ungrateful for everything. He was baiting them, but none of them ever took the bait and that only annoyed him even more. The rest of his time was spent staring out toward the vast sea with cap in hand when he wasn't trying to find something wrong with the place.

Anya noticed that he even spoke to her less, and when he did, he always told her to be careful, and to remember the Ark's ways. She began to wonder whether he had another reason; maybe it pained him to see her looking up to Rosita and requesting her advice over his?

Anya's mind had wandered far from the Ark, and even farther from the Oasis. The thing that brought back again was the arrival of a kayak on the morning of the third day. Aboard was her brother Jake, his blond curls half wet and blowing in the wind. The sight of him brought Anya great relief. Jake had brought with him a child named Patrick; he was pale and gaunt and had been one of the first to fall ill.

In the early morning sun, the last souls raised the rowing boat to the tanker's deck. Jake was dressed in his sea-leather poncho, which contrasted with Anya's blinding white gown.

"Sea-sister, what the hell are you wearing?" he asked as he stepped onto the deck.

"I'm so happy to see you," Anya replied with a sigh of relief, and though he hesitated for not wanting to ruin her clothes, Anya held him tight.

"Look at you, you look … you look so clean it's disgusting!"

"And you smell like fish-guts."

"Eh, I've smelt worse. How are you?"

"I'm great, actually. There's so much I want to show you, they have trees and fruits and beds—"

"Where are the others?" he asked without care for such comforts.

"Simone and Cayden are well, but Wilson is tired of this place. I think it reminds him too much of the 'old' world," Anya replied.

"Actually, I've never been better," Wilson interrupted, approaching from behind.

"Why don't we have Jake row you home?" Anya asked, folding her arms.

"Not until you, Cayden, Simone, and Fiona are off this ship for good."

"How is it here?" Jake asked.

"Good," Anya replied, having stopped Wilson before he answered. "They've treated us well and there's so much that you have to see."

"I don't want to stay here for too long; I fear I'll be dressed up in white, like you. I only came to check on you, and to bring Patrick here to see the doctor."

Behind Jake was the frail and rather shy eight-year-old. He had stayed quiet whilst hiding in Jake's shadow. "He's got the sickness," Jake whispered, and then Patrick began to shiver.

Anya knelt down to Patrick's level. "It's okay, we'll get you the help you need," she said, before the boy hid behind Jake once more.

"How's the baby?" Jake asked.

"Fiona is her name, and you must see her before we do anything else, come!" Anya led the way, and watched Jake move with hesitation. He was off balance, and so was Patrick at his side. She had forgotten how quickly she had got used to the movement of the ship.

They made their way around the deck and Jake soon ended up carrying Patrick on his shoulders. They crossed the tanker and headed inside the creaky metal corridors. Here, a last soul led the way in his raincoat and Jake touched the walls to keep his balance. They soon arrived at the door of Cayden and Simone's room, where another of the last souls was standing close by.

Anya knocked on the door three times. "Prepare yourself, Cayden's gone rather soft."

"Soft?" Jake asked, and then the door opened.

"Jake, Anya, Patrick! Come in, come in, just wait until you see my beautiful wife and my new-born," Cayden with open arms.

Everyone froze. Anya saw that he was dressed in a button-down shirt and grey trousers. His Viking beard had been shaved, his hair was cut short and he was wearing spectacles. The room had two bunk beds, a cot for a child and its own cooking area, which was covered in leftovers and a stack of dirty plates.

"Did they take your leathers too?" Jake asked.

"Do you like them? Pin-stripe! I needed a change.

Oh, and these? These are spectacles; the doctor had a spare pair. Turns out I'm rather short-sighted."

Anya thought it strange that he was already dressing like the last souls, but then she looked down at her own gown and realised that she had done the exact same.

Cayden led them to the sitting room, where Simone was on the couch with Fiona in her arms. She too wore a long white dress. "Welcome Arkies," she said.

"Would you care for a bite to eat?" Cayden asked, and he threw an apple at Jake, who withdrew his hunting knife and caught it mid-air. Then he stared at the strange, bright red object with suspicion.

He smelt the fruit. "It smells of nothing." He licked it. "It doesn't taste of anything."

"You're supposed to bite into it," Cayden replied, but Jake flung it free from his knife and into the pile of dishes which fell and smashed on the floor. No one moved to clean it up. "Anyway, have you seen my little girl? Isn't she adorable?" Cayden asked as he sat alongside his wife and took Fiona in his arms.

"I see you've gone soft," Jake laughed.

"Me? Soft? Call me soft again and you'll see what a master hunter thinks of the word."

"He's only joking," Simone interjected.

"Ha-ha, only joking."

"He's very soft."

"Yes, very soft now. I've been talking to Doctor Phillips; he's been coaching me about my anger issues and my problems with seaweed wine."

At that point, no one else knew what to say. Cayden had gone from being a seasoned hunter drinking gallons of seaweed wine to a polite family man in only a few days.

"I'm glad to hear it." Jake said, breaking the silence. "Sorry for jumping right to the point but, when do you all want to go home? I'm sailing before sunset, so I can take you back today."

"Oh … I see," Cayden replied, and then he passed Fiona back to Simone before folding his arms. The happy couple turned to one another and then they whispered with each other.

"You don't have to decide right now, you have a few hours, I've come to take Patrick to the doctor is all, but if you're ready …"

Cayden took a moment to think things over. "Look, I was never a man of many words. I loved to fish and I loved to hunt. I was a Master Hunter, but that place, the harshness of it all; I did things I wasn't proud of." He turned to Anya. "I know what I did: I supported Tyson, and I sailed you to the middle of the ocean and cast you off the side. I know that you say you forgive me, Anya, but I don't forgive myself. The dishonour will forever be on my name, and so—"

"What Cayden's trying to say," Simone interrupted. "Is that the Ark isn't where we want to raise our child. We want to stay here, and we were wondering if you would give your blessing, Anya, and ask Rosita?"

Anya didn't know what to say. She looked at her brother in his fish leathers, the dark and broken child at his side, at little Fiona, and then the happy couple. She had seen at first hand the world they wanted for their child, and all the reasons for staying, but as the Ark's leader she had to stand up for her home.

"I understand, but the Ark's a part of you. It's our home."

"Cayden and I are more than thirty years old. The Ark was never our home, it is, and always has been our prison, and a cold one at that," Simone said. "We've spoken about it a lot, and we don't ever want to go back. You *must* speak to Rosita for us."

Anya wasn't expecting such a strong response, she wondered how many other Arkers would be thinking the same thing, and what right did she have to deny them. Even if the tanker was a better place for any child, the Ark was their home. "I'll speak with Rosita, but I can't guarantee her agreement."

"Thank you," Simone said, and the couple smiled at one another with satisfaction.

It was at that moment Patrick began coughing and wincing again. He stepped back towards the door and struggled to breathe, turning rather pale.

"Patrick, look at me," Jake said as he tried to calm him. "Anya, where's the doctor?"

They left the couple's room as quickly as they could and made their way to the medical bay, where Doctor Phillips was writing in his journal. When he saw the child, he guided him to a bed.

"Move along everyone, give us space. Is everything alright?" he asked. "Sit down, sit down." Doctor Phillips guided the boy to the edge of the bed. "Breathe," he continued, "just breathe. That's it, in through the nose and out through the mouth, on the count of four, yes, yes that's it."

Doctor Phillips checked his vitals, he looked at Patrick's arms, his ragged sea leathers, and then he took a picture book from the cupboard on the side and gave it to him. The distraction caused Patrick to take his mind off his breathing and catch his breath back. Patrick calmed himself down, "Lie back now, that's it. Close your eyes and rest, you're safe here."

Doctor Phillips sat with him for a while until the boy grew tired and fell asleep. Then he stood and approached Anya and the others.

"What is it, Doctor?" she asked.

"May we have a word in private?" he replied, and so the pair of them walked back down the corridor.

"What's wrong?"

"The boy has no physical ailments. He's fit as could be, I'd bet my life on it … but he does have severe anxiety." Anya gave Doctor Phillips a clueless look, and so he thought it right to define such a term. "It's easier to diagnose than to define, it's a state of worry, fear and panic."

"But what about the rhyme?" she asked.

"What rhyme?"

"I-I don't know the words off by heart … but the ill on the Ark, they all say strange words."

"Well, I can only diagnose what I see, and what I see is anxiety," Doctor Phillips replied. "All he needs is a good night's sleep and some therapy. On the tanker we talk about our feelings; we try to live free of stress. Do you do the same on your Ark?"

"No."

"Well, I can only imagine how stressful it is. I'll teach him some breathing exercises. Now, who's this young man ?" the doctor asked as he led Anya back to the hospital bed.

"This is my brother, Jake."

"Ah, I see; well, it's a pleasure to meet you. Any brother of Anya's is a brother of mine."

"Aren't you a little old to be my brother?"

"It's an expression …"

"Oh," Jake replied, scratching his head.

"Have you come to row the others home?"

"I have."

"I don't know if I will go," Anya said.

"Well, I'm rowing before sundown," Jake replied.

"Six o'clock, then?" the doctor asked.

"No, *sundown*," Jake reiterated.

"Never mind. Anyway, its time I gave you some supplies, as Rosita promised. Paracetamol for pain, amoxicillin for infections. Is there anyone on your Ark with medical experience?"

"Yes, Tiff the master carer," Anya replied.

"A master what?"

"A master carer. Tiff is the best at caring for the old and the sick, I think she was … a nurse, no, someone's wife or something."

"Ah, a midwife. Well I would very much like to meet her some time soon when I go to the Ark! That reminds me, Jake, you'll be taking supplies and gifts back with you. I've called through for Barnaby to help you load a rowing boat, which should fare better than your kayak."

"Whatever you say," Jake replied.

"And Anya. Just between us, I know how hesitant you are to trust us, that you have a lot on your plate, but believe me, there's a lot riding on this. Please, do speak with Rosita. Why don't you both leave Patrick to rest, and I'll have a word with him when he perks up a bit?"

Jake found it hard to disagree with the doctor's suggestion, but at that moment Patrick began to grow restless again. "Get away!" he shouted as he pointed at the group of last souls approaching his bedside.

Jake put himself between them; "It's okay, Patrick, everything's okay." He insisted, but then Patrick fell back again.

"What the hell just happened?" Jake asked as Doctor Phillips came to the boy's side.

"He just had a nightmare, that's all."

"You can't pretend that that was normal," Jake said in disbelief. "You lot, you must have done something to startle him," he continued as he pointed at Barnaby, Nameless and a few more last souls.

"Now now Jake, I know this is hard, but we must let him rest," Doctor Phillips said, "you have a long day ahead of you."

"Come on, Jake," Anya replied. "You have to ready the boat."

"The boat," Jake reminded himself as he looked around at all those present. "Are you coming with me?"

"No, you go on ahead, I have other things to do first."

The group of last souls escorted Jake, and he didn't say a word as they did. Anya turned to Patrick, she waited for him to wake, to say or do something to show Doctor Phillips the extent of his condition, but he didn't rouse.

"Doctor, what causes anxiety?"

"Oh, it can be anything: a person's surroundings, stress and pain, their upbringing. There can be many things—one's own way of thinking, perhaps. Do you have any idea what the cause might be on the Ark?"

"I-I don't know, but I've seen it myself: they look like they're possessed. Is there anything, any creature that can make a person behave like this?"

The doctor laughed. "I don't understand what you mean?"

"A sea creature, or something."

Doctor Phillips stopped laughing, and for the first time he dropped his polite smile. "I don't understand what you're saying, Anya. Have you ever heard of Occam's razor?"

"No."

"Well, it's the idea that the simplest explanation is usually the right one. What do you think the simplest answer is here?"

Anya had to think for a moment. "That he has anxiety?"

"Very good."

"So, what fixes it?"

"Well, talking about it, for one; confiding in others,

meditation, exercise, lifestyle changes, and sometimes medication—but only as a last resort."

The word 'meditation' stuck with Anya. She thought back to her days with Neptune and all that he had taught her, and she considered it would best to clear her mind. "I see, I think I need some fresh air."

"Very well, lets continue this conversation later on."

Anya made her way back up to the very edge of the tanker and looked out to sea. She sat cross legged as Neptune had taught her as she felt the sea breeze and the clouds above. She considered her inner demons and her struggle. She considered the water dwellers, and why she hadn't gone down to see them.

"What is stopping me? Life before the Shallows was so much simpler, all I ever wanted was to become a hunter, but when I drowned, everything changed. I put so much pressure on myself to return to the Ark that I missed so many beautiful moments down there, and what did I get when I returned home? Failure. I should have gone back to the Oasis, I should have gone back a long time ago. Why did it have to happen to me. I died and I came back, only to die and come back again—and for what? What was it all for? Why me?"

Anya stared down at the forty-foot drop, and in that moment she had an epiphany. "I've been running away, I ran from Pearl, from Kai and Hali. I'm not going to run anymore." She knew that the tanker had been nothing more than a distraction, a brief period of bliss, and she couldn't help but feel it was making her weak.

Anya looked at her hand; she turned it green and inspected her scales. Then she turned it back to soft, bronze skin again. She knew what she had to do: she would fix the oil rig, then she would return to the Ark and say her goodbyes. She would go back to the water dwellers and make amends, swim with Oracle and be gone forever—leave to map the entire ocean, the whole world. She didn't belong anywhere, or to anyone, and for that reason she wanted to be with the only being that could ever understand her. The craving to swim was growing stronger, and no matter how much she tried to subdue it, she had to go.

Anya got to her feet, she turned, and ran for the ship's bridge, scaling the massive structure with ease. Up and up she went, and near the top she could hear someone shouting, but when she approached the door, the shouting had stopped.

Anya saw that Rosita was standing with Nameless and Barnaby. She waited for them to walk away and for Rosita to be on her own. Then she knocked on the door and saw Rosita wipe her eyes before coming to let her in.

"Anya, it's good to see you."

"Is everything alright?"

"Yes, it's just that we're on our reserves now. We need fuel, and if we don't have it soon, our lights will go out, our crops will die, and everything will go with it."

Anya knew that she and she alone had the power to fix everything, that she was the only answer for the last souls and their way of life. She couldn't bear to let their world become like the Ark, not if she could help it.

"I'll do it," she said.

"Do what?"

"I can fix the pipeline."

Rosita shook her head. "It's thousands of miles under the ocean, you couldn't possibly—"

At that moment Anya revealed her true self, her green scaled body dressed in white, her glowing yellow eyes and fang-toothed smile.

Rosita jumped back. She was afraid at first. "Anya, you're—you're green!"

"I am."

"I … I don't know what to say, I have so many questions. What does this mean?"

"It means that your people will never go without oil again."

"Anya, you can't be serious. That's incredible, we'll do anything to show our gratitude."

"In return, I want you to supply my people with medicine, with food and even with shelter for the sick when they need it—oh and I want you to house Simone and Cayden."

"Of course, anything," Rosita said as her mascara ran.

"What's wrong, I thought you would be happy?"

"I am, it's just … so much to take in." Rosita gave a teary-eyed smile as she embraced Anya. "You're like a sister, I don't deserve this."

"You do."

Rosita crossed the room to her cabinet and returned with a bottle of champagne. "I've been keeping this for a very long time."

Anya sat and drank with her new friend, and felt the cool bubbling sensation. It didn't taste good at first—

bitter and too fizzy—but on her second glass, she found it to be a little better.

That afternoon the last souls prepared a cooked meal for their guests. Rosita sat next to Anya, and Wilson and Jake sat at the other end of the long table. They shared a late lunch of fresh fish and bread, and there was laughter as Rosita and Anya told each other stories, but Anya noticed that Jake and Wilson weren't laughing. They weren't even smiling and were showing little respect for their hosts.

Soon after, Anya put on her fish leathers and said her goodbyes to Simone, Cayden, and little Fiona. Next, she went to see Jake at his rowing boat, as Barnaby was helping him load everything in.

"Did you spill something on your bright whites, sea-sister?" Jake asked as he lifted a rather large box off a trolley.

"No, I'm just more comfortable in my leathers."

"You look more comfortable laughing with Rosita than anywhere else."

"Jake, don't be like that."

"Like what?" he said, before putting down the box.

"It's hard enough with Wilson, I don't need this from you," Anya said.

Jake looked at Barnaby, who turned the other way whilst continuing to load the boat, and then he went to sit alongside her. "Chin up," he said.

"That's easy for you to say."

"I know it must be difficult; I know you have to make decisions for all of us. You're smart, sea-sister, and strong, and if you want to lead, the Ark will follow if you just believe in yourself." Jake paused for a moment. "But I know you, Anya, I really know you. You don't want to lead, and ever since you came home, all you wanted was to get away again. The Ark is a heavy thing to keep afloat, so when you finish your voyage to the tanker, promise me one thing."

"What?"

"Swim. Swim far and free."

Anya looked up at him and smiled, "I love you, brother."

"I love you too," he said as they embraced. "Now, I think there's someone else who wants to speak with you."

Jake pointed to Wilson, who was hanging around near where the speedboat was sent down in the water. It was time for Anya to go, so she embraced her brother once more.

"I'll miss you, Jake."

"I'll miss you more," he replied. "Now go!"

Anya walked towards the bridge and looked back to see her brother moving boxes, and the sight made her smile. She headed for where the speedboat was docked, looked over the side and saw Rosita and Nameless readying the vessel. Anya then turned to Wilson; he looked rather unapproachable with his trademark scowl, but Anya knew him well enough to know that he wanted to speak to her.

"The great Anya of Ark, to what do I owe this honour?" Wilson asked as he took a bow.

"Don't call me that."

"That's what they all call you!"

Anya wasn't feeling comedy at the moment. "Are you going with Jake?" she asked.

"Nope. I'm not leaving until you come back, although I don't think you should be going there in the first place. These people, these last souls, they can't be trusted."

"I have to go to the oil rig; I have to fix it for them."

"Don't be stupid, Anya, this isn't right, the Ark needs you."

"Needs me? It doesn't need me, it never needed me."

"These aren't your people, Anya, and there's something wrong with them."

"With them?"

"Only a fool could miss it."

"A fool? These people have opened their hearts, they've fed us, they're giving us food and medicine, and all you've done is scowl and moan. Maybe I am a fool, but it's better than being a nasty old man."

"I'm only trying to protect you, and to help you see who they really are."

"Protect me? All you did was try to instil fear in me, to prepare me for war, for enemies and danger."

"We don't know them; you have a choice."

"What choice do I have? The choice to let them go cold and hungry and end up just like us?"

Wilson paused for a moment; he looked around at the last souls nearby, but he decided to lower his scowling façade for a moment. "I just don't want anything bad to happen to you, that's all. If you don't come back, if they're up to something … I care about you, Anya, I really do."

Anya didn't know what to say; he had never said anything like that to her before. She went towards the old man and placed a warm hand on his cheek. "There's still good left in this world, Wilson, I just wish you could see it."

"I do see it; I see it in you." Wilson took her hand and held it tight. "I'll be waiting right here until you get back, no matter how long you're gone. If you think I'm going back to the Ark before then, you may as well throw me overboard."

"I'd like that," Anya replied, and then, to her surprise, Wilson hugged her tight.

"I've missed many goodbyes in my days, Anya, I can't miss any more, not at my age."

"Goodbye, Wilson."

"Farewell."

Anya returned the gesture and shed a tear in the old mentor's arms. "I'll see you on the other side," she said before letting go. She turned out to sea to feel the wind fresh against her, she hovered for a moment with her toes over the edge, and then she dived off the side of the ship. Free-falling for a moment, Anya soared, she felt free, and then came the crash. She broke the surface close to the speedboat, and with ease she pulled herself aboard, splashing Nameless in the process.

"Are you ready?" Rosita asked.

"As I'll ever be," Anya replied.

Rosita gave the signal, Nameless started the engine, and the journey began.

Anya had many things on her mind as she crossed the horizon toward. Rosita's light-hearted conversation kept her distracted from the cold stare of Nameless. Soon enough she saw a speck in the distance, and that speck quickly became a structure. It was unlike anything Anya had ever seen, an orange and black skeleton with four huge legs planted in the sea.

When the vessel ventured closer, Anya saw the rusted paint and heard the creaking, the hiss and roar, as it moved with the wind and water. It was a strange sight to behold, another remnant of a lost world, and as they got closer, the structure loomed over them as if it were a beast staring down at her.

"What is this?" Anya asked.

"It's a semi-submersible oil rig; it floats in the water."

"But what *is* it, what does it do?"

"People lived here, and they pumped oil from the

seabed. The oil was refined and then it powered people's homes, their cars and boats."

"Are there people here now?"

"No, not anymore. It's a lonely place plagued with harsh weather, so we come here only when we really need to."

The sea was rough and the clouds dark as they made for one of the four floating legs. Soon Anya was within the shadow of the beast's underbelly. It started to rain, Anya felt a cold shiver, but when Rosita put a friendly hand on her shoulder, the shiver went away.

The boat came to a halt as they approached one of the ladders. Rosita led the climb, and Anya looked back to see Nameless taking his time to secure the boat, his cold stare unbroken as their eyes met for a moment. Anya shook off the chilly feeling left by his glance, and then she began to climb.

The ladders were cold and wet, and Anya could feel the movement of the structure as she had felt the movement of the Ark. Ladder after ladder, platform after platform they made their way until they reached the top of the rig. Here Anya saw a grand world of metal, now a ghost town of cranes, with one high middle tower, which whistled in the wind. There were shipping containers and doorways to indoor areas where the drillers had lived. Anya realised that this place was big enough for another community to live on—but there was nothing here, only the shadows of dark clouds, the creak of the metal and the crash of waves, until a rumble of thunder echoed across the sea.

Anya had never believed in ghosts, but she considered that any non-believer might reconsider on the rig. Despite the eery feeling, wasn't afraid of anything anymore, and so she had a look around. She witnessed the long drop below the grates on which she stood. She peered through some of the old windows, to see dark rooms where high-visibility jackets hung on pegs. There were photos, calendars, monitors and chairs—just like the office, but above water.

Anya realised that she had lost track if Rosita. She heard a strange noise, stepped back and then the whole vessel lit up.

"Sorry, I had to turn on the generator!" Rosita shouted.

Anya used a hand to shade her eyes as she looked everywhere for her.

"Over here, Anya, follow me to the east side." Anya followed Rosita's shadow to the side. She looked down at the huge drop and stayed close to the edge as Rosita casually leant her arms over.

"These rigs have two pumps or pumping stations, and neither is pulling anything up. We would've gone down to see why, but ten feet is too far, let alone hundreds." Rosita then revealed the blueprints. "According to these, if you follow the grey pipes all the way down, two yellow pumps should be fixed to the sea floor. You might have to go all the way down to see what the problem is."

"If it's on the seabed, it'll take me a while," Anya said. She remembered the last time she had been in such dark uncharted waters, and the kraken and other strange creatures that could be found down there.

Rosita leant in toward her. "Do you have the knife I gave you at the feast?"

"No, sorry, I forgot. I won't need it; I've got my claws."

At that moment, Rosita's expression changed ever so suddenly as her smile disappeared, but then it came back, and Anya questioned whether she was imagining things. "I wish I didn't need you to do this, but I do." Her words were heartfelt, but she didn't make eye contact with Anya, instead she looked past her toward the centre of the rig. "I promise I'll take care of the Arkers for you; I'll look after everyone while you're gone, I promise."

"Rosita, it's okay, I'm not going to be gone that long, trust me." Anya smiled and patted her on the shoulder. "There's something I wanted to say before I go …."

"What is it?"

"Thank you."

"Thank me, for what?" Rosita asked. She appeared to shiver for a moment, maybe due to the cold. There was a fierce breeze here after all.

"For reminding me of what it means to be human."

"That's—that's quite alright."

Anya embraced her, and after a moments hesitation, Rosita hugged her back. When they parted, Anya climbed over the rail and dived into the sea. She felt free, free from the worries of both the Ark and the tanker. She thrust down into the depths, following the pipes into darkness. She passed beautiful schools of fish, and then saw a huge dark trench, which stretched as far as the eye could see. Rosita was right: the seabed was a long way down; even at Anya's swimming speed the journey would take a good portion of the day.

Anya used the grey pipes as her guide, swimming as close to them as she could. As she went, she couldn't help thinking about how peaceful it was below. It was so quiet, so tranquil; none of the noise from the world above could be heard. She was alone and finally free of the Arkers' woes. Soon her mind drifted to the dwellers, to Pearl, Kai, Hali, Guillermo, and Polka. She missed them, but down here, all alone, her worries seemed insignificant. She wondered what she would do upon her return, when her side of the bargain was complete. She might even go to see the dwellers, to see if they were all okay.

Hours passed as she swam into the murky abyss. Soon she was deeper than she had ever been before, and she felt the cold and the pressure. Finally, she passed into the trench, dark walls of rock rose around her as the bright colours that could be found above disappeared. The water was much colder here; it reminded her of the first time she had got lost, just after turning into a dweller for the first time. Then she remembered the kraken, and she shuddered.

Anya propelled herself with her webbed claws as she continued her journey into the abyss. At the start of the trench were eels, crabs, and coral, but the further down she went, the less life she found. Despite how lonely these waters were, she still didn't *feel* alone. It was hard to describe … as if something, or someone, was watching her, but where she would have once been afraid, she wasn't, for she was the strongest dweller in the sea.

Her gills took in water; her claws pushed her forward with ferocity. As Anya wandered, so did her mind. She felt free in a way her brother or uncle might never understand. She began to wonder what they would look like if they were dwellers, and the rest of the Arkers too: if she could swim with them, hunt with them, be free with them and have all the fish in the world. No one would ever go hungry, no one would ever fight, or get sick.

Finally, Anya saw the pipes' ends floating in the water, and she swam down to see what was wrong. The pipes were floating free. One was larger than the other, its end orange, whereas the other was thin and grey. She was wary of getting too close in case they sucked her in, but she felt no suction, and so she examined the sea bed.

On the sea floor there was a strange device built into the rock. There were holes in the device, circular holes —that might house a pipe. Anya guessed that the pipes were supposed to be plugged into the device, so she dragged them over before assessing the situation again. The pipe that was orange at the end seemed to fit perfectly, and she forced it in before clamping it into place. Then she clamped the second one in, and wondered how, or what, had pulled them loose. Maybe a humpback whale had collided with them, or a kraken?

Anya turned to make for the surface, it took her hours to retrace her swim, and then she saw the rig. The gargantuan structure looked much simpler from beneath: a dark blotch resting on the ocean. Anya swam along the pipes and took her time to appreciate the underside of the rig. She couldn't believe how easy her task had been, and at the surface she found a ladder and climbed. It was darker than before, and the rain had started coming down, but that didn't bother her: she had saved the last souls as well as improved the lives of her own.

Anya changed back into human form. She wanted to get going as soon as she could, say goodbye to Rosita, return to the Ark, and make an overdue visit to the water dwellers. She was excited that her trip to the depths had done her some good. She climbed onward and upward, but when she reached the platform, the lights were off, and all was dark.

10

THE NAME

A cold wind blew through the oil rig, and the sky was clouded over. Anya could hear a strange humming in the distance. Something wasn't right, and when she reached the railing, she saw Rosita crossing the ocean in her speedboat. If Anya called out, Rosita wouldn't hear her.

"Where is she going?" Anya asked herself. "Maybe I took too long," she reasoned, and it had been a good few hours after all.

Her first instinct was to dive into the water, to swim and catch up with her, but then she felt the same familiar chill she had felt many more times over the past few weeks: something or someone was watching her.

Anya peered across the rig into the darkness. She saw a shadow, and then she noticed that it was Nameless. If she hadn't been so confident in her abilities, she might have been afraid of him standing there in silence. He walked forwards, and upon closer inspection, Anya saw that he looked different—he wasn't wearing his long-sleeved jumper—and for the first time Anya saw that his arms and torso were covered in hundreds of scars. She didn't know what to say; she had seen people and monsters of all shapes and sizes, and she was so strong that nothing of this sort would scare her, but his appearance did catch her off guard.

"Nameless, where's Rosita gone?" she asked, but Nameless said nothing. "I fixed the pipes, have you got another way to get out of here? I can always swim my way."

At that moment, Anya saw something completely out of character, a sinister smile on the face of the man before her. It was the first facial expression Anya had seen from Nameless, and she felt rather on edge.

"Rosita isn't coming back," he whispered.

"You can talk."

"I can."

"I don't understand—everyone said that you can't talk, that your tongue—"

Nameless stood with a hand on his hip as he inspected the nails on the other. "People presume all sorts of foolish things. Consider this a lesson, one that your old fool could never teach you: always fear the silent man, for he often knows much more than those who talk. I always thought you would be far more observant, but you only ever disappointed me." Nameless stepped toward her, the shadow of his scarred body looming over her.

"Disappointed you? I don't even know you; I didn't even know you could talk."

"I do much more than talk, unlike you and your

Arkers—that's all you ever do. Your voices smother the surface; there's never any peace." Nameless stopped himself; he tried to calm his rage and remain composed. He shook his head and Anya looked on, unsure of what to say or do.

"I don't understand."

"The way the cold wind blows, water echoes and flows, when you're alone, I'll find you. What you've done, you know, you reap what you sow, for this, be sure I'll drown you. Do you understand now?"

Anya shuddered in disbelief. "Those words, I've heard them before …"

"A fine poem, wouldn't you say?"

"Who are you?"

"I never thought it would be this easy to get you all alone, *Anya of Ark*, but here you are, tricked with such ease. Surely you can work it out?"

Nameless took a step toward her, and Anya backed up against the railing. "Don't take another step. Tell me who you are and what you want."

"I just want you to know how it feels …" said Nameless as he advanced.

"I'm warning you," Anya said as she peered over the rail behind her to assure herself of an escape route.

"Go on, swim away. I can see the fear in your eyes —but if you do, know that I'll come for your brother, your uncle, and your aunt."

"No one threatens my family."

Anya stepped forward and made a fist as Nameless smiled once more. "That's it, get mad."

"I won't tell you again."

"We'll see where your warnings get you when your Ark is nothing but scrap, when the children drown and the ocean swallows everything you ever loved."

"That's it," Anya said as she ran forward, "I've heard enough." She jumped into the air and came crashing down upon Nameless feet first, but he effortlessly stepped to the side. Anya landed on a floor grate with such force that it bucked under her. She threw punch after punch, venting her rage, and expending every ounce of energy without care for technique. Nameless moved back, evaded each assault, and then he caught her fist in his hand.

Anya struggled to break free and she couldn't believe his strength. *It cannot be*, she told herself upon the realisation of what Nameless was.

"Feel familiar?" He asked. Nameless was strong, so strong, and before she could consider her next move, he grabbed her by the arm and threw her through a nearby window. The glass shattered, and Anya found herself in a dark control room.

She staggered to her feet as the door burst open, crashing from its hinges. "What are you?" she asked as she struggled to her feet.

"Better than you," Nameless replied as he kicked her in the side and sent her into the lockers. "Come on, is this the best you can do? Get up and fight me, don't hold back. If you do, you will lose."

Anya rose to her feet and threw a flurry of punches,

some of which Nameless dodged but others he let land in his side and his chest. Despite Anya's best efforts, her attack did little and he countered with a harsh right which sent her into one of the large old computer screens. Anya picked up another monitor and smashed him in the head, knocking him backwards. She considered following up the blow, but instead she ran down the corridor.

"You can't run from me!" His voice echoed as Anya reached a door. On the other side she found herself on a metal walkway overhanging the sea; she ran forward and tried to jump the long distance down to the water, but Nameless caught her hand and threw her back up.

Anya knew then that this was it: she couldn't mess around anymore, she had to fight him, and she couldn't hold back. She threw punches as well as Wilson had taught her to, one of which missed and busted a hole in the concrete wall.

"Yes, that's it," Nameless goaded. She hit him again and again and her blows made him stagger, she landed one on the chin, and then he spat blood. It appeared as if he wanted to be hit, that he wanted the pain, and then he returned them with his own attack. Each vicious blow pushed Anya back along the walkway and then she had to retreat up another set of stairs, to the helicopter platform.

There they clashed again, testing one another like gods, smashing through metal grates, pipework, and fencing. It went on and on until Nameless grabbed a hold of Anya by the arm, spun her round and slammed her down on the harsh metal. Blood began to trickle from her forehead and her lip.

"Who are you?" she asked.

Nameless snarled. "I'm nature, the next step in evolution, the same as you." With his words, his eyes turned blood orange.

"You're a dweller," Anya said.

"That I am."

Anya stayed low to the floor as she tried to process his revelation. She was tired, and he was too strong. She had to attack, and so in one final act of desperation she pulled a metal grate from the floor and hit Nameless as hard as she could. He flew into a stack of oil drums and Anya thought it was over.

A violent screech sounded, and Nameless came flying back. He snatched the grate, and with one powerful blow caved in her leg, which buckled beneath her. His teeth flared into fangs, his skin turned to scales, and his eyes glowed blood orange as he continued his assault. Anya could do nothing more than try to cover herself with her arms as her elbow shattered and her forearm splintered.

"Please, stop," she whimpered, without the heart to take any more.

"Pathetic. I expected more from you, much more. All you've ever done is disappoint me."

Nameless was in full dweller form now, but Anya's vision was blurred. She tried to crawl away toward the side of the rig, as Nameless paced back and forth in anger. She tried to call for Oracle, but she couldn't hear her friend.

"I can feel you trying to summon her, but she won't answer. You won't see your precious killer whale ever again."

"No?" Anya murmured. "Why?"

"Because you—you could have been something! You were the future, the only one strong enough to protect my people, and you betrayed them. Instead of learning to lead us, you left us, you left me! You made me look like a fool, and in your wake, you spread a weakness, a weakness which led my people to question who they are. Even the young fins tried to go above the surface, and even I had to in the end, despite how much it sickens me. You could have been my heir; you could have had everything."

Anya recognised him now; he had saved her life and freed her from the kraken. "Neptune," she whispered. She looked up in disbelief to see his blood orange eyes as he crouched down at her side.

"The very same."

"I thought you cared about me."

"And I thought you cared about the water dwellers," he replied before grasping Anya's good arm and pulling her along the walkway. "We were gods, the next phase of evolution, and we had *everything* you could ever dream of. Humanity was done, beneath us—all except for your cursed Ark. I tried to starve them, to give them a natural end, but you had to put an end to that, didn't you."

Neptune continued to drag her along and up a metal staircase as Anya tried to grab onto anything she could, her claws sparking against the metal as she resisted.

"You thought you were strong, stronger than me. I could have given you everything, power beyond anything you have ever known. The power to influence minds, to control the weak, your young, your old and sick. I'm strong enough to mould minds, dwellers and human alike, but now you, you will never know that power."

Anya tried to hold back her tears.

"Stop it, you did this to yourself. I remember when the Arkers first came to the shallows, the way they looked at us in fear, as if we were some horrible thing, the same way you look at me now. You know what humans are don't you? A *disease*."

"That isn't true."

"Did you really think that Rosita wanted to learn from *you*? That she would help *you*, knowing what *we* are? You're a fool, and you've proven yourself unworthy of your own strength. You left me no choice—and to think that it would be this easy to get you on your own."

Neptune continued to drag Anya up and up. She clung to the rail, but he pulled her off. With her last ounce of strength, she inched her mother's emerite necklace free from her forearm brace and let it fall down through the metal.

"You're evil."

"No, Anya, I'm a god, I'm above good and evil. And as for you, I treated you like a daughter, and you betrayed me. To think that I wanted to make you my heir. All the dwellers do is talk about how much they miss you, how strong you are, but look at you now. All you are is weak."

Anya didn't know what to say; she was in so much pain that all she could do was cry.

"Tears won't save you now," Neptune continued, dragging her to a platform which overlooked a huge metal vat. "I want you to know that not a single part of me is enjoys this, I only do what I have to."

"It was you, wasn't it?" Anya asked. "You killed Cray, and you made the others disappear. You're the darkness that Serus warned me about."

"That old man and his foolish premonitions. Those three were in my way, and Cray, let's just say he was my little experiment. I wouldn't waste any more time thinking about them, I'd worry about what's going to happen next. Your Ark will sink, and that fool Rosita, who's stupid enough to think I'll let her miserable tanker stay afloat, will sink too. When it's all done, only the dwellers will live on. I'll be free of the untamed voices, the plague upon the surface … As for you, I've spent much time thinking over the best way to kill you. Dwellers are hard to kill. after all, but what would be more fitting than seeing you burn?"

Neptune took hold of Anya's arm and threw her into the vat below. She tumbled to the bottom and sank into the oil. She tried to crawl out but found herself slipping straight back down. When she looked up, she saw Neptune light a flare.

"Please," Anya whispered.

"That's all you have to say?" Neptune let the flare

go. It tumbled down into the vat where it sparked, and Anya was engulfed in flame.

Soon the sea was alight too, and Neptune dived into the ocean. He swam far and fast, and when he turned back, he saw an image of hell, as smoke billowed and flames fluttered, as they fought against the darkness.

The largest fire in the world flickered out, the final candle in the wind extinguished, and Anya of Ark was no more.

11

THE OLD MAN

Wilson stared out in the direction of the oil rig. He stood with one hand in his pocket and held his old white sea cap to his chest in the other. He had a bad feeling as the last souls loaded Jake's rowing boat for his journey back to the Ark. Wilson noticed that there were more last souls than he had ever seen watching him. He could feel the weight of their eyes, and he hoped that Anya would return soon.

"Well, that's nearly everything," Jake said. "Come on Wilson, it's time to go."

"I'm not going anywhere until Anya returns."

"There's no telling when she'll be back, it could be hours, days or weeks," Barnaby said as he loomed over the old man, his voice more stern than polite.

Wilson knew by the look in Barnaby's eyes and his inability to hold eye contact that something was wrong. "I said I'm not leaving until Anya returns. I gave my word. I don't know what a man's word means on this vessel, but it means something to me."

"Very well," Barnaby said as he folded his arms.

"Then I guess this is goodbye," Jake said as he approached Wilson.

"Will you at least give an old man a chance to say goodbye in private?" Wilson asked as he turned to address Barnaby. The big man nodded before taking a few steps away, although not nearly enough.

"Tell your uncle I wish him well. I'll miss you, Jake."

"I don't understand … I'm not going far."

Wilson unfolded his arms and made a cross on his chest—the diving signal for danger. "Just tell him what I said. I'll return with your sister as soon as I can."

"Very well; take care, Wilson."

Wilson watched Jake make his way down to the vessel and row his way back to the Ark. Though he wished he was aboard, he had to wait for Anya. He waited and waited. The last souls were all around him, the vessel was quiet, and the evening was cold. Hours passed but Wilson didn't move. At first, he had faith, and then he grew concerned about the way the last souls kept watch on him. His fears were only deepened by the appearance of thick black smoke on the horizon, rising high into the air. And when he saw the speedboat with only one figure aboard, he knew that Rosita was on her own.

The last souls hoisted Rosita up in haste and Wilson saw that her mascara was running; she was unsettled, and neglected to look him in the eyes. His worst thoughts were coming to fruition, and the plume of black smoke only reinforced them. He pushed his way past the protective line around Rosita. "Where's Anya?" he demanded as tensions rose.

"There were complications … Anya isn't going to be back for at least a few days."

Wilson looked to the smoke in the distance, and then he locked eyes with Rosita. Her expression was one of honesty, but beyond it, her eyes were full of heartbreak. He saw through her façade, and when he peered at Barnaby and the others, his worried were confirmed by how timid they were. "What's all the smoke from?" Wilson asked.

"The rig's chimney."

"Oh, is that right? Well no semi-submersible I've ever seen gives off smoke like that, you think they run on coal? You're lying."

"No I'm not."

"I know a liar when I see one," Wilson insisted but Rosita said nothing in return. He could see that the last souls were closing in on him, but he remained vigilant in the face of danger and stood tall. "If you're telling the truth, then look at the rig."

Rosita had to keep up the act, so she forced herself to face the tanker, and sank down under the weight of her guilt. She couldn't look Wilson in the eye any more. "You would never understand, you don't know what he is, you don't know. Take him to the brig!"

Barnaby was the first to Wilson's side. The old man hit the muscle-bound beast square in the crotch, and he fell down in anguish. Wilson moved through the ship as the last souls closed in with hatchets and harpoons. When the first came close enough, Wilson punched him in the nose. "Come on, then! You won't take me alive," he said as he ran toward the tanker's side. He tried to launch himself, but the last souls grabbed hold of him and pulled him back. He looked over the edge and hoped, just hoped, that there was someone or something that could get a message to the Ark—but all he saw was black water. The last souls pulled him down to the floor and he felt a needle pierce his arm.

"Take him to the brig," he heard Rosita say before he was out.

12

UNCLE

Uncle Isaac had watched Anya and the others sail into the most picturesque sunrise with all his hopes, as all his worries remained behind with him. He didn't dare take his eyes off the boat as it soared toward the tanker. When everyone else was going about their day, Isaac remained at the dock. He sat on a nearby bench and thought things over. Despite his niece's strength, he feared for her; though she had faced hardships down below, he knew too well that there was nothing worse than people, real people. People who would fight to the death to survive, who had been to the brink and back in the flood.

Isaac shuddered; he tied back his long bushy hair and stroked his beard in contemplation. He didn't eat, and only when night came did he return to his shack to rest. It was hard to sleep; he should have gone with them. If something were to happen to any of them, he would bear the guilt until the end of his days. Isaac tossed and turned; he turned to Lyn and saw that she was fading. He expected her to mutter that strange curse he had heard from her lips night after night, but she didn't.

He spent the next few days waiting at the docks, and only when a rowing boat appeared on the horizon did he feel some sense of ease. He was excited to see his nephew and niece, but when the small rowing boat returned, Jake and Patrick were the only Arkers aboard.

"Jake, what news do you bring?" Isaac asked whilst he offered a hand to pull his nephew aboard.

"I bring food, medicine, and many gifts from the last souls. Doctor Phillips even gave me something to ease Aunt Lyn's pain."

That raised Isaac's spirits a little. "You've make me very proud. Where are the others?"

"We must talk in private, there's much to discuss."

More Arkers came by to unload the boat, and the pair made their way to the grand stage, where they could speak alone.

"How is Simone?" Uncle Isaac asked.

"She has had a baby girl, and she named her Fiona; she'll be a strong Arker one day, just like Anya, but she's already done something very strange."

"What?"

"She's turned Cayden soft."

Isaac laughed. "Good. When will they be ready to return?"

"That was what I wanted to talk to you about. They don't wish to return to the Ark, they want to stay on the tanker."

"What did Rosita say?"

"She said yes."

Of course, she did, Isaac thought. "What about Anya?"

Jake nodded.

I should've known this would happen. "What was it like?"

"There was electricity; it was warm; they had bright lights—too bright. It was all metal, inside and out, but no rust, no draughts. Oh, and apples."

"Apples?"

"Yes, apples."

"How were the people?"

"Kind, but they never left us alone."

"And how was Wilson? I trust he tried to get a reaction out of them?"

"He tried, but he failed. Wilson didn't want to stay on the tanker, he wanted to come back …"

"But?"

"Anya made the decision to go to the oil rig."

"What?"

"And Wilson refused to leave until she returned."

Isaac felt nervous, but the fact that Wilson remained reassured him a little. "When will she return?"

"I don't know. When I asked the last souls, they kept giving different answers: hours, days, maybe weeks. They dodged my question; I didn't like how they looked at me."

"What's your gut telling you?"

"That we shouldn't trust them. It's a strange place where most don't speak, with weird clothes, small rooms and too much metal. I didn't like it; they were always watching, and always close by."

"Do you think Anya will be okay?"

"I hope so, but I barely had chance to share a word with her. I didn't speak with Wilson either, but he shared a message with me when I was leaving: he made a diver's cross on his chest."

Isaac knew what the cross meant: it meant danger, and now he felt even more on edge. He knew that Wilson would never use such a sign lightly. He didn't know what to say to his nephew, but he tried to hide his worry to avoid making him panic. Then he reminded himself that Jake wasn't a child anymore. He was growing up, they both were, and he himself was growing old. He worried for Anya, but then he remembered her strength; she would return.

Isaac paused and tried to calm himself once more. He reminded himself that he had already wasted good time fearing Anya dead once before, back when Tyson ruled the Ark. He couldn't face losing her again—but he knew her strength, and he had to have faith.

"I fear for her," Jake said.

"Your sister is strong, and so are you. You need to rest; you've had a long day. I'll think over our next move. I'm sure Anya will return soon."

Isaac's hopeful expectations dwindled, as a few more days passed, and Anya didn't return. Isaac got little sleep, and though he tried to stay positive the weather seemed to foretell his fortune—as it always had. It was grey, cloudy and a light rain drizzled the Ark for days.

Lyn didn't do much but sleep, and Isaac didn't do much but sit in her chair. The council called its meetings without Anya, and he didn't wish to attend. He felt he was in a rut, and the only relief came in the form of an unexpected knock on his shack door.

"Anya is that you?" He asked."

"Spare a little time for a former lord," said the voice, and Isaac knew that the man who once called himself 'Lord Turtle Head' was knocking on his door.

"Go away, I'm busy."

"It's about Anya." Isaac stumbled to the door and opened it just enough to see Terrance. "You don't look well, and that's coming from a man who used to live in a barrel and wear a turtle shell on his head."

"Then I must look terrible."

"Let's take a walk; there's much to discuss."

"I don't know if I want to, I'm tired."

"We're all tired, come on."

Isaac followed Terrance. They walked the length of the Ark, passing hunters who were getting ready to spend the day fishing, and makers who were busy mending the raft as best they could. They stopped to speak on the South dock where no one else was around.

"You know, I looked like you in the early days," Terrance confessed. "Yep, just like that. Then I started having dark thoughts. Next, I was talking to myself, and then I started hearing the voices. Then came the barrel and the turtle shell … I've still got them if you would like to borrow them."

"We don't have time for jokes. Something isn't right,

Terrance. Anya made for the oil rig, and it's been two days since Jake returned."

"I see. Perhaps you're just being over-protective?"

"No, I know my niece. I wouldn't normally ask, but I need your help."

"What is it that you want me to do?"

"Anya once told me that you can …"

"Say it."

"That you can talk to turtles," Isaac said with a sigh.

Terrance smiled; he could indeed speak to turtles, but he had kept his gift close to his chest and had discussed it with no one except Anya. She had taught him much about his gift, about mind-speak and the unique bond that Terrance shared with the sea.

"I might be able to put a good word in."

"How would you go about it? Can you send them a message or something?"

Terrance tapped him on the shoulder and guided his eyes out to sea. To his disbelief, he saw a number of sea turtle shells bobbing at the Ark's edge.

"What do you want me to ask them?"

"I want to know if Anya is safe."

Terrance approached the Ark's edge. He closed his eyes, made tight fists and shook himself to the core. When he opened his eyes, he smiled and almost jumped for joy. "Good morning to you too! To you, and you, and you! How are the little ones? Splendid!"

Terrance's eyes creased as he smiled; he seemed happier than Isaac had ever seen him before. When they first met, in the flood, Isaac remembered how sombre and quiet he was, but now he was happy. He looked on, careful not to say anything to disrupt the turtle whispers; he merely stroked his grey beard and re-tied his fuzzy hair , which expanded again beyond its bun. Then he considered that the name Lord Turtle Head didn't suit Terrance anymore—no, for now he truly was lord of the turtles.

"Can you ask them?"

"Shh, I'm making casual conversation. I'm warming up. Oh … oh yes. Yes, beautiful, wonderful. No … no he didn't, no. Yes, I bet it is, though I'm sure he didn't mean it." The conversation went on that way for a while until Terrance felt confident enough to ask his little friends. "Well, I hate to call in a favour like this, but I need your help. There's a girl from the Ark who rides with an orca and who can make herself green. Oh, you've seen her around? Really?"

"What did they say?"

"They've seen her, and they saw her go to the rig," Terrance said, "but …"

"Well, what are we waiting for?" Isaac asked, feeling his energy come back.

"I said *but* …"

"But what?"

"But she didn't come back. They say there's a great darkness in those waters and that anyone who goes there will almost certainly die."

"I must go."

"Alone, its suicide."

"Then *we* must go," Isaac insisted.

"*We*? But the turtles said it isn't a good idea."

Isaac started walking. He already had a plan to help his niece, to find out what the last souls were planning and to stop them.

"Where are you going?" Terrance asked.

"To save Anya."

"Did you not hear what I said? A great *darkness*? They also said that it can mould the minds of men. We mustn't go."

"I have to."

"Isaac, at least wait for me to find another way, a better way."

"No, this is war."

"I'm begging you, don't go to the oil rig, if you do, you won't return."

"Then I'll go to the tanker. Rosita has my niece, and now I'm going to get her back."

"What are you going to do? Swim to their boat and throw spears at steel? There must be a better way."

"No, Terrance, Rosita has left us no choice. We leave at once."

The message was passed only to the most able and trusted Arkers. Not one of them could accept that Anya was dead. She was a legend, a myth come true. The bringer of fish, the queen of orcas, and though she had felt she was not accepted, she had become a symbol that her people told many tales about.

It was a hard day for Isaac; he felt as he had the day he lost his niece to Tyson. He tried to summon his courage, the kind of courage that Anya had summoned to return to him. He looked towards the tanker, sent word to Jake and met his hunting party at the South dock.

"Uncle are you sure you want to do this?" Jake asked.

"We have no choice."

13

CAPTURE

Wilson awoke behind bars within a large, white-walled room. The light flickered and buzzed above his head as he tried to take in his surroundings. Through the bars, he saw that a large member of the last souls was fast asleep. He was resting in a chair and leaning back against the wall. The chair bowed under his weight and his snores echoed around the room. Wilson looked down to see that his usual clothes were missing and that he was dressed in an orange jumpsuit. The clothes smelt fresh and they were too soft and clean.

What happened? he asked himself, and then he felt his arm and recollected his sedation. "Oi," he said in an attempt to get the guard's attention. "Oi!" The sleeping guard didn't wake; he continued to snore until he choked on one of his wheezing breaths. The guard took a moment to remember where he was and then shot a disgruntled glance at Wilson before he attempted to return to his slumber.

Wilson put his hands on the metal bars and tested

their strength. "Where's Anya?" he asked, and the overweight guard opened his eyes. "I need to speak to Rosita and Doctor Phillips."

The guard leant forward, uncrossed his arms and squinted at his prisoner. Wilson took note of the abundance of keys on his belt, which jangled as he stood up and stretched. He scratched his bottom. Upon standing, his large cheeks turned to red balloons. At first Wilson didn't know what to make of him, but then the guard smiled.

"Garr, matey," said the guard, but his words were met with silence. "Get it? You look like an old sea captain ... Your hat? Your coat?" Wilson said nothing and held his blank piercing stare. "The name's Yan. Now, I'm not really supposed to talk to you, but I love new people! I have so many questions about your Ark, by the way, I'm a big fan. Looks cold, though, and I guess there's no cake, or beds, or appliances ..."

Wilson continued his solemn silence as Yan picked his nose with a fat finger and gave his brain a good scratch before inspecting his booger and wiping it on his shirt.

"Oh no, I've said too much, haven't I? They warned me not to make friends with prisoners, but we just never have any guests. I miss having guests." Yan hunched over in disappointment, and then he appeared to remember something—a grand idea of sorts—and made his leave.

"Where are you going?" Wilson asked.

"Not far; just to tell them that you're awake. I suggest you get comfortable; we're going to be spending a lot of time together—like, every day; oh, I can't wait! Do you like playing cards?"

"No."

"Oh, well, we can just tell each other stories."

"No stories," Wilson said. Soon he was alone again, and the sedative began to wear. He hated being inside, away from the sea. Being trapped inside reminded him of the old days, of the days before the flood, and most of all, of her.

"What I wouldn't do to be outside, up in the clouds in my nest, and as close to you as possible." Distant memories started to take over, but he batted them away. "Focus. I need to get out of here, to get back to the Ark, to warn them." Wilson scanned his surroundings. Outside his cage was a vent, a fan, and some light switches. There were coat pegs next to the door where his old clothes were hung up—but they were out of reach.

Above him, the bars of his cell ended short of the ceiling, but the tops of the bars were also out of reach. The only thing in his cell was an old thick pipe, but what use could that be? He had no choice but to sit back down, and no matter how hard he fought it, his mind started to wander again.

"I should be with you now, Clara," he said. "But I'm here." At least on the Ark he served a purpose, and he could lose himself by looking out to sea. The ocean calmed him, and her eyes were the same sort of blue that changed with the weather and time of day. He would often lose himself in the ocean as he had lost himself in those eyes, for those were better days.

Right now, though, all he saw was the bars of this wretched metal cell. "I should have gone with Jake, why didn't I go with Jake? No, *focus*, you stubborn old fool."

Wilson thought over his interactions with the last souls, the few he had had. Aside from their constant overbearing presence, they had been nothing but polite, overly polite, even when he had shouted and scorned just to test them. There was a lot he didn't know, and so he tried to connect that which he did. Why hadn't they killed him? And why did Rosita appear guilty and upset upon her return?

"She said I would never understand, that I don't know what *he* is, who is *he*?" Wilson had many hours to think over the notion, and he arrived at his conclusion. "Maybe, just maybe, Rosita isn't pulling all the strings. She was crying when she returned, and maybe that whatever has happened to Anya, it wasn't her intention. Anya was too strong to die in a pipe, so why would Rosita lie?"

He considered who, if anyone, would be strong enough to force Rosita to do what she was doing; and not only that, but also to draw Anya far away from her friends. "It had to be planned, it had to be an ambush, and it had to be someone who was holding something over the last souls—but who? Either I'm a mad old fool and Anya is fixing the pipes, or there's something far more sinister at play, and someone pulling the strings. Even if they were, it could be no Arker, it has to be someone else."

Wilson waited and waited; he counted the bars half a dozen times, but he soon found himself back in his own mind. Hours went by, but no one came. It was quiet except for a drip coming down from the fan in the far corner of the ceiling, and the hum of the light. *Clink ... clink*—there it was again. Wilson tested his ear all about the place; he checked the ceiling, the walls, and then looked at the pipe in the corner of the cell, which ran from the ceiling all the way down and into the floor below. He got down on all fours, placed his ear against the pipe and heard what he could only describe as some sort of muffled speech.

He looked around the room for something with which he could open the pipe. He reached through the bars for the chair, and then realised that he was never going to get it through. Losing hope, he looked past the chair, to the coat pegs, where he saw the gold pin on the front of his hat shining like a gem. If he could get it, he could puncture enough holes in the pipe to hear. The old man tried to reach for it, but it was too far away. He took a step back and took off his overalls to reveal a clean white vest and bottoms, which made him shudder. He knotted the orange overalls, extended his hand though the bars and tried to swing them up and knock off his hat. One, two, three—nothing. One, two three —nothing.

"Hopeless. I'm too damn old for this." Wilson took a moment, then tried once more, and to his delight the cap fell off the peg. With a few more throws of his overalls, he clawed the hat close enough and had soon detached the badge from the front.

He dressed himself incase of Yan's return, and then he drove the pin into the old worn pipe with all his might making hole after hole. When he heard the thudding footsteps of Yan, he hid the pin in his overalls and threw the hat at the peg, narrowly missing, before lying back down.

Yan entered the room with a heavy wheeze. "You look comfy," he said whilst catching his breath. "Making yourself at home I see? The Captain will be sure to commend me when she sees how good you've settled in. I just got a promotion, I did; I was working sanitation, poo everywhere, as far as the eye could see, as much as the hands could hold. You'd think I'd spent enough time away from it to forget the smell, but I can't."

"Lovely," Wilson mumbled.

"Oh, look, your hat fell off the peg." Yan bent down, revealing his bottom, and when he stood, he put on Wilson's sea cap. "Suits me, doesn't it? Garr, I be from the Ark, dress like an old sea captain, I do!"

Wilson gave him a look of prolonged disdain. "I don't sound anything like that."

"Yes, you do! Now, I brought you some soup, bread and water." At that moment Wilson smelt the most putrid smell. "Oh, sorry, that's me. Too many beans!"

Wilson shuddered. *Ten years on the Ark would do this soft soul some good.* He watched Yan struggle to bend over and push the water container through the bars, along with the bread and soup. "Anyway, good night Wee-Willy-Wilson. I'm shattered, it's been a really busy day."

Wilson gave his cold-eyed glare.

When the guard left, he ate the bread and soup. He

waited a little while longer to be sure no one was going to return before tackling the pipe again with his badge. He made a few more holes, and then he pressed his mouth to them and began to speak. "Hello, is anybody in there? This is Wilson. Anya—Anya is that you?"

Wilson waited for a response, and then came a faint female voice. "I'm sorry to disappoint you but this isn't Anya. My name is Stix," she whispered.

Wilson didn't respond for a moment. "Is this some sort of trick? You're going to try and befriend me, so I'll spill the beans—well you won't hear another word from me you vixen."

"No, it's not a trick, I promise. It's just good to hear a new voice."

"Then tell me something useful, something I don't already know."

"That Rosita is in trouble, and she is only trying to protect her people."

"How long have you been in here?"

"Six months. Our tanker's been held prisoner for six long months, and then you came . I know all about you, Wilson, about Anya and your Ark."

"How?" he asked.

"I was Rosita's second mate. I studied you from the brig with the telescope; I read your lips and all. Wilson, the old man in the tower. I know how much Anya means to you—"

His eyes widened at the prospect of inside information. "What's Rosita's second mate doing stuck in the brig?"

"It's a long story, one I've never told, and one I don't

know how to begin ... It's complicated." Stix took a long pause.

"Well, you'd better get started."

"We're a tough but kind people, and we fought to survive, just like you. Our lives were far from perfect, but far from bad, until one day someone ... or something ... came to our tanker. A creature from hell itself, a darkness, a monster, scaled and green. At first the creature promised us fish, endless fish, and he delivered, but then everything changed. I could tell by the look in his eyes that he was bad news. He spoke of another civilisation, and he led us to your Ark. Then he made us watch you, learn from you and report on your movements every day. He told us that you were our enemy, that you were vicious and primitive, but we saw a kind and loving people—just like us. We questioned him, and that's when he snapped."

Wilson took a moment to take it all in. "What happened then?" he asked.

"He told us we had to go to war, but Rosita refused. She stood for what was right, but then he bent our spears and broke our hatchets. His strength knew no match, and he killed five of Rosita's best with his claws before sinking our oil reserves. He said that the oil was a lesson, and that we would have more, but if we ever went against him again, he would sink our tanker. Rosita had to give him what he wanted."

"And what does he want?"

"*Anya.* He knew that Anya would be naïve enough to go to the rig to fix the pipes."

"It was all starting to make sense. What is his obsession with her?"

"He fears her, we don't know why."

"Who is he?"

"He's Nameless when he walks with those above, but he must have another name down below."

Wilson couldn't believe why the last souls would be stupid enough to trust him. "Why is Rosita helping him?"

"She had no choice. He said that if we could get Anya alone, that we could go free."

"He will never set you free."

"You think I don't know that? But this vile creature threatened to claw our tanker in two and feed us to his sharks. Where were we supposed to go? What were we supposed to do?"

As Stix vented, Wilson fixated on one word. He remembered what Anya had told him about the world below, and everything clicked into place. "Sharks?"

"Yes."

"Neptune. His name is *Neptune*."

"Neptune, what kind of man names himself after a God?"

"Only the delusional. I've a lot of questions, but questions that only Anya could answer. Stix, may I ask how you ended up here?"

"I was going to kill him, but Rosita was afraid that I might fail, so she locked me in here."

"So she he imprisoned you?"

"She did it to protect me. Rosita and I: we're in love,

but even love won't stop me from killing that thing. He put his hands on her, and that I can't forgive."

"I see … Tell me, what was his plan with Anya."

"We were to get her to the oil rig, to make it look like it needed repairing, and then he would set us free," Stix confessed, and Wilson could hear that she was crying.

"I see."

"There's something else … something horrible. He said he was going to destroy the Ark."

"What? There are children, there are families, on the Ark."

"I'm sorry Wilson, I'm so sorry. He doesn't care for humans; we're beneath him. Our minds clutter his, one he can't tune them out and he hates it."

Wilson sighed, he was too old and tired to be hearing any of this. "You said you wanted to kill him— how would you do it?"

"There's a weapon onboard, a weapon from the old world: a gun."

Wilson hadn't heard that word in a long time. He didn't know what to say. He knew that he had to get to the Ark to warn them, but then, to his dismay, he heard the heavy footsteps of Yan. "I've got to go," he said, and he moved away from the pipe and back to the middle of his cage.

14

NEGOTIATION

Twelve strong and skilled Arkers set off on their secret mission to the tanker when it was dark. They made their way in kayaks as to not be spotted in anything bigger. Isaac knew that they would be watching the Ark due south, and so he planned to loop northeast around the tanker, and to take it from the other side. Isaac stood at the helm of his vessel, and behind him, in formation, were the strongest men and women he had, each with a spear on their back, and grappling hooks made of knotted sea ropes to climb the tanker's high walls.

The Arkers crossed the sea in silence, and when Isaac approached the mighty mass of metal his throat went dry. Such a reminder of the past struck him with the reality of the situation. It had been a long time since he had seen a ship up close. Still, he didn't panic, and he would make no mistake that might risk the small advantage which surprise gave him.

When they reached the wall, the Arkers threw their

grappling hooks and began their ascent. Isaac appeared calm, but his heart was racing; he hadn't seen such a structure in so long, and the adrenaline kept him moving. He made it over the side first with Pierce the master hunter close by, and from there they gagged and tied the two last souls on watch.

As Isaac looked across to the large number of last souls patrolling the other side, he knew that he was right. He had their backs, and he would take each of them one by one. The Arkers moved swift and quiet on hardened bare feet. They used the shadows of supply crates, and the creaks of the tanker to provide them with cover. One by one they took down each last soul on their side and made their way to the bridge.

They were close, but then fog lights glared all around them, so bright that Isaac and the others were blinded. It took them a moment to adjust to the brightness, and then came the sound of a creaky metal doors opening, and forty last souls appeared from all different directions. They formed a circle around the Arkers and the bridge; each was armed with an axe, a shiv, or a pipe.

The Arkers readied their spears. "Rosita!" Isaac shouted, and a moment later Rosita showed her face on the balcony of the bridge.

"Why have you come here, Isaac? Why have you tied up my men? I've given you food and medicine."

"I wish to see my niece, and Wilson, Cayden, and Simone."

Silence followed. "Now is not a good time. Anya and Wilson have gone to the oil rig. As for Cayden and

Simone, it's late and they're busy with their new-born. I can't disturb them now, but if you come back in the morning, without your spears you can see them all."

"Don't trust her Uncle, she's lying, Anya went to the tanker without Wilson," Jake insisted.

Rosita hesitated. "She did, but then the old fool demanded that he go with her to check that she's okay."

"I don't wish to play games, Rosita, bring Wilson to me at once."

Rosita felt tense and tired. Nameless, or rather Neptune, could return from the water dwellers at any moment; he might be listening, watching and waiting for her to slip up, for any reason to sink the tanker and the Ark. As frustrated as she was, she had to lie.

"Wilson went to the oil rig; I give you my word."

"I doubt the worth of your words. We don't want to fight you, but the Arkers I bring before you are warriors."

"You board my ship, tie up my people and make outrageous accusations. You had my respect, Isaac. All I've done is give you gifts, and now you threaten to me? Leave this place, leave now and there will be no bad blood between us."

"I can't leave my people, or my niece."

"Your niece will return to you."

"When?"

"In a week's time.

"You're lying." Isaac considered giving the signal to his men; they were heavily outnumbered, but their skill with a spear would be unmatched. He thought back to the flood, the violence, and he considered giving the order, but then Barnaby appeared alongside Rosita, and mounted an old heavy machine gun on the bridge. Such a reminder of the past sent a shiver down Isaac's spine, and those with him felt the same. Isaac knew what would happen if they opened fire: there was no protection from such a weapon, they were sitting ducks.

"Leave now, right now, and you will live," Rosita said, but Isaac didn't falter.

"Uncle," Jake interrupted.

"She's bluffing, she won't shoot our prisoners."

"We don't know that," Jake said as he grabbed his uncle's shoulder.

At that moment Cayden ran out in front of them. "What the hell is going on out here?" he asked as he caught his breath.

"I've come to bring your family home, Anya and Wilson too. Where are they?"

Cayden folded his arms. "They both went to the tanker. I don't understand, last I heard was that Simone and I would stay here? What's really going on out here?"

Isaac saw that Cayden looked well, and that calmed him down. He looked back at Rosita with want to reconsider his next move. "This? This is just a little misunderstanding. How is Simone, and your child?"

"They're wonderful, I hope you can see them soon, but maybe not tonight! This place is good, they're really taking care of us. They're good people, Isaac, all of them."

Isaac nodded and considered his next move very carefully. Even if he launched a good spear or two, the machine gun would cut him and his people down as if they were nothing.

"I'm glad we've cleared up this little understanding," Rosita said.

"Me too," Isaac replied. He cut the restraints of the captured last soul at his feet and let him go; the other Arkers did the same with their own prisoners. "We'll leave today, but if I don't hear from Anya and Wilson within a week, I'll return."

Isaac and his crew retreated to the tanker's edge, one by one they dived off the side until only he was left. Then he turned to look at Rosita one last time. "Remember how easy it was for us to board, I'll see you soon," he said before diving off the side and making his way back to his kayak.

"Do you believe them, Uncle?" Jake asked as they sailed back toward the Ark.

"Not in a million years."

There were so many things that didn't add up, Isaac wondered why Wilson crossed his arms if there wasn't an emergency. He also wondered whether they were really at the rig given Terrance's warning. Something wasn't right, but the last souls were treating Cayden and Simone well. Though he wanted to storm the tanker and find the truth, the last souls had something which rendered his spears useless.

If only Isaac could see Rosita at that moment, he would have seen her collapse on the bridge under the weight of her mistakes as Barnaby tried to comfort her.

"He could have come," she sobbed, in fear of Neptune.

"But he didn't," Barnaby replied.

"They think I'm a monster."

"It doesn't matter what they think, only that our people survive. We all know that you would never fire the gun, and that you would never hurt them."

Rosita looked up at Barnaby as the strain of her mistakes kept her down. She thought of Stix, and then she thought of Any. She had left the poor girl to die by the hands of a true monster, and she might have been the only one strong enough to stop him.

15

FOR ANYA

Isaac didn't say a word as the *kayak's* made its way back to the Ark. Everyone respected his silence as he wondered what his brother, Richard, would do. And what Wilson, or Anya, or even Tyson, would do. He knew that Tyson would have climbed aboard and taken the ship by force, and that he wouldn't have hesitated before the machine gun was mounted—but somehow Isaac knew there was a better way.

It was getting late, and Isaac didn't wish to go home to his shack, for Lyn would ask about Anya's return. Instead, he sat by the dock and tried to think. He thought about his niece, about where she could be and why Rosita would lie to him. He didn't have any idea why, and that only made things worse. Exhausted by his failure, he felt older than ever before, but then he saw someone hovering at the Ark's edge.

"Great, Terrance. Just who I need to scold me for not listening," Isaac said, but upon closer inspection he saw that Terrance was smiling when he came to his side.

"How did it go?" he asked.

"How do you think it went?"

"Judging by the lack of Anya's reappearance ... not too well; and judging by your worried face ... terrible."

"Right and right again, turtle man."

"Not to worry, I think I have an idea," Terrance said as he raised his eyebrows in excitement.

"Does it involve more turtles?"

"Well, now that you mention it, it does. Take a walk with me."

Isaac followed Terrance to a quiet spot at the Ark's edge, and there Terrance boarded a kayak. "Follow me out into the water in that canoe and I'll explain more when we're there."

"Why do we need a kayak and a canoe?"

"Now isn't the time for questions."

Isaac did as told, and followed him out to sea, guiding the large canoe as best as he could. "Are you going to tell me why we need both?" he asked.

"You will see, my friend, you will see."

A few hundred metres from the Ark, Terrance stopped rowing and sat cross-legged. He raised his hands at his sides and closed his eyes. A ring of turtles gathered around them showing just their shells above the water. They swam in a circle; round and round they went.

"Terrance, this is—"

"Shh," came the reply, and a moment later Terrance began to laugh. "Yes, yes, she's here." He stood up in his kayak, and saluted Isaac before pencil-diving off the side. On his way down, his grasped the side of Isaac's canoe, capsizing it and forcing him under. Isaac felt a hand grab hold of him and force him back up, and there he coughed and spluttered. When he opened his eyes he was in darkness, for his head was inside the upturned canoe.

"Terrance, what the hell are you doing? Why did you capsize me?" Isaac asked as he locked eyes with Terrance and they both trod water.

"Shh," Terrance replied as he pointed behind Isaac.

Isaac felt a faint glow of orange light coming from behind him, and when he turned around he almost scared himself to death. He closed his eyes and opened them once more to see big orange eyes staring back at him.

"Anya?" he asked, but then he saw a hint of blue and understood that it wasn't her. "Who are you?" he asked.

"This is Hali, Anya's friend," Terrance replied.

Hali kept bobbing at the surface to keep her skin hydrated as her blood orange eyes stared into Isaac's soul.

"Hali, I've heard all about you. Thank you for coming, thank you for all you have done for my niece. She speaks very highly of you, and I wish we could have met under different circumstances, but now I fear for her safety." Isaac waited for a response, but none came. Hali bobbed under the water and back up, and then she signalled to her throat whilst making a strange hissing sound.

"I know you can't speak to us, but I know you can hear me. I fear that Anya is in great danger. There's another group of humans on the oil tanker ten miles north of our Ark. They asked Anya to help fix their rig. They say she hasn't left, but I think they're lying. Will you help us get there?"

Hali dived under the water, and she was gone. The two men looked at each other in surprise, and then Hali shot back up and scared Terrance before carving something on the boat's planks with a sharp stone.

TANKER FORBIDDEN. DARK WATERS.

"Please, Hali, we need your help. Anya needs your help."

Hali appeared unsure, and then she began to write something else: FOR ANYA.

Isaac nodded. "For Anya."

16

THE TRENCH

Thousands of leagues under the sea, in the deepest, darkest trench, lay a large metal vat. Sand had risen when it hit the floor and the fish had scuttled away into darkness. Days and nights went by, but on the third day Anya pulled herself to freedom with one scaled claw. When she emerged, her green head was bruised and swollen, and she had a tremendous headache due to the pressure. It took a moment for her to comprehend her surroundings. It was almost pitch-black; the only light cast was from her yellow eyes and the faintest glimmer of moonlight. It was cold, colder than anything Anya had ever felt, and as she gently released herself from the barrel, she hit her leg.

"Argh!" she cried, and then she knew it was broken. She looked to see her other arm, which was floating free no matter how much she tried to keep it to her body; it was dislocated.

Around her she saw the bottom of a canyon, a crevasse with walls miles high. She could see that there was nothing above her on the surface, and she knew she had drifted far from the rig and the Ark.

"Where am I?" she asked herself, and it hurt to try to remember. "I need to get out of here, to swim up," she said, but as soon as she started to swim, the pain was too much. She made her way to a large rock, and there she forced herself down. Now that she was anchored, she tried to think, and the last thing she recalled was Rosita. She remembered turning green and journeying with her to the oil rig. Her head started to hurt again, and then she remembered every strike, every blow—the hatred, the fear, and the helplessness. His scar-covered body, his vengeful eyes, and his sole motivation—to end her.

"Neptune, *why?*"

Anya had no answers; all she knew was that he had once saved her from the kraken, but somehow, she had driven him to hate her and to take everything she held dear. She made a fist and tried to focus.

"Oracle," she called, but she received no response. She tried to call for Hali, Kai, and Pearl, but no one came. Anya gave up as she remembered that no matter what she threw at him, Neptune sent it all back twice as hard. Despite every obstacle—drowning, turning back into a human and fighting Tyson—never in her whole life had Anya been betrayed by someone she loved. She had admired Neptune; he was complicated, cold, and stubborn, but she loved him and the world he had created, but as she lay motionless on the ocean floor, she began to cry.

There was very little for her to think about except

her failures. "Stupid," she called herself. "How stupid can you be to think that Rosita wanted anything more than to betray you?"

She should have listened to Wilson. For all she knew, everyone and everything she had ever loved was already gone. Neptune would take it all in a heartbeat as the Ark tried to defend itself in vain.

Hours went by as she stewed in resentment. She cursed those who had betrayed her and wept for those she missed. Her leg was in excruciating pain. On the surface she could keep an injured bone still, but under water it continued to move and provided a constant reminder of the break. She had to do something about it, so she scoured the seabed for anything that could be of use. She found a long piece of old metal, and then she took some seaweed to use as a binding and made a splint.

Even with her leg in better shape, she couldn't survive down here for long, and there was no way she could swim up with a dislocated shoulder and a broken leg. She didn't have the energy. She tried to summon fish to eat, to regain her strength, but she couldn't: her powers had left her.

Day and night melded into one as she remained near the seabed. The few fish that glowed in the night steered clear, and she felt the threat of predators watching from above. The dwellers used to say that the bottom was another world, and a darker one at that: well, they were right. Life at the bottom was death itself, and it consumed anything that came this far down.

There was barely any plant life and nothing worth catching.

Anya could do little to ignore the hunger, and the only distraction was the pain in her leg. She swam back to the rock, with no choice but to try and lie down and stare up at the huge rock walls around her. For hours she swore she was seeing blue lights, and she feared that Neptune was searching for her. But her eyes were getting heavy, her body was exhausted, and she had no choice but to sleep.

Anya slept for a whole day, and when she awoke, she had hunger pangs. She tried to find fish, but she was too weak to call them. She had to move despite how slow her movements were. She pulled herself along the ocean floor where there was nothing but rocks; but then she saw something hard-shelled, a giant crustacean, and so she took a bite of its soft underside. The creature tasted vile, but she had no choice other than to swallow it down.

The next few days were the same. It was so cold that Anya thought she would freeze to death, she was finding it hard to cope with the pressure, and she knew that if she didn't do anything soon, that she would die. She thought about her family, she looked up towards the surface and knew it would be a long journey, one she didn't have the strength to make. Then she saw the same flicker of blue, and she had the strangest feeling that something, somewhere, was watching her.

"I know you're out there; I can sense it!" she shouted out of distress for her situation, and she received no response. "Are you just going to watch me struggle? Tell me who you are, tell me what you want!" Anya kept staring, waiting for the blue flickers of light to reveal themselves again.

"Who am I?" a strange voice replied. "How can you ask such a question when you appear so uncertain of yourself."

"I know who I am. My name is Anya, Anya of Ark."

"All I see is fear, no name."

"I'm not afraid of anyone."

"Then my eyes deceive me …"

"You're a water dweller," Anya insisted.

"A what?"

"A water dweller!"

"And the way you shout is supposed to teach me the meaning of such a term?"

"You are, you must be."

"Forget about me. I see what you are—a broken fish in a very big pond."

Anya didn't have the energy to think clearly, for the weight, the pressure and the cold were taking everything from her. But then the mysterious blue eyes came closer, and with them came warmth.

"I'm not broken."

"Well you look broken, now tell me, what are you doing in my home?"

"Do you think I want to be here? I'm lost and *clearly* hurt."

"Tell me what you want."

"What?"

"In life, tell me what you want more than anything."

Anya was losing her patience, she was freezing to death in great pain, and now some stranger was trying to ask her strange questions. "I'm not telling you anything about me unless you show me who you are."

"Well this is my home, and if you hadn't noticed, I'm the only thing out here that might be able to help you. If you don't want to answer my questions, and answer them true, then I bid you farewell …"

The creature's eyes disappeared and Anya was left in darkness, to deal with the cold and the pressure in her head alone. "Wait! I want to be better … I want to save the Ark and the tanker, to say sorry to the dwellers, and then I want to go away."

"Away?"

"Far away, and never come back."

"Hmm, an honest answer …" And with the stranger's words its blue eyes lit up again and Anya used her good arm to shield herself from the brightness.

"Tell me, Anya, what do you love?"

"I love my brother Jake, Aunt Lyn and Uncle Isaac. I love my people."

"What about yourself?"

Anya lay still and helpless as she looked up to see the shining blue eyes, which seemed to move all about the place. "How can I? I tried so hard, but I let my guard down. I was played like a fool, and now I've lost everything."

"We all make mistakes … Tell me, Anya, what do you fear?"

"I fear no one."

"Now, that was a bad lie … Goodbye."

The eyes closed and there was darkness once more. "Wait!" Anya cried, "Wait! I fear death, I fear losing those I love, I fear drowning, I fear being alone. I fear— I fear Neptune." She sank down in self-pity and sobbed. "Please, don't leave me, I don't want to be on my own anymore."

The cold blue eyes appeared once more; they narrowed and came closer. "Fair answers, each of them. Now I only have one more question ... Tell me why you are here."

Anya told the story from the beginning, recounting the tale for the first time aloud. She started with her sixteenth birthday, the trials, the shallows, drowning, coming back, and waking up in another world. It was strange to say it aloud, tragic even, but when she spoke of her adventures as a water dweller with Kai and Pearl, she laughed. When she told of her bond with Oracle, she smiled, and when she spoke of Cray's death, she cried. Soon enough she addressed her ordeal with the tanker, with Nameless and Rosita. She finished with the oil rig, with fire and betrayal. Anya felt better for getting it off her chest, and as she went on, the bright blue eyes seemed to widen with interest.

"Quite the story ... but how can I be sure that you're telling the truth?"

"I don't know."

"Bring forth your orca."

"I can't."

"Bring forth the fish."

"I can't!"

"Then turn human."

"I don't have the energy …."

"If you reveal your human form then I shall reveal myself."

Anya thought over the request for a moment; she needed the warmth of his blue eyes, for without it she would die. So, she summoned all her strength, and then came her hair, her eyes, her skin—only for a moment, however, for any longer and she would die at this depth. The change hurt and she felt faint, so she closed her eyes and turned herself back into her scaled form.

"I don't believe it," the stranger said as their eyes came closer. At that moment, warm blue light burst from the being, and Anya saw scales, luminescent neon scales. Anya shielded herself in disbelief. "You're a dweller, a blue-eyed dweller. Who-who are you?"

"My name, my sea name, is Enki."

17

THE HEALER

At nightfall, Hali made for the oil rig with a rope in her claw as she towed Isaac's kayak. She thought about her destination—a place that had already toyed with her heart. It reminded her of someone she loved. Someone who had once made her laugh and cry … but that person had betrayed her trust and done something she had never thought him capable of. That dweller's name was Enki: Neptune's dishonoured brother. And Hali remembered the day of his disappearance like it was yesterday.

Deep under water, amidst the bright and beautiful coral of the dwellers' kingdom, the sun shimmered and fell upon the old art gallery. Though the paintings were ruined, the building itself was the real masterpiece: cream stone, still so strong after being submerged for so long. The rooms were dark and crooked, and most of the art had withered away, but its best attraction had always been the museum's centre. The courtyard had once been a garden, but now it was an aquarium, a beautiful place of crabs and coral which shimmered in the daylight and sparkled at night.

Hali swam through the maze of rooms and into the courtyard with eager anticipation. There she found her love floating in its centre. As usual, he appeared casual, carefree, as if in mid-flight. His name was Enki. Finding love underwater was a strange thing; they had lived most of their lives as humans, but there was nothing like a dweller's love, an animalistic thing that, when it took hold, never faltered.

"Isn't it beautiful?" Enki asked.

"You ask me that every time we're here," Hali replied as she swam to meet him.

"Well, isn't it?"

"It's as beautiful as it was yesterday and the day before."

"Or is it not more beautiful each day, like you?" Enki extended a hand to meet her; he pulled her in and then began to spin her round as if they were in a ballroom.

"Enki," Hali sighed, before flaring her nostrils due to her nerves.

"I've been thinking about us, about our future …"

"You're always thinking."

"There's an oil rig not too far from here. It would make the perfect human settlement."

"But we aren't human."

"Not, not yet, but maybe we can find a way."

"You and your big ideas," Hali said. "I thought you had everything you ever wanted right here."

Enki swam forward and kissed her, and she began to glow blue for a moment. "I do, you know I do ... but maybe, just maybe there's a way."

"Do you miss it?" Hali asked.

"Miss what?"

"Being human."

Enki took a moment to think. "There are some things I miss: hiking, fresh air and sandy beaches; on the other hand, how could I miss something so cruel as work? As evil as illness? As horrid as hunger? I suppose there's one thing and one thing only I would give everything to see ..."

"And what's that?" Hali asked.

"Your beauty. You're beautiful now, but once, just once, I'd like to see you, us, in human form." Enki nestled his nares up against hers and looked deep into her eyes. "If we were human, I would build us a home on the oil rig, and we would live out the rest of our days watching the sun rise every morning, and see it set every night."

The pair were lost in the moment, until another dweller interrupted them. "Brother," said a voice from below. The pair looked down to see Neptune, and then they separated just a little, for their relationship hadn't yet been announced to the rest of the dwellers.

"Have you ever considered knocking?"

"You don't knock under water," Neptune replied. "We must go, now."

"Where are you going?" Hali asked.

"We wanted to keep this quiet, really quiet. There are humans; Neptune has heard them."

"Where?"

"Close by," Enki replied, and then he summoned Fin, his beloved hammerhead, who had been lounging amid the seaweed. When the beast came forward, he revealed the happy and smiling axolotl on his side. The shark stopped right in front of Hali, lowered his nares, and she retrieved Guillermo.

"Must you leave now?" she asked. "Maybe we should talk about this a little more."

"There's no time, I'm too excited."

"Well, maybe I should come with you."

"Hali, you're our only Healer; if anything happened to you, I couldn't bear it. You and the others must wait for us on the forbidden cliff edge, we don't want anyone in town. We both have our sharks and our strength; we should be fine."

"Hurry, brother," Neptune said.

"Alright, alright, I'm coming," Enki replied. He rolled his eyes and smiled at Hali before kissing her once more. The world around them ceased to exist—just for a moment—as Hali began to glow, and specks of Enki's skin glowed, too.

"Well, would you look at that," he said. "I won't be long, there's something I wanted to show you today, down at the rocks."

"*Now*, Enki," Neptune insisted.

"Go," Hali said. "Just promise me you won't do anything stupid."

"I promise on all my love for you." Enki took a bow,

before he swam down at speed, mounted his hammerhead, and flew up through the courtyard opening. Neptune followed close behind and Hali watched them go.

⁓

As Hali swam toward the oil rig, she remembered what he had promised, and she remembered how that promise had been broken. But still she remembered the good things: the way Enki used to smile and laugh; the way he looked at her. The way he used to float as if he were in a dream, soaring through the sky, and how he used to see the best in everyone and everything. It hurt to return to the oil rig after all this time, and it hurt to remember him. That day had played on her mind a thousand times: the kiss goodbye, his smile … and then he was gone. He had died that day when he went to see the Arkers.

"How could he do what he did? How could he kill a human being and leave in such a cowardly way?" But Hali shook off such feelings; she could waste no more energy on him, for she had wasted enough.

She pushed Enki from her mind and remembered Anya. She was strong and brave, and more powerful than any other. But Hali remembered how she had left them, how she had been the first to burn herself with the sun's light and become human again. She recalled that Enki had said that there was a cure, that there would always be a way—but how was he to know that it would be so painful.

Hali heard Isaac moving up above in the boat. It was a cruel thing to be unable to speak to him. If only she could talk about their communities, their differences, then maybe they could come to understand one another better. What she had come to understand without the power of speech was serious enough. The worry in his eyes for his niece could not be mistaken, and if Anya was truly in danger, then so was she. Hali had to be careful. Even now, she could feel a darkness in the water, and a slight feeling of dread took hold. If Isaac was right, she could only imagine what might be strong enough to hurt Anya, and Hali might not be strong enough to stop it.

As Hali made her way to the rig, she could taste something foul, and soon enough she realised what it was: oil. The putrid taste made it difficult to go on. She saw no fish, and no other signs of life from here on in. She stopped a hundred metres from the rig and then surfaced.

"What is it?" asked Isaac. He passed her a piece of driftwood and she began to etch something on the side.

OIL. YOU GO MUST GO ALONE.

Isaac nodded, dived into the oily water and began to swim. The pungent fumes irritated his eyes and affected each breath, but he had to keep going for Anya. The closer he got to the rig, the more he appreciated the size of it. The last gargantuan structure of man creaked away as if it were alive. When he reached the giant's legs, he pulled himself up on the ladder and began to ascend. The ascent took time, and he tired quicker than he thought.

"I'm too old for this," he said as his hands felt the constant cold of metal, and his forearms felt the burn. When he reached the top, he felt the wind and heard the creaks and judders of metal moving all around him; he was alone, and he knew right away that he shouldn't be there, for it was a place of ghosts not meant for a man who had left the old world behind him. He moved from wall to wall, peering round corners whilst staying light on his feet. He walked past cabins and cranes, remnants of man's old ways, and there he saw that the metal was black. Some of the rig was still smouldering, red hot with embers. He knew then that it wasn't safe, that it could give way any minute, and that it would be best to leave, but he had to push on for his niece.

Isaac was careful with his footing, so the damaged grating did not give way and expose him to the huge drop below. He looked around for any sign of Anya in the moonlight. The grids were badly damaged by the fire, but some were still stable. He found one that was all bent and mashed, almost folded in two; no human being could have folded it. He bent down to find a dried substance between the grates, and so he tasted it.

"Blood; where are you, Anya?" He asked himself as he inspected the dents that told of a hard impact. He turned to the control room windows and saw that they were smashed. He made his way in and saw the broken screens, the bent lockers, and knew that they were signs of struggle.

Isaac followed the corridor to a stairwell and along to a walkway. There were marks on the concrete wall, even the mark of a fist; but here the signs of struggle ended. He made his way to more stairs and saw claw marks scraped across the structure; something or someone had been taken, and they had resisted. Isaac followed them, fearing that someone had been dragged to the exposed metal staircase. He ascended the stairs and at the top he saw more evidence of struggle: scratches on the railings, more blood, and then the missing piece of the puzzle: half of a used flare. He picked it up and inspected it. Then he looked around and noticed a sign that indicated this was an area used to fill oil barrels. He was puzzled.

"If Anya had been in a struggle, it would mean her assailant had superhuman strength ... but Anya was the only dweller who could surface, maybe there was another."

Isaac tucked the flare into his sea leathers and was about to leave when he saw something else. Something glimmered green in the moonlight below him on a ledge. He pulled up a grate and climbed along the structure, careful of the drop into the sea far below.

He reached out a hand as far as he could, stretched a little more, and retrieved Anya's necklace. The green and gold emerite necklace she would never take off—unless she had intended to leave it behind. Isaac wrapped it around his wrist and began his descent. He made his way back to the kayak, and when he returned, Hali threw him back over the side before bobbing up and down on the surface to keep herself hydrated.

"One of yours has her," Isaac insisted, "there were signs of struggle, and broken metal that no human could break. It has to be one of yours." He withdrew the flare and passed it to Hali. After a short inspection, she took the sharp stone to the driftwood again.

FLARE = HUMAN.

"I'm telling you, Hali, whatever it was, it wasn't human. There are claw marks and torn grates thrown around as if they were nothing. Something or someone has her, and whoever it is has to be stronger than her. There must be someone out there … there must another Anya. Did anyone have a grudge against her?"

NO.

At this, Isaac revealed the emerite necklace, which was glowing. Hali took it in her hand for a moment; she felt its warmth, and she could feel how Anya felt just before she was burned. She felt her pain, her suffering, her fear. She looked worried as she took a moment to collect her thoughts and consider what it meant. Though she wished to dismiss Isaac's speculations, she couldn't dismiss what she had felt. But why would any dweller take Anya? Most adored her, though they would never say it. She watched Isaac for a moment and saw how sad he was.

"Anya was here, but there's no way of knowing where she is now. I guess this is goodbye," he said, and Hali etched one more message into the board:

WE WILL FIND HER.

18

BROTHERS

Anya awoke upon a rock; she was tied down from the waist to a makeshift stretcher, and the stretcher was weighed down with rocks to keep her from floating away. Ahead of her, she saw the dweller's eyes glowing blue as he foraged on the seabed. AShe remembered his name: *Enki*. A name she had heard before, but only once.

"You're Neptune's brother, aren't you?"

Enki stopped what he was doing for a moment. "I don't have a brother," he replied.

Anya could detect the pain in his voice as he said these words. "You do, and he did this to me. They always said you were the evil one, now I know the truth. Why are you helping me?"

"Because."

"Because?"

Enki swam to her. He had a rusty old bucket filled to the brim with sea snails and crabs. "You needed help. Now, enough questions, you need to eat and rest."

"I don't have time for either: the Ark is in danger, I need to help my people."

"Well, you can't save whatever the 'Ark' is on an empty stomach. Eat. Try to suck them from their shells."

Anya did as she was told. The taste was awful, but she persisted and quelled her hunger.

"How do you turn blue?"

"A simple trick: bioluminescence is a gift that I believe many possess but few have learnt to master. Dwellers have many talents, many we are yet to understand, and they only seem to come forth when you need them most. Someone special used to glow like this, and down here I would've died without such light, so I somehow made it happen."

"How do I do it?" Anya tensed and closed her eyes as if that would make a difference, and when she opened them Enki was giving her a cold blank stare. "You don't smile much, do you?" she asked.

"I haven't really been around children for a long time."

"Children? I'm an adult."

"Oh."

"How long will it take me to heal? Today, tomorrow?"

"Weeks, maybe months."

"Months! I can't wait that long; we need to find Oracle and the water dwellers and then together we can stop your brother."

"We? Let's get this straight, there is no we, and that monster is not my brother. You or anyone else who goes against him will lose, he's too powerful. He will cloud the minds of anyone you hold dear. He will take your power and your heart; if you're smart you will run and if you're stupid you will perish. You need to regain your strength and then you can be free; you said you wanted nothing more than to go far away—well, you can have that now: swim to the ends of the earth."

"I-I can't, not yet, not until I beat him."

"You can't."

"You're afraid of him, aren't you?"

Enki went quiet for a moment and turned away. "He took everything from me. He took my bond, my shark Fin, my love, and my people. I can't even move fish anymore. I should have seen it coming, I should have seen it all, even back then. We were brothers, we had families, cars and jobs, but the ocean took everything. I came to terms with what I lost in the great flood, but not my brother—no, there was a darkness growing inside him even then. I should have seen it; I should have sensed it."

"How did he get those scars?"

Enki struggled to look at Anya for a moment as he recalled his darkest memories. "In the early days of the flood we climbed aboard a ship to survive. It wasn't just any ship, it was a hellish place and we were enslaved by the crew. My brother and I were starving; he stole a tin of beans, and do you know what they did to him?" Anya shook her head. "They tied him down and tortured him, cut him hundreds of times so everyone would know he was a thief. That's why he has those scars, and that was when he changed. I begged for his release, but only when he was at death's door did they let him walk the ship, displaying his marks of shame. Most would have jumped overboard, but not my brother. He could never let it go. Do you know what he did to them?"

Anya waited for him to go on.

"He sank the ship. He took everyone on it to the bottom of the ocean: men, women, and children, the guilty and the innocent. We drowned together, and, unlike everyone else aboard, only the two of us became water dwellers. We were given another chance."

Enki looked down; he appeared almost ashamed of himself, guilty for telling the story. "Together we found our sharks, built our kingdom, and lived a life without humanity, free from starvation and cold. A life of peace —or so I thought. The day your people came was like any other day, but I should've known, I should've seen it coming …"

Years prior, Enki said goodbye to Hali at the old art gallery, and he mounted his shark alongside his brother. Enki was distracted and neglected to focus on what was ahead of him, for today was the day he would see humans for the first time since his transformation. As Fin soared away, he kept looking back at the art gallery and thinking of Hali. There was so much he wanted to say to her, and in truth he didn't want to leave, especially not today.

"The humans are close," Neptune said.

"You can hear them better than I."

"Of course, I can; you were never as sharp as me, brother."

Enki laughed. "And you were never as funny or as charming. If you really think you're so good, how about another race? I left something at the statue, something important."

"Very well, but you will lose."

"Three, two …" Enki counted down, but Neptune's hammerhead propelled forward before the final count. "Cheater!" Enki said as he tried to catch up with his brother. They swerved around grand old broken buildings and soared through the reef. It took a moment or two, but soon enough he caught up with his brother and now they were neck and neck, weaving through the water together on their hammerheads.

"Surprised to see me, brother?" Enki asked.

"I'm surprised that you haven't quit," Neptune said, before slamming his mount into his brother's, knocking him off balance and forcing him to slow down. Neptune was in the lead now, far ahead, and Enki was no longer sure he could make up the distance. He assessed his options on the path ahead, and then he saw a half-covered sign to the subway. This was his chance, and he soared down into the darkness. He trusted his instincts and moved to the left to avoid an old broken train, before crossing right to escape another.

"Come on," he said, urging his mount forward, and with all his might Fin pushed on. They soared through the tunnel until they saw light at the end. As he pulled up into the open, Enki turned his head to see his brother just behind him. Now he had the lead, and he wouldn't give it up for anything. Soon he came to a halt at the foot of a statue of the old sea god Poseidon; in his hands was the golden trident. Enki dismounted his shark, and soon after, his brother arrived, rather disgruntled about losing. The two sharks swam off together to hunt as the brothers stopped to stare at the statue.

"Why do you look so glum, brother?" Enki asked as he faked a smile. To tell the truth, he was worried about his brother, incredibly worried. He had become so quiet and distant as of late, and all Enki wanted was to have him back.

"You cheated," Neptune replied.

"*I* cheated? You pushed into me!" Despite Enki's initial reaction, he calmed himself and went to his brother's side. He wanted to ask a question that had been on his mind since Hali had asked him earlier today, and he didn't know how Neptune would respond. It was so hard to get him to speak about the old world, about what had been lost.

"Do you ever miss it?" he asked.

"Miss what?"

"The surface."

"No," Neptune replied.

"I thought not, but what about the rolling hills, the sunsets and the warmth of fire. Do you remember when Dad used to take us camping?"

"The old man grew to hate anything but watching television."

"You're not so different really, are you? Mom would have wanted you to smile."

"Don't."

"I … I need to know if you're okay, brother." Enki's words came with careful consideration; there was so much more he wanted to say, but he didn't dare speak of the flood, of Neptune's lost daughter or his torture on the ship.

"Why wouldn't I be?"

"You just seem quiet, a little off is all."

"I'm fine," Neptune insisted.

Enki swam down behind the statue and withdrew a large piece of slate and a sharp stone.

"What's that?"

"This is going to be my pen and paper so we can start communicating with the humans—so we can learn from them."

"And you think those things are going to sit down and talk?"

"Why wouldn't they?"

"The gods never spoke to us, why would we want to speak to them?"

"Because they *are* us. You of all people know how tough it was."

"What if I don't want to talk to them?"

"Then I'll go alone."

Neptune flared his nares, shook his head, and swam up to the statue. He examined the trident for a moment before prying it loose.

"What are you doing?" Enki asked.

"I'm taking it."

"Brother, that's an artefact. It's—"

At that moment, Enki noticed his brother's demeanour change. He flared his nares, lowered his brow, and raised a hand as if to silence Enki.

"What is it?" he asked.

"They're here."

The pair mounted their sharks and began their ascent to the office block. They saw the underside of the *Iron Lady* and knew that the humans had arrived. They swam up to the hole in the roof and from there they watched four pairs of feet meet the office block roof for the first time in over thirty years. Enki reminded himself to be on his guard as he watched the humans edge forward with eager anticipation.

"What are they saying?" he asked, knowing too well the power of Neptune's hearing.

"They're talking about treasure, about food and medicine."

Enki readied his pen and tablet, and began writing the word "Hello." But Neptune was having none of it: he shook his head in frustration, flared his nares and swam forward into the foot or so of shallow water upon the rooftop.

"Neptune, what are you doing!"

Despite Enki's plea, Neptune continued, and Enki had no choice but to put down the tablet and follow him. When Neptune rose from the water, the four Hunters stepped back in fear and raised their spears. They began to shout in panic, so he gave a screeching hiss. The Hunters didn't retreat as he intended, and he fell back down into the water again to bathe himself before rising once more. This time he was closer. He hissed again, but the Hunters didn't move.

When Enki rose alongside his brother, he tried to step ahead of him, to present a more peaceful and welcoming stance, but the damage was done: the Hunters held their spears high and ready, and Neptune hissed again.

"What are you doing, brother?" Enki asked.

"Is this what you wanted? Look at them, they think we're monsters," Neptune replied in mind-speak, all the while screeching to the humans' ears.

Enki pushed him back. "Get a hold of yourself, maybe they can help us, maybe they can help us turn back."

"Is that what this is about?" asked Neptune as his fury grew. Then came a spear. It flew through the air with precision and power from Gregory's hand, but Enki caught it right as it teased Neptune's chest. They both looked down to see the sharp point bring the slightest trickle of blood, and Neptune bared his teeth and screamed.

"No!" Enki shouted. His brother had already dived into the foot of water before launching himself toward the hunters once more. The Hunters were retreating, their backs turned and running to their ship when Neptune rose from the water in front of Gregory and forced his claw through the man's chest before tearing out his heart. Gregory was lifted into the air before being cast aside by Neptune, who picked up his trident and readied his aim at the others. Just before he threw,

Enki put himself between them and raised his wooden spear.

"Step aside," Neptune instructed.

"Have you gone mad?"

But all Neptune wanted to do was pass him. He tried to sidestep his brother, but the spear followed his every move, and so he raised his golden trident and the fight began. Back and forth they went, clashing with their weapons as water splashed all around them.

"I don't want to do this, brother," Enki said, but Neptune said nothing. They fought along the rooftop, back and forth, strike after strike. "Why are you doing this?" Enki continued.

"Because they're a plague," Neptune replied as they exchanged blows once more. "Enough games," he continued as he snapped his brother's wooden spear in two.

"Yes, let's stop this and go home," Enki said, and he dropped the broken spear into the water below. He turned as if to leave, but to his dismay Neptune drove the trident through his chest and lifted him into the air as the brothers locked eyes, frozen upon the edge of the world.

Thee third prong snapped off and Enki fell into the sea. Neptune remained on the surface for a moment, and soon felt the fire and the heat—but he also felt good. Enki, meanwhile, swam down from the dark side of the office block to the darker side of town. He swam for safety as quickly as he could despite his injury, and he made it to the bottom.

Above him, Neptune fought the fire brewing in his

mind at the sound of human shouts and voices as they retreated. He fell to his knees for a moment to process what he had done. Then he dived in to follow Enki.

"Why, brother?" Enki asked, as he remained hidden at street level.

"Because you had everything, you had it so easy. They all look up to you, laugh at your jokes; they love you, but nobody cares about me. I was the one who bled for our survival, who sank a ship for you, and now you're trying to take us back to that mess."

Neptune made his way down to search for his brother. With his trident in hand, he was ready to finish the job, and Enki looked at him eye to eye as he had done many times before, although this time he didn't know what to say except, "You've lost yourself, truly lost yourself."

Neptune raised his trident, ready to deliver the last blow, but Fin came roaring by and slammed into his side. He fought the shark's jaws for a moment and let go of the trident. He punched the beast in the snout before wrestling it into submission. His eyes shone red for a moment, and then the shark stopped flailing and became docile at his side.

"Your shark is mine, brother. Your power is mine. Now reveal yourself."

Enki had used Fin to buy him time, and he had used that time to enter an old sewer. From here he witnessed his bond leave him, his connection dwindle and disappear. He could feel the power leaving him, and in its place he felt only darkness. He saw his brother retrieve the trident, and now where there had once been one obedient shark, now there were two.

"You can run, but if you come back, if you ever come back, I'll feed Hali to your own shark piece by piece, do you hear me?"

Enki heard his brother's words, but he didn't wait to respond; instead, he kept moving through the sewer pipe. He thought over his brother's threat and looked down to see the prong embedded in his chest. With great anguish, he had to pull it free before he could carry on.

Enki remembered that day like it was yesterday, and as he relayed those events to Anya, it was hard to finish the tale. "I didn't see my brother's hatred until it was too late, although it was always there. I should have seen it, but I turned a blind eye. I wanted to befriend your people, but you came with spears, and my brother had other intentions. I spent many nights wondering why, but the truth was that he only ever saw your people as they saw him."

"My people are kind."

"But are they kind to monsters?"

Anya said nothing.

"My brother died on that ship when he was tortured, and the man, the thing that stands in his place, isn't the brother I loved. He's something else now, and he's only grown stronger."

"Why didn't you go back to the water dwellers and explain?"

"It was too late. I had to escape, and so I came here."

"I would never run."

"That's easy to say, but when those you love are in danger it's a different story. You said you too have a brother, Anya, what would you do differently?"

Anya thought of Jake, and then she knew that such a betrayal would break her heart. "I don't know."

"If I ever returned, he said that he would hurt her, so I stayed away."

"What was her name?"

"My love—her name was Hali."

"Oh my god! She never mentioned y—"

Enki almost laughed. "Why would she? I tried to get to her, to get to the art gallery, but he got to her first. He covered his tracks by moulded their minds into believing that I had hurt the humans."

"But if she knew the truth, she would forgive you."

"She's under his spell, they all are."

"It all makes so much sense now: what Serus was saying about the darkness, about Cray's death and the other disappearances. It was always him; he was just covering his tracks. You can't blame yourself, and you can't waste away down here without making this right. We can fix this."

"No, we can't."

"Don't you want to see Hali again? If you don't fix this, you're just as bad as your brother. I can't stop him on my own, but together we can do it."

Enki shook his head and laughed. "We? There is no *we*; look at you. I've more use for a sea snail."

Anya looked down at herself and saw the stretcher and her dislocated arm floating lifeless at her side. She was about to cry, but she held back the tears, and when she looked back at Enki, he was at her side. He took hold of her arm and forced it back into the socket as she screamed.

"Oh, get over it. It couldn't have hurt that bad—is your leg the same?" Enki pushed down on it and Anya screamed even louder this time. "No. That's not dislocated, it's definitely broken."

Deep under water, within the water dwellers' kingdom, was the stadium. A place overgrown with seaweed and coral, washed by the sands of time, it was an amphitheatre used only for the young to play water wheel, and in the time that had passed since Anya's visit, much had changed. The young fins had grown up. They were taller now, stronger, and there were even some new members: little brothers and sisters who swam around the side-lines. The young fins did not have a leader, but if they were asked to choose one, they would all say the same name.

He swam with speed and precision, his speed and strength untested in the game, even against the larger players such as Cliff and Crash. His name was Kai, and he had long been undefeated; in fact, he had been undefeated for so long that he had begun to lose interest. He scored point after point, flying back and forth. It didn't take long for him to grow bored of the game, so he swam back down to the seating area where Pearl was watching.

She had little want to play the game nowadays and was more content to sit and listen to all things. "Are you not going to finish the game?" She asked, her silver eyes shimmering as she spoke.

"I don't feel like it," Kai replied.

"Want to talk about it?"

"Not today."

"Why not?"

"I just have a bad feeling; I can't explain it."

Pearl seemed rather nervous herself and chose her next words with care as she didn't want to unsettle her friend. "I have the same feeling Kai, I can feel something in the water, something not quite right."

Kai shivered. It was easy for him to see how Pearl's eyes resembled those of Serus, the ancient one. "Stop it. You're giving me the creeps."

"Well, I sense darkness, every day. I can feel it everywhere, it's all around us and it doesn't want me to see."

"Or maybe it's just you?"

"It can't just be me. I keep thinking of Anya too. I keep thinking she's in pain, and that she needs our help. I know she's never answered our attempts to speak with her—but I could always feel her presence before, and now I can't."

"Do we have to go over this again? She left us; she doesn't care about us."

"Anya cares, I can feel it, and one day she will return. You're only saying that because you miss her."

Kai paused for a moment; he looked at the water

wheel pitch and the children playing. Then he looked up, way up, to the great divide, the clear line between air and ocean. "I do miss her—why else would I let you talk me into surfacing?" He remembered the rush, the fear and then the pain of the sun on his scales.

The pair went quiet for a moment until Kai took off. "Oh no!" he shouted.

"What is it?"

"I'm late." He swam out into the open where Polka soared to his side.

"Late for what?"

"Training with Neptune," he replied as he swam away.

"Be careful!" Pearl shouted, but Kai was gone.

He darted east towards Neptune's playground. Upon his arrival it was quiet. The old park's sand-covered basketball court, was still. He was nervous, afraid even, for Neptune hated him being late. All he wanted to do was make him proud, but all he ever seemed to do was fail to live up to his mentor's expectations.

"Hello!" Kai shouted, but his voice fell to silence. He knew Neptune would sneak up on him—he always snuck upon on him and then droned on about the element of surprise. "Is anybody out there?" Kai asked as he saw fish scatter from a part of the forest to his right; and as he took his eyes from his left, Neptune's large hammerhead shark Grey came rushing towards him.

"Ah!" Kai shouted as he rolled to get out of the way.

Then came the second shark, Fin, and Kai dodged again.

He took a moment to try and compose himself, but a scaled claw landed on his shoulder from behind and he flinched before turning to see that it was Neptune.

"Are you afraid, Kai?"

"No," he replied.

"You are, I can sense it."

"I'm not."

Neptune lunged forward and sighed in disappointment when Kai shielded his face. "How many times must we do this?"

Kai bowed his head.

"If you want to be anything like me, or her, you have to change. How could I ever entrust the leadership of the water dwellers to someone so meek? What if another tribe attacks, what then?"

"I-I …" Kai tried to think of something to say. He knew he wasn't as strong as Anya; he had spent enough time swimming laps, moving boulders and fighting sharks to know that for sure.

"You're weak."

"I'm not weak!" Kai shouted, losing himself for a moment in anger.

"Ah, there's the spark that I've seen before. Remember this feeling, channel it, and maybe, just maybe, you will be able to move more than one mighty creature." Neptune raised a fist, the water began to ripple, and then a large group of sharks thundered by as Kai watched Neptune's eyes turn blood orange. Kai swam out into the open, and here tiger sharks hurtled toward him. Back and forth he went, trying to evade them. Meanwhile, he had instructed that Polka flee for safety.

"You're being too defensive; you must attack them. I won't stop them until you do."

More sharks came at Kai. At first he was able to dodge, but then more came and he had to increase his speed. He hurtled through the ocean, dodging each one and batting them away, but then one latched on to his arm.

"Argh!" he cried as he pried the shark off. But then came another and another. Finally, he could take no more. He propelled himself towards them and batted them aside one by one with his fists. In the end, all the sharks swam away, having been released from Neptune's grasp, and Kai was left alone, fuelled by anger and ready for more. After the adrenaline started to wear off, he looked down to see the bite marks on his arm. They stung just a little.

"Ow."

"Good," Neptune said. "Remember this pain. Now try to summon your dolphins."

Kai raised his hands in the air, closed his eyes and struggled with all his might. He tried and tried but no dolphins came forth.

"You aren't trying hard enough."

"I'm trying my best."

"Try harder!"

Kai was exhausted and he felt like a failure, but perhaps that wasn't the reason the dolphins came. He knew that if they did, they would have to fight, and although he wanted to please Neptune, he didn't want to hurt them. Torn between the two, he was about to apologise to Neptune, but then he heard something strange: the faint cry of a whale.

"What was that?" he asked.

"Never mind, you're supposed to be concentrating," Neptune replied, seeming rather agitated. "I've had enough of you today, we're done."

Kai nodded. "Will we continue tomorrow?"

"When your wounds are healed," Neptune replied before swimming away. Kai excused himself. He made his way back to the water dwellers; he told no one of his training, not a soul. He took time to patch up his wounds, and took off his bandages before meeting with the young fins when it was dark.

20

BEHIND BARS

W ilson stared at Yan as he snored away beyond the bars of the brig. This was his chance, his only chance. He rattled his empty metal cup on the bars and Yan jolted forward as he awoke to his surroundings.

"I need water."

"I'm coming," Yan replied as he waddled toward the bars and poured Wilson a drink from his canteen. "You know, I haven't ever seen you smile—it doesn't hurt to smile, you know." Yan chuckled, but Wilson didn't; instead, he dropped his cup, grabbed Yan by the collar and pulled him against the bars.

"Woah! Don't hurt me, please, you'll get into trouble, big trouble!"

"Shh!" Wilson hissed as he pushed the sharp pin against Yan's neck. "One more word and I'll do it, I'll pop you. Now give me the keys, nice and slow."

"I'm too young to die!"

"I said give me the keys."

Yan trembled as he reached down to take the keys

from his belt. His hands were shaking, and so he fumbled and dropped them on the floor. "Sorry, I'm so sorry," he said as Wilson crouched down to retrieve them.

"Can you not do anything right?" Wilson asked as he opened the cell and forced Yan inside.

"On the floor, now," he said, and when Yan was down, he hog-tied him with his own handcuffs.

Wilson made his way out, then turned back to see the prison guard's tears above his gag. "Oh, and Yan, just so you know, you're the worst prison guard I've ever seen."

Wilson headed for the stairwell and scanned the ship's fire-exit map. He knew where he had to go, but there was somewhere else he needed to visit first. Down and around the stairs he went, to another cell, beyond the bars this cell had posters on the walls, a dressing table, and even a CD player. It was like walking into a time machine, and at the end of the bed was a blonde woman in her mid-thirties brushing her hair.

"Wilson?" she asked.

"It's me," he replied, and though they had only shared one conversation through the pipes, he felt he knew her better than anyone else aboard.

"What are you doing in here?" she asked.

"I'm breaking out, I'm going home."

"You didn't hurt Yan, did you?"

"No, but I should've. Anyway, I'm short on time and I have to warn the Ark. If you come with me, I can keep you safe."

"Oh, I wish I could but I can't," Stix replied as she shook her head.

"You have to."

"No, Rosita needs me."

Wilson sighed. "You don't have to stay here for her."

"I do. I'm in love, have you ever been in love?"

Wilson nodded. "Very well," he said as he turned to make his leave.

"Go down the hall, take the first left and there's a passage that leads to the other end of the ship. From there, take the stairwell all the way up and there should be a rowing boat."

"Thank you."

"Wait … There's one more thing you can do …"

"What?"

"The passage leads to near the bridge. In Rosita's desk there's a lockbox, and in the lockbox there's a gun."

Wilson turned around. "Thanks, but I have to return to my people, I can't get caught again."

"But you can end this."

"So can you, goodbye Stix."

Onward he went, quiet and careful. He made it to the passage that stretched all the way from one end of the ship to the other. He passed storerooms, the oil store, and then he heard the noise of the engine. Soon enough he had made it all the way to the other end of the ship and there he climbed the rusted stairs. At the top he found the rowing boat that Stix had mentioned, and freedom was at his fingertips.

Wilson lowered the boat into the water in haste, and then it was time for him to dive. The night was dark, the air was cold, but he knew he could make it, and he turned to take in the sight of the tanker one last time. He wanted to say good riddance to the tanker, but his eyes fixated on the bridge. He couldn't do it, he just couldn't leave after what Stix had said, and so with a massive sigh he made his way to the command centre.

The lights were off. It was too early to sleep, but Wilson knew that Rosita could be within. He was nervous. *Get the gun and go*, he thought to himself over and over as he looked through the glass and confirmed that no one was there. He lifted the latch and very slowly opened the door. He made his way through and found the desk. He checked each drawer and found an old blue lockbox. Using the pin of his badge, he pried it open, and there was the revolver. He felt the weight of it, checked the cylinder and ensured that it was loaded. He tucked it into his old weathered trousers and made for the door. Then, to his dismay, the light came on.

Wilson hid behind the desk as Rosita made her entrance, kicked off her boots and was about to sit on the couch when she saw his footprints. She reached for the hatchet on her belt and raised it high. "Who's in here?"

Wilson revealed himself, his pale blue judgemental eyes colder than ever as he raised the revolver. "Don't make a sound and get on the floor."

"I'll scream …"

"Scream and I'll kill us both—you don't want to test me."

"Maybe I do."

"I wouldn't, I'm an old man with nothing left for me in this world."

"What do you want old man?"

"I want you to redeem yourself. I know all about you, Rosita, I know about Stix and all the excuses you make to protect her; but more than that, I know th danger you're in, that you're afraid, so afraid that you would rather kill a sweet girl than stand up to a monster."

Rosita's eyes filled with tears. "You think I wanted this? Any of this? You would never understand …"

"No, I do. You chose the wrong side, but it isn't too late."

Rosita shook her head. "It *is* too late, Wilson. He will tear this ship in half and destroy your Ark. I've lost soldiers, friends, brothers and fathers to him, do you understand?"

"I can take you somewhere safe."

"Don't you understand? Nowhere is safe."

Wilson cocked the trigger. "Enough talking. We're going to the Ark, now." He led her outside, but he saw that Barnaby was at the bottom of the stairs, so he ushered Rosita out of the other door and onto the bridge's balcony. Then the fog lights came on. Wilson was prepared to fight his way out, but as he turned to Rosita he saw the fear in her eyes when a deafening screech filled the air.

"He's here," Rosita whispered. A shadow came down from above and landed just ahead of them; a dark green being, and its claws crunched into the steel of the deck as Wilson beheld Neptune for the first time. The dweller stood strong, with a look of menace and pleasure in his vengeful blood orange eyes.

"Well, well, well: the old man; we finally meet."

Wilson showed no sign of fear, but met the beast eye to eye. "Nameless—or should I call you by your sea name, *Neptune*."

"I did wonder whether anyone would ever figure it out. I'm not surprised the girl told you my secrets, she betrayed me."

"Anya told me all about you, your sad swing and your pathetic sharks. What will your people think when they find out what you're doing?"

"They'll follow me to the ends of the earth."

"No they won't."

"Anyway that doesn't concern you. Rosita here told me many things, and she told me that Anya took quite a liking to you. She begged, you know. She called out your name and she begged for you to save her."

"You're lying."

"What reason would I have to lie?"

"Because you're a coward. A conniving spineless worm and I'm sick of listening to you drone on and on." Wilson lifted the revolver high and took aim at Neptune's skull.

CLICK. The revolver failed to fire, and Neptune slid toward him in a second before throwing a mighty punch to his rib cage. Wilson felt the cracks as the air left his body and the force threw him at the bridge's outer wall.

Neptune went for him again. Rosita put herself between them but he effortlessly pushed her aside.

"No!" she screamed as Wilson caught a glimpse of Neptune's advance; his deadly claw was in reach now, but then a metal spear point burst through the monster's chest.

Neptune looked down at the wound in surprise, and then he fell to his knees. He turned his head and saw Barnaby holding a harpoon. He staggered back to his feet and pulled the spear free from his shoulder as he screeched. Then he launched it back at Barnaby and pinned him to the wall of the bridge.

"No!" Rosita screamed. She tried to pull the spear free, but it was too far in. She fell at Barnaby's side and held him in her arms. "Barnaby, Barnaby—no …"

"At sunset tomorrow you drive your tanker through the Ark and then you make for your oil rig. If I *ever* see your ship again, I'll sink it. Do you understand?"

"Yes," she wept.

Neptune nodded. He looked at Wilson once more, and then approached a flaming torch on the bridge's balcony next to the tanker's large beacon. "Oh, and, old man, before you go, I want you to know that I burned Anya alive."

With this, Neptune turned to make his leave, and then Wilson began to laugh. The laugh soon turned to a wheeze and a cough.

"What's so funny? Neptune asked.

"Looks like I know more about dwellers than you do. You don't burn."

"What did you say?"

"Fire won't kill her, you idiot."

Neptune scowled and put his hand into the flaming

torch. If the dweller could have blushed, he would have, and as Wilson laughed again, Neptune launched himself high in the air and dived into the sea where the hammerheads were waiting for him. He panicked and made for the rig to hunt Anya down once and for all. He swam at pace, ignorant of the oil spill, and he stopped at nothing as his sharks searched for any hint of blood. When he saw just how deep the trench was, he knew his sharks would not make the journey, and without daylight, neither would he. He turned back and made for the water dwellers empty-handed as the fear of Anya being alive plagued his mind.

21

DWELLERS

Hali retuned to the water dwellers with caution. The oil rig was on her mind, and so was the feeling of touching Anya's emerite necklace. She had felt such pain, such darkness, and she couldn't help but consider what Serus—the ancient one—used to say. She remembered the day she had tried to free Cray from his illness, and how that in trying to heal him, she had felt such evil. She had made herself believe that such darkness had died with Cray, but when she touched Anya's necklace, she knew that it hadn't. It had always been there, but she had never been able to see it. Her journey to the rig had given her clarity, and now she knew that whoever had used Cray as a vessel, now they had Anya. As she made her way back across the sand-covered outskirts toward her home, what was once a magical place, a bright and colourful underwater world, was now dull and grey.

The thought of the rig reignited her old feelings of loss, she had the sudden urge to consider memories long since buried, and to visit somewhere she hadn't been for a long time. Now she needed answers, and so Hali made her way to the art gallery, as she could not get Enki out of her mind. She remembered that he had wanted to show her something when he returned, but he never did. There was little she could do to shake it from her mind, and she needed closure. She had to go there, she had to see it, and so she passed through the stone arches and through to the once rich red lobby. She stopped in the archway as feelings flooded back, and then she entered the courtyard. This was her place, her home for a time with the only person she had ever loved ... and he had thrown it all away.

When Hali swam in, the place was just as beautiful as she had left it. A shimmer of light still met its cream-grey walls, but the rock garden at the bottom was now filled with thick fronds of seaweed. Hali thought back to the day when Enki had left with his brother. She should have asked him to stay, but then she might not have discovered what he was really capable of. She swam down between the reeds to the rocks, and there she found herself between the two boulders. She remembered how he had said not to look until he got back, and how she had promised; but he was never coming back, and so she swam past the reeds and saw his work of art, his masterpiece etched into the rock.

It was a beautiful carving of the pair of them, holding hands and surrounded by fish, and she read the words, 'Hali, my love, will you marry me?'

She swam backwards and covered her nares to control her emotions as everything came flooding back.

Every day with Enki seemed to flutter by before being washed away by the sorrow of being without him. She put a hand on her heart, and for the first time in far too long she could feel its warmth. She remembered just how much she loved him, as if some dark feeling was being purged, and then she remembered when the dark feeling was first placed.

~

At the time of Enki and Neptune's fight upon the rooftop, Hali had been out swimming with Guillermo, Marina, and Patricia, far from the water dwellers' kingdom. She had felt something was wrong and so she shot back towards home. When she tried to find Enki, when she called out to him, he was nowhere to be found. She then crossed into what would soon become Neptune's domain, and there she saw him sat alone on the swing where he had spent so much time remembering his daughter.

"Neptune, where's Enki?" she had asked as she approached, and then she saw the pair of sharks, the sorrow and despair written all over him.

Neptune didn't answer at first as he struggled to make eye contact with her. "Hali," he said as he swam to meet her. "He loved you, you know that, don't you? He really did."

His strange and unexpected words made Hali think the worst. "Neptune, you're scaring me. Has something happened? Tell me."

"The humans, they attacked us with spears. They

almost killed us both … My brother, he—he killed one of them with his claws, and then he fled."

"No," Hali said in disbelief, "no, no. I told him not to go, I told him not to go. How could he do this? I—I don't believe you."

Neptune swam towards her and placed a hand on her cheek. Hali felt a hint of darkness and cold. She wanted to let go but she couldn't. She wanted to scream, to fight and to flee, but she couldn't move, and then he said the words:

"My brother is a murderer. He killed an innocent man and fled like a coward."

Hali's will to fight back had disappeared at that moment and she was left with a feeling of calm. Neptune had entered her mind and manipulated her, despite her powers. She was helpless, and in that moment—a moment which she had completely forgotten until now—she had accepted every word.

Hali remembered that day, those words, and the feeling of darkness. Now she had been liberated, and Neptune's words had worn thin at long last. She was almost in a trance as she stared at the mural, the beautiful piece of art Enki had made for her. She didn't know what to say or think, nor did she know why the darkness had lifted; but then she the water turn cold … He was coming.

Hali stayed perfectly still, as, to her disbelief, the two sharks—Grey and Fin—swooped in from above.

Then she saw Neptune, and she prayed that he couldn't see her as she remained hidden by the long reeds.

"Insects. Weak pathetic insects!" Neptune swam with one arm as blood mingled with the water. He had his hand upon his chest and appeared to be tamping a wound. When he turned around, Hali saw that something had gone right through him: a stingray, or a spear. "I'll show them who the last souls really are. I'll take their souls, all of them, mark my words."

Hali remained still as she observed him, and she wondered whether his pain was causing him to lose his grip on her mind. *Good*, she thought, *let him hurt, let it sting.*

"She can't be alive," Neptune insisted. "I watched her burn in a vat of oil."

Neptune turned his gaze to Hali's direction, and she wondered whether he had seen her. He swam down towards her at speed. Hali didn't move a muscle as Neptune stopped right in front of her, before tearing a few reeds free and swimming back up and out into the open. There, he bandaged his wound.

"I can still hear the old man's laughter. I should have finished him right there. Never-mind, he'll be quiet soon, they'll all be quiet, mark my words. She *must* be dead, but what does it matter, we don't have time."

Time for what? Hali wondered as she struggled to stand the sight of him. Her emotions began to weigh her down as she closed her eyes and tried to breathe, to stay calm. Soon enough, Neptune left, but Hali was so afraid that she remained hidden in case he returned. A little while later she took her leave as she tried to connect all the dots. She wondered how long things had been like this, and why it had taken her so long to see through him. Throughout the day she recalled conversation after conversation as she tried to pick up on anything out of the ordinary. It appeared that the only person acting strangely was her; the young fins were playing water wheel and the grown-ups were all getting on with things. She wanted to speak to Neptune and raise her concerns, but he had casted a dark cloud over her mind once before, and so whatever she was going to do, she had to do it right.

There was a meeting that afternoon at the town hall. Hali swam in and floated down to take her seat with Guillermo in her arms. He was being more affectionate today as if he knew her pain, and he hadn't left her side since she had returned. It was as if he knew something, but he was unable to tell her what.

Hali saw Marina ahead of her, accompanied by her octopus, Patricia, and Hali took a seat alongside them.

"Hali, how have you been?"

"I'm fine, Marina. Thanks for asking."

"Well, you look tired, dear—make sure you're getting enough rest."

Hali turned her attention elsewhere and saw the large dweller Russell scratching the chin of his equally large walrus. Next to him was Ray with his stingray— Sting (Ray was never the most imaginative of dwellers). Many more followed with crabs, porpoises, lobsters and eels, an endless stream of dwellers and their bonds in a myriad shapes and sizes. There were of course many adult dwellers who could not bond, such as Dorian, who Hali remembered had saved Anya from the sword-fish attack at the water wheel pitch.

Hali kept a close eye on everyone who entered, and now she felt the subtle chill moments before Neptune arrived with his sharks. When Hali saw him, she noticed the wrap around his chest which covered his injury.

Hali knew why he hadn't asked her to heal him, and as the meeting began it was all she could think about. The meeting droned on as different dwellers spoke of fish and slight changes in currents. All Hali wanted to do was confront Neptune, but she wasn't that stupid. The conversation changed to the subjects of stone monuments and young fins expected to be born soon. It went on that way for about half an hour as she obsessed over Enki, Neptune, and the possibility of Anya's murder. She held her tongue for as long as she could, until she could take no more.

"And so, that brings to a conclusion our discussion on tuna ," Dorian said. "Do we have any other business?"

Hali floated out into the middle and everyone was silent.

"Hali, do you have something to share?"

She took a moment to collect her thoughts. "I must confess that, like most of you, I tried to surface …" The crowd gasped, and everyone shared a look of surprise and then denial. "I tried, but, like you, I failed."

"Hali …" Dorian interrupted.

"We shouldn't be ashamed of it; we should be proud of who we are and of who we once were. Everyone in this room was human or descends directly from a human. They may not sparkle in the water or possess our strength, but deep down we are human, and Anya proved that."

"Hali, are you feeling alright?" Marina asked.

"I went to see Anya. I met her uncle, and I heard the noises of their raft, of the children playing, their songs and dances." The crowd didn't know what to say or how to react; no one had spoken of Anya in a long time and their initial reaction was to not say anything.

"Is she alright?" Marina asked.

"Anya is in danger, but she wouldn't have been if she didn't have to choose between our world and her own. She was the bridge, and now she is missing."

"Missing?"

"Anya has been missing since her naming ceremony, when she left us never to return," Dorian interrupted.

"Hali, you admit that you went to see her with complete disregard for our decision to never see humans again?" Russell added.

"We made that decision in fear of our past; we shouldn't make any decisions out of fear. I met with Anya and I met with her uncle. They are kind people."

"We agreed to have no involvement with humans— none," Neptune said, short, sharp and to the point, and the whole room fell into silence. Hali noticed just how quiet everyone had become as Neptune snarled. When he sat back and waved his hand, everyone erupted into chatter again.

"She's one of us. She will always be one of us, and now she is missing. There's another civilisation close to the Ark, an oil tanker. Little is known about them except that they have electricity and oil, and that Anya disappeared whilst helping them."

"So that explains the oil spill? First, Anya brings shame upon us by choosing their side, and now she betrays our ways by polluting our ocean!" Russell shouted, and his passion was gained the delight of the crowd.

"I believe Anya was attacked at the oil rig and possibly killed."

"Human business. It's not right for us to care what goes on above the surface."

"Is it human business if the only one strong enough to take on Anya is another dweller?"

The room went quiet as everyone looked at each other.

"What are you trying to say, Hali?" Russell asked.

"That someone in this very room can turn human, and that someone in this very room meant to kill her."

The crowd erupted into chaos. Hali watched them with eager eyes, those who were shouting and those who were quiet, and then she stared past them, at Neptune: the man she had healed time and time again, whom she had trusted and rallied behind on many occasions and cried upon his shoulder at the loss of his brother.

"Order!" Neptune shouted. "What evidence do you have?"

"None, but—"

"Then how do you know that it's the truth? You've been through more than most, Hali; do you not think your eyes might deceive you?"

"He is right," Dorian agreed.

Hali went silent. She wanted someone, anyone, to speak up.

"Anya is one of us," said a voice from behind, and everyone turned to see who had spoken. At the back of the meeting were the young fins: Pearl, Kai, Cliff, Crash, Bow and River.

"Pearl, honey, now's not the time," her mother said, but Pearl was already swimming forward to meet the adults.

"Anya is one of us, she's always been one of us, and if she's missing, if she's in trouble, then we have to help her."

"Come on, Pearl, it's time to go, this conversation is for the adults."

"We're not going anywhere," Kai added. "Not until you help Anya."

"Anya saved my child," Marina said.

"And she swam with Orca," Dorian added.

"And she reminded me that we are all, deep down, human," said Hali.

"Okay, I see where this is going, but how on earth are you going to help her?" Russell asked.

"Enough of this," Neptune said. "I'll send my sharks to search for her , but we've lost too many in recent years, and I won't risk any of you. If Anya returns, we'll hear her story, but I won't sit here and listen to you accuse our people of murder: you of all people would sense if there was such a dweller amongst us, would you not?" he asked.

Hali bit her tongue. "I would …"

"Hear, hear," Russell echoed.

"From today, we're on high alert," Neptune said. "No one is to go anywhere alone; stay close to home and my sharks will patrol the waters. Meeting adjourned."

As everyone swam away, Hali tried to swim toward Neptune, but many seemed to block her path. When she finally pushed through, he was gone. Hali felt that everyone's eyes were on her, and so she made her leave via the stage side door rather than the main entrance. She stayed close to the derelict shops, but no matter which alleyway she passed through, or how fast she swam, she felt she was being followed by a dark and powerful force. She kept moving, until t she ran right into Kai and Pearl.

"Hali, what's going on?" Pearl asked as she saw her look of worry.

Hali put a clawed finger over her lips to ensure their silence before gesturing them to follow her. She swam into an abandoned shop where old clothes were still hanging on their hangers; the place was dark and as they entered, all the fish quickly left.

"You're scaring me a little, is everything alright?" Pearl asked.

"Someone has hurt Anya," Hali whispered.

Neither Kai nor Pearl knew what to say, for Anya had been their best friend. They had taught her how to be a dweller, how to swim, to dance and bond. They missed her every day, but Anya had left them, and that had hurt.

"I wish you said you were swimming to her; we

would've gone with you," Pearl admitted. "Kai and I, we wanted to see her too, we even tried to surface together. We struggled, but the pain was too much … We miss Anya but I knew that deep down she wasn't happy."

"We all knew that she would have to leave one day; this isn't her home," Hali replied, and then she saw the mark on Kai's arm. "Is that a shark bite?"

"No," Kai replied as he folded his arms to hide it.

"It is, isn't it? How did you get it?"

"It's nothing, honestly."

Hali tried to take a closer look at his arm, but Kai moved backward. "It is, when did this happen? Was this a part of your training?" She asked, having known that Kai was being trained by Neptune. The pair met eye to eye for a moment, and Pearl tried to hold Kai's claw until he shrugged her off.

"I said it's nothing."

Hali nodded, she wouldn't push him to tell her the truth, not now. "Pearl, can you find Anya? If anyone can, it's you."

"No … I haven't felt her presence for a long time. Everything is clouded and dark, like I can't see."

"Can you sense Oracle?"

"No, I wish I could."

Hali looked at Kai and noticed his guilt as he tried to cover up his arm. "Speak Kai, people are in danger, if you know something, you have to tell me."

"When I was practising with Neptune, I heard something to the east, past the town. It sounded like the cry of a killer whale."

Hali knew that Neptune and his sharks were to the

east. "I believe Neptune has done something … something evil," she said. "Stay together, keep Polka close and don't leave each other's side. Speak to no one about this, do you understand?"

"But Hali—"

"No buts; do you understand?"

"We do," they sighed in unison, and then Hali embraced them both for a moment before backing away.

"Where are you going?" Pearl asked.

"To solve this once and for all," Hali replied before swimming off in haste. Every moment that went by was a risk, but Hali couldn't be careless, she was angry, and instead of going too close to the shark-infested waters, she swam low, with Guillermo cradled in her hand; he looked tired. "It's okay, you get some rest," she said whilst giving him a stroke, but he didn't smile.

Hali went north, she hid within in the shade of buildings for a mile or so, and then, when she was far enough away at the end of the town, she circled back around, careful not to alert any of the many sharks. She passed a forest of abandoned shops, broken and half-smothered with sand.

It was at that moment Guillermo made a sound that only she could hear. "I know, I know. It's going to be okay, little one, everything's going to be okay."

22

STRENGTH

In a deep dark trench, Anya watched Enki glow bright blue. He had tried to teach her how to glow, how to make oneself warm, but Anya was failing to grasp the lesson. It was easy for her to be frustrated, to be angry at herself. Enki's lessons reminded her of Wilson's, and she imagined he would get on with the old man—although he might be the first.

"Cast your mind back to when Hali first healed you, to when you first felt the warmth and the light."

Anya tried with all her might to remember, and she could picture it, the glow on Hali's claws. She clenched a fist and expended every ounce of energy, but no matter what she could not fathom how it worked.

"It's useless, only Hali can save me."

"Well, Hali isn't here, it's just you and me," Enki sighed. "And if you're as powerful as you say you are, if you have bonded with an orca, then healing should be no problem."

"Why do I get the impression that you don't believe me?"

"Do you know what being a dweller is really about, Anya? Do you know why you can move fish? How you bonded with an orca?"

"I don't really know."

"I suppose my brother never taught you that lesson … It's about letting go. I see the pain in your eyes, the worry. If you can't let go, then you go the other way. Negative thoughts take over, they change your view of the world, and you are compelled to control rather than to bond. You question rather than accept and hate rather than love—just like my brother."

Anya felt hopeless: here she was at the bottom of the ocean, beaten and broken, betrayed by new friends and hated by old. The Ark was soon to be destroyed, and everyone with it, and right now she was being lectured by someone who couldn't face his own problems.

"It's useless," She admitted.

"Useless, is it? Hopeless? You're right, Neptune is going to sink the Ark, and it's all your fault. Let it go."

"Why am I even listening to you? You're a coward, you lost your powers, you ran from your brother, and from Hali, and now you think you can tell me to let go? Well, I can't; I can't let go!" Anya's tears began to build as she fuelled her anger and frustration. Enki didn't say a word; instead, he looked all around, including up above, and there he saw it: every creature was frozen in place, every crab and every fish.

"Let it go."

"I hate this place, I hate Neptune, I hate the tanker and I hate Rosita for what she did to me. I hate how everyone always relies on me, how everyone expects me to do the right thing, to be perfect, to look a certain way, to smile, to be good and kind. I hated drowning, I hated burning, and I hate that Hali brought me back." Anya stopped to recover her breath and to process her frustrations.

"I asked you before to cast your mind back to when you were healed; you said it was when you were poisoned, correct?"

Anya thought back and realised that she had repressed that first moment for so long. It wasn't when she was poisoned, it was in the office block—when the roof came down and the beam pinned her to the office floor. She could picture the warming blue glow of Hali's eyes, and the warmth on her chest.

Anya focused on these memories and began to feel that warmth as if it was happening now, and when she opened her eyes, they were glowing blue. When she looked down at her hands, they were glowing, too.

"I'm, blue!" To her amazement, her claws were glowing like Hali's had, and as she observed them, they began to flash like a light about to be extinguished.

Enki flew towards her. "Keep concentrating!" he shouted as he took her hands and guided them down to her broken leg. When she looked up at him, he was glowing, and she could feel the vibration, the warmth—it was as if he was charging her up. The glow travelled into her broken bone and was absorbed.

Anya flexed her leg, she broke the splint and tore herself free from the stretcher. To her amazement, she was able to swim out into open space, and from there she looked back at Enki and smiled.

"Well, I'll be damned," he said. "It worked."

23

THE HEALERS' CURSE

On the edge of the water dwellers' territory, Hali swam the long way round to where Neptune would often rest with his sharks. It was a dark and desolate part of the town, and she soon passed the abandoned buildings which surrounded the park where Neptune would sit and think of his daughter. Hali was beyond worried, but she knew that if she was quick and quiet, she would be fine. Onward she went, steering clear of the shadows of sharks.

After making sure that Neptune wasn't nearby, she looked around for anything that might provide a clue as to where the killer whale may be, anything at all, but her search was proving rather pointless. Even so, Hali scanned the seabed for anything amiss, for she could not give up on Anya or Oracle.

It was at that moment that Hali heard a faint cry, and then she saw something out of the ordinary: down below were large marks in the sand where two cars had been dragged toward each other. Hali swam down and realised that the cars were blocking the entrance to a sand-covered structure—a car park. She swam to the old rusted wrecks blocking the entrance, and then through the gap and into the dark concrete space. Every car was overgrown with algae and covered in rust. The building had an eerie and claustrophobic feel to it, but Hali didn't care, for ahead of her was Oracle. The whale was malnourished and covered in scratches from her captivity. Hali felt the pain of the beautiful creature as it nestled up against her.

"Shh, girl, it's okay. I'm going to get you out of here, I'm going to get you out so we can find Anya."

Oracle sighed as Hali swam back to push the cars out of the way. "Come on, come on," she said whilst exerting herself. To her relief, she managed to make an opening large enough for Oracle to get through. Hali waved her arms as she tried to get the whale to move. "Go! You're free, go!" Oracle, however, didn't move. Instead, she stayed in the darkness as if she was afraid of something. Hali didn't know what it was until she turned around and saw that Grey and Fin were floating above her, and alongside them was the one responsible.

"Neptune, how could you do this to us after everything?"

"I've only done what was necessary."

"First your own brother, and now Anya?"

"My brother was weak, just like the rest of you."

"I should've known it was you; Enki would never hurt anybody. It was you, wasn't it! And you—you killed him. Say it, I want to hear you say it."

"I did what I had to do."

"Enki was kind. You're half the man he was; and Anya, she trusted you."

"She betrayed you, Hali, she betrayed *all* of us. Anya took our secrets; she chose to be human."

"What secrets? Anya is human *and* dweller. She looked up to you."

Neptune's eyes turned a darker blood orange. "No, Anya stole from us, she left us."

"What happened to you? You're not making any sense. Come with me to the town hall, you have some explaining to do."

"I'm not going anywhere," Neptune replied.

"I'll tell everyone what you've done, you can't stop me, Neptune."

"Oh but I can." At that moment Neptune swam forward, and so did his sharks, but before they could reach Hali, Oracle came crashing past the cars to protect her.

"Stay back, girl, I don't want you to get hurt," Hali said. To her dismay, Grey and Fin began to charge. They darted toward her bearing razor-sharp teeth. She froze, but just as they were about to tear her in two Oracle batted them out of the way. Hali looked on as the three beasts fought with ferocity. Oracle was powerful, she butted and smacked the pair, grabbing one by the tail and throwing it into the other.

When Hali returned her attention to Neptune, he had retreated behind the car park, and so she gave chase. When she caught up to him, they began to grapple. Hali was stronger than he thought; they battered each other, dragging each other down and along the seabed while landing vicious blows, and throwing each other into cars. Hali threw Neptune through a glass window, but he was back in an instant and tackled her into the car-park wall. She threw him off and they went at each other again bearing teeth and claws.

Hali managed to scratch his face from forehead to cheek, leaving an open wound, and then they separated. "You will bear my mark for the rest of your days," she said.

"You fight well for a woman, better than she did."

"And you fight well for a worm."

Neptune grinned. "The difference between you and me is that you don't know what you're fighting for. I do, I have a plan, I've had a plan all along."

Hali wondered what he meant at first, and then she knew. A piece of her was missing, and as Neptune revealed Guillermo in his left hand, Hali's heart stopped.

"No!" Hali screamed as she swam toward Neptune at full speed. She tore a chunk from his neck, but he drew a rusted blade and forced it into her side. She felt the pain as black poison began to sear through her. She froze, hollow-eyed, despite her wish to fight. She tried to breathe, to speak, but all she could do was utter the word "poison."

"Strange isn't it?" Neptune asked. "Having all the will in the world to move but being unable to do a thing about it. You'll feel nothing for a while until it hurts more than anything you've ever imagined. ."

At that moment Oracle charged full force to save

her in one last defiant act, but Neptune drove his blade into the beast and it cried out before slowing to a halt.

He turned his attention back to Hali, and gently placed Guillermo on her shoulder before carrying her toward the car park. "You can't fight me anymore, no one can. I'm sorry it had to be this way, I really am, but when the Ark and the tanker go down, I can't have you trying to save them."

Hali looked on, helpless as Neptune let her float free into the middle of the car park. In the corner of her eye, she watched the sharks drag Oracle to her side. She could see the pain in the orca's eyes, but she could do nothing about it. She looked at Neptune one last time before he moved the last car across the entrance and shut out the light.

24

SILVER EYES

Pearl, Kai, and Polka were hiding within a discount clothes store. Pearl was keeping watch; she didn't want to attract any attention, and she was deeply distressed by Hali's display of concern. Her worry only increased as Polka kept trying to swim away and Kai had to hold her back. She had the strangest feeling, a headache almost, and all she could think about was whether Hali was okay.

"Shh, what's with you today?" he asked as he tried to calm Polka, but no matter what he did, she wouldn't settle. "What is it, girl?"

"Something isn't right," Pearl replied.

"Everything's fine."

"No, Kai, it isn't fine. Something big is going on, you know it, I know it—Hali was right. I know she said not to move, to wait until she came back, but I think we should go after her."

"No."

"What do you mean, *no*?"

"We should stay here."

Pearl could see that he was afraid, and she knew that she would have to be the one to fight, so she followed her heart out into the open.

"Where are you going?" Kai asked.

"I'm going to help Hali."

"But you aren't strong enough."

"It's not about strength. It's about having courage." Pearl swam to where Hali was heading, to Neptune's playground. It wasn't easy leaving the safety of the store; sharks had always made her uneasy, so she kept a close eye on them as she swam across the streets, hiding behind cars and in old storefronts.

"Why are the sharks on patrol?" she asked herself when the coast was clear, and she was right to ask, for there were sharks circling each and every block the further she went. She journeyed across the dwellers' territory, remaining close to the roof tops above Neptune's playground. Then her intuition took her down to the half-buried car park.

Just outside of the car park was a great white shark. The beast had razor-teeth, cold black eyes, and it hovered in place as if keeping watch as Pearl approached.

She wondered why it was there. As she approached the creature, it appeared lost in a trance, but when Pearl got too close, the shark charged. The beast came at her head on, snapping its teeth. Pearl didn't know what to do, she swam away, manoeuvring around cars, lamp posts and anything else she could put between her and the creature as it snapped it's mighty jaws. The shark crashed into the sides of cars, knocked over post boxes, and then Pearl realised she had nowhere to run. She turned to face the beast as it hurtled toward her, and then she threw one mighty punch at the snout. The beast tumbled over her head and into a nearby shop front. The impact had freed it from the spell, and so the shark fled.

Pearl then retraced her steps to the car-park entrance. She hesitated at the opening, for fear of what she might find. She wanted to turn back, but despite her instinct, she swam on. When she ventured past the rusted cars, she couldn't believe what she saw. Oracle was lying on the ocean floor looking malnourished and weak. Then Pearl saw a dweller alongside her whose scales were dark and matte; she knew who it was, but she wished it wasn't her.

"Hali, hang on," she said. At first Pearl didn't know what was wrong, but then she noticed the wound in Hali's side and the poisonous black ink seeping out of it. "Who did this?" she asked, and then Hali's eyes opened. They no longer held their golden shine but were dull and grey. Pearl remembered when Anya had been poisoned by the kraken's ink.

"Can you hear me?" Pearl asked.

"I can," she whispered.

"Who would do this to you?" Pearl asked.

"Neptune."

"Neptune? How? How could he?"

"He has deceived us all … he has hurt Anya, and he plans to kill the humans, but he hasn't won yet."

"How can I stop him?" Pearl asked.

"You can't, it's too dangerous."

"Why not?"

"You have Serus's gift Pearl, your eyes are the same silver. I can't let you go after Neptune, but that doesn't mean you can't help. Now do you know where Anya is?"

Pearl didn't want to be like Serus. She could see more and more every day, but she didn't understand what was happening to her, and that scared her. "I don't know ..."

"Close your eyes and think of Anya. It'll be okay."

Pearl closed her eyes. She tried to think, to see, and so her mind scanned the vast ocean. When her eyes opened, they were a bright and blinding white. She remained within a trance for a moment, and then she broke free.

"Woah. That was weird, I feel ... I feel strange."

"What did you see?"

"She's in a trench, the deepest darkest trench close to the oil tanker. And you're right, I'm not supposed to go, Kai is, Kai and ..." Pearl turned her attention to the injured orca.

"Here, place my hand on Oracle's wound," Hali said.

Pearl guided Hali toward Oracle. She placed her hand on Oracle's wound, and then came the bright blue glow that she had used before to heal many others.

The whale transformed from being discoloured to being healthy, slick black and white. Pearl knew that everyone had a chance now—but Hali was still injured.

"What about you?" she asked.

"I wish I could heal myself, but I can't. Don't worry about me."

Oracle swam out of the car park and disappeared into the distance. "Oracle, wait!" Pearl shouted. "I'll go after her."

"No, you know what you have to do."

Pearl sighed. "Fine, i'll spread word to the other adults and tell them what Neptune has done, I'll try and break his spell, okay?"

"That's my girl."

Pearl held Hali close, and their foreheads and nares met as they gave a dwellers' goodbye. "There's one more thing, when Kai returns, tell him to follow the turtles. We won't let you down, Hali," Pearl said before turning and swimming out of the car park.

25

COURAGE

Kai felt trapped as he remained hidden in the discount clothes store. He hadn't wanted to leave Pearl, or Hali, but here he was, afraid and alone. He replayed his time with Neptune over and over again in his mind as Polka nestled into his side. His mentor had taught him so much about his bond, about power, and Kai had confided in him. Though Neptune was harsh, all he had ever wanted was for Kai to be stronger —or so Kai had thought. He remembered every moment of fear and insecurity, uncertainty and loss. He remembered that Neptune had always compared him to Anya, and he felt such anger, such pain, about all the times his mentor had pushed and pulled him. He knew what he had to do.

Polka wriggled free, turned to him, and smiled. "What is it, girl?" he asked. "I don't want to go outside … because I don't think it's a good idea!" Kai shouted as Polka attempted to reason with him. "Okay, okay. It's because I'm scared. What if Hali's right? What then?"

Polka made for the exit. Kai knew that she would go on her own, and so they swam out of the shop and into the open alongside her. Polka raced ahead above Neptune's playground, and Kai did the same. From here he surveyed the entire place, every broken rooftop, every car, the rusted playground and coral-covered beauty, and then he felt a sudden chill. He didn't spot the markings in the sand from the cars, but when Polka shot down towards them, he soon followed.

"Pearl?" he called out. "Pearl are you in there?" After receiving no response, he made his way further into the car park, and there he saw a body: it was Hali. He swam to her side and held her. "Hali, are you okay? Who did this to you?"

"Neptune."

"I don't believe it," Kai said as his world began to fall apart.

"It's the truth, he hurt Anya, and I'm sure he's done much worse."

Kai didn't want to believe it. "Here, let me go and get you some help."

"No. I know you're afraid, Kai, but you have to be strong."

"I don't want you to die."

"Don't worry about me, worry about our people, about Pearl and Anya."

"Anya left us and Neptune would never hurt her."

"Neptune tried to kill me, and when he did, I felt his pain: he worries that Anya is alive."

"Where is she? Where is Pearl?" he asked.

"Pearl went to warn the adults, and Neptune, well, he could be anywhere."

"He said he was going hunting," Kai remembered, and then he began to panic.

"I know you're fond of Neptune, Kai, but you don't know him. Anya is in trouble and you're the only person in the world who can help her."

Kai gulped as he realised then that the world was on his shoulders. "How will I ever find her?" he asked.

Hali smiled, she gave the slightest nod and looked past Kai. When he followed her line of sight, he saw three turtles. "Follow them," Hali said, but Kai didn't move.

"What if … what if I'm not strong enough, what if I freeze?"

"Anya needs you, and we're stronger than Neptune thinks—together."

"What about you? I can't just leave you here!"

"You must. Promise me."

"I promise." And so, Kai and Polka set off together as the turtles led the way.

26

BROKEN SOUL

The spirit of the last souls was broken and the world weighed down upon Rosita's shoulders. Barnaby was dead, and Rosita had Wilson handcuffed to the pipe within his cell. Though she had rationalised every action for her people's safety, she had lost one of her best. She knew that when Neptune returned, they would all be doomed.

Without time for a proper funeral, the last souls wrapped Barnaby up in tarpaulin and weighed his body down before throwing him overboard. Rosita didn't say any last words as Barnaby floated to the bottom; all she could think about was the tanker crashing into the Ark. She didn't know what to do, and though she wished she could sabotage Neptune's plan, it would only secure the demise of her own people. She would do all she could to ensure their survival, and so each of the lifeboats was well stocked with essential supplies: food, blankets and medicine. Everyone onboard the tanker had an exit strategy if anything was to go wrong and every last soul was accounted for.

To Rosita's disbelief, Wilson had survived the vicious blow to his chest from Neptune, so she had Doctor Phillips check on him every hour in his cell. When Rosita heard that he was awake, she approached his cell and waited by the door until she finally summoned the courage to speak with him.

"Oh, you again," he wheezed.

"I need your help," Rosita admitted.

"My help? Look at me, just let me die in peace."

"I see the fear in the eyes of my crew. The way they tremble and stumble as if they know that this is the end. Am I the only one who thinks we can make it through this?"

"The time for 'making it through this' is gone. If you think that monster is going to let your tanker float on all merry and jolly after it destroys the Ark, you're in for a real treat."

"I know that now."

"The truth is there for you to see Rosita, you're just scared of looking. Anyway, you're not here for my wisdom—what's the real reason?"

Rosita frowned. "I came to say I'm sorry," she said as she leant upon the bars of Wilson's cell and began to cry.

Wilson didn't know what to say, and he gave a short sigh which quickly reminded him of the pain in his chest. "If you wanted forgiveness, you came to the wrong place," he whispered. "Look, you chose the wrong side, but I get it."

"Do you?"

Wilson shrugged. "I do. It takes a special sort of someone to make a true leader."

"I'm not fit to lead."

"No, but Anya was. She would have beaten him on her own terms, and I still believe that she will."

"Anya is dead."

"No, she's alive. I saw the way he boasted when he said he burnt her, and the way he shat himself when he put his hand in that fire. That fool will be swimming all over the place out of desperation to find her. You can't just kill Anya, she comes back, she always comes back—mark my words."

Rosita didn't know whether she wanted to be here if Anya did return, for how could she ever face her? She had granted the poor girl a death sentence and walked her right into a trap.

Amidst the silence, there came a clank of heavy footsteps on stairs until a stocky greaser named Latch entered and said: "He's here."

"There's still time you know," Wilson said.

"Time for what?" Rosita asked.

"Time to redeem yourself."

"No there isn't, but there is time for revenge." Rosita turned to the plump guard daydreaming in his chair. "Yan, when this is over, you let Wilson free, do you understand?"

"No," Wilson interrupted. "If the Ark goes, I'd rather drown."

Rosita rolled up her sleeves. "No one's going to drown," she replied before making her leave. She made her way to the bridge, but when she arrived, Neptune wasn't anywhere to be seen. It was only when the other greasers came running up the south stairwell that she knew he was in the engine room.

The tall broad chief engineer approached her, her name was Helga, and she was out of breath. She had a short blonde bob, and her overalls were half covered in oil. "He knows how to start the ship; even on his own it's just a matter of time," she said.

"Where is he?"

"He's shut everyone out and he's twisting metal around the doors so no one can get back into the engine room. He knows how the ship works."

Rosita saw glowing blood orange eyes appear from the darkness of the stairwell. Neptune walked out onto the deck to face the last souls as the engine workers put themselves in front of Rosita. She saw that Neptune was injured: he had a scar on his face and a mark on his neck. He had also had a hole in his chest from where Barnaby had harpooned him.

"Step aside," Neptune warned.

"We're not moving," Helga replied.

"How admirable, now Rosita, I'm not going to warn them again. Tell them to step aside, or I'll go through them."

The men parted. Rosita locked eyes with Neptune, then she dropped something metal on the floor, which clinked and rolled toward his feet. The last souls closed their eyes, the flash-bang grenade exploded and caught Neptune by surprise. Without sight or hearing he was vulnerable, and so the last souls screamed as they charged with pipes and wrenches and beat him down from every angle.

Neptune screeched as he battered them back in a blind, delirious state. The last souls threw a weighted net that wrapped him up and kept him down. He was entangled in the net, and when he struggled, a de-restricted cattle-prod was jabbed into his sides. He screeched in pain before he finally stopped resisting.

"Good effort," he said as he tried to regain his composure. "But it's going to take more than that."

"I know," Rosita said, and then she whistled. Neptune looked up, and to his dismay he saw a group of last souls on the bridge, where the .50 calibre heavy machine gun was being set up.

"Are you sure you want to do this?" he asked, and then they prodded him once more.

"Am I sure? You're a plague, a menace, and if you think I'm not going to stand up to you, then you've got another thing coming. Any last words?"

Neptune watched the machine gunner load the ammunition, it clicked into place, and he was careful not to make any sudden movements. "None. Do you?"

The last souls stepped back. The gunner's finger hit the trigger as Neptune dug his claws into the floor grate just ahead of him. He lifted it up and batted the cattle-prod-wielding last soul into the ocean. Then he used the grate as a shield as the machine gun rained down hell. It took only a moment to slip free from the net, and then he leapt into the air. Neptune threw the grate at the gunners and landed on the bridge. He took the gun and bent it in two before throwing it far into the ocean, then headed for the control room. Rosita could hear him smashing the room to pieces, she didn't want to go up there, but she had to.

When she arrived at the bridge, Neptune was already programming the autopilot. "I don't blame you for trying," he said as he wiped the blood from his eyebrow. "In fact, you have nothing but my respect."

"Oh, go to hell."

Neptune slid toward her; he took a tight grip of her neck and lifted her off the ground. "Another word and I'll rip your throat out. Now, you're going to do exactly as I say, or I take five of your youngest."

He loosened his grip and Rosita fell to the ground.

"That's what I thought … Now, disable the manual override," he continued.

Rosita did as he asked, the whole time hoping there was another way.

"I've already disabled the trick-wheel, if that's what you're thinking." Neptune raised one arm before bringing it down to smash the nearest screen to bits. Then he continued to destroy every other piece of electronic equipment onboard as sparks flew and monitors smashed. Rosita tried to stay as still as possible, but on the inside she was broken. With every swing of Neptune's fist, she tried not to flinch.

Neptune stopped, and picked up the intercom and gestured for Rosita to take it. "I said no harm would come to you, Rosita. I'm in a mind to kill you and everyone else for what you just tried to do, but I'm a man of my word. I want everyone onboard to head for the food store. I'm locking you in so you can't change course."

Neptune passed the intercom to Rosita. She told everyone to go to the food store quickly and quietly, and so they did. Once inside, the last souls huddled together as Neptune closed the huge metal doors and sealed them in from the outside.

Their course was set, and every single variable had been taken care of, but then Neptune heard the strangest thing: a whisper in the wind, one that he had heard before. In the water, below the tanker, he saw a turtle, and Neptune could have sworn it was staring right at him. He knew then that the whisper was that of another with a bond, but it was no dweller that he knew. Whoever it was, though, they were watching.

Neptune jumped off the tanker and into the water. The turtle tried to flee, but with his mind Neptune held the little creature in place.

"Now, now, little one, where do you think you're going? I think you have a lot to tell me."

27

SHARKS AND TURTLES

The Ark was quiet, the ocean calm, the sky free of cloud and the moon was shining bright. Terrance sat upon the edge of the Ark, where he had remained since meeting Hali. His turtles would come and go, venturing through the ocean and stopping to share the little they had discovered along the way. Bit by bit he was piecing together the puzzle, connecting the dots and trying to make sense of everything. He had been watching the dwellers, the tanker, too, and he had even been trying to find Anya.

He would sit for hours and meditate. Speaking to turtles was one thing, but a mastery of guiding them, shaping their movements and behaviour, required more energy and focus. Here he remained as time went on, gathering snippets no matter how big or small, until a dark figure grasped hold of one of his turtles and banished his influence as if it was nothing.

Terrance opened his eyes. He had seen Neptune himself, and now he was worried that his foe knew of his abilities. At that moment, everything made sense, and he rose. He made his way to Isaac, who was in the storm shack with Elder Frederick and Vanya.

The past few weeks had aged Isaac significantly; his strength was fading with age, and his sense was fading with lack of sleep. Having heard nothing from Hali, and fearing Anya was dead, he said little to most, and he didn't so much as look up when Terrance approached him.

"Isaac, I haven't seen you in too long."

"Terrance, what news?" he asked in the flickering light of a forever flame candle.

"I bring answers. It's my turtles."

Elder Frederick rolled his eyes. "Go on then, spit it out," he said.

"I wish I knew where to begin … One of my turtles has been watching the last souls. Their leader was forced to lure Anya to the oil rig, her intention being to get her on her own. You were right in thinking it was someone like Anya. There's another dweller known as Neptune. In human form he was called Nameless—the one who came aboard the Ark with Rosita and Barnaby. He wanted to kill Anya; he wants to kill us all."

"We need to warn Hali," Isaac said.

"It's too late, he has her, and he has Oracle." Terrance waited for a moment as his words sank in.

"Then we're done for."

"No, not yet … there's something else. Anya is alive."

Isaac's eyes regained their shine. "How do you know?" he asked.

"I found her, she's unharmed, deep at the bottom of the ocean, but unharmed."

"Well, then, what are we waiting for? We need to get to her."

"We can't; we aren't dwellers."

"We must help her."

"If we go into the sea, all we would do is hinder her. We'd be at risk from Neptune's sharks; he would use us as bait."

"Then what do you suggest?"

"There's another who might be able to stop Neptune, a friend of Anya's, a young dweller named Kai."

"So there is hope?"

"Maybe; but there's something else, something much worse."

"What?"

"Neptune plans for the tanker to crash into the Ark."

Elder Frederick gasped. "We must raise the alarm," he said.

"No," Isaac interrupted, "all that will do is cause panic, and we have nowhere to go. There has to be another way."

Terrance thought for a moment. "I know we don't trust Rosita, but maybe, just maybe, if we can get onboard the tanker, we can fix this."

Isaac thought over their next move, the last souls could not be trusted, but if help was what they needed, then maybe something could be done. "Elders, not a word of this to anyone, swear on it."

"We swear."

"Walk with me, Terrance," Isaac said, and they left the shack at pace. "Can you make it to the tanker?"

"Maybe—but look at the water, do you see the fins?"

Isaac looked out to sea and saw the grey shark fins in the water. "I've never seen anything like this …"

"They're here for us."

"Sharks or not, you must go to the tanker and stop them from destroying the Ark before it's too late."

"Me?" Terrance asked, knowing too well he wasn't strong or fast or brave.

"I can't go, I must stay on the Ark. I was here when it was crafted, and I'll be there if it sinks. It's up to you, Terrance. Take the *Iron Lady*, take Jake and Tomas with you; with the wind behind you, you will make it there in no time."

At that moment, a stranger leapt down from a nearby rooftop. "I will go too," he said, and when he stepped out of the shadows, Markus saw that it was Miles, son of Tyson. Miles had been living in hiding; he was ashamed, though Isaac would argue he shouldn't be ashamed of his father's actions.

"Let me regain my father's honour," he said.

Terrance looked out to sea once more. The tanker was but a small shadow on the horizon, and in between were hundreds of sharks, but he had to swallow his pride. "Let's do this," he said, and so they readied the *Iron Lady* and set sail.

〜

The sails were full and the wind was in their favour. Jake stood at the wheel of the *Iron Lady* in his brown sea-leather poncho, his long blond hair tied back. He didn't shake or falter or show any sign of fear, but Terrance meanwhile was feeling rather squeamish and seasick.

"Are you okay back there?" Jake asked him.

"Me? Oh, I'm fine," replied Terrance as he realised that this was as far as he had been from the Ark since the flood.

"Tomas, what about you?" Jake asked.

"I've got a bad feeling about this," he replied. "Nothing good happens when Miles is around."

Miles chuckled. "Oh, shut it you. We've only been off the Ark once."

"One time, and we nearly died; you're bad luck."

"And you smell, but you don't hear me complaining." Miles' remark caused Tomas to his armpits before scowling at him.

"We're sailing towards a forty-foot tanker filled with enemies, and there's an uncomfortable number of sharks in the water, so get your head in the game," Jake insisted.

"Do they always do that?" Tomas asked.

"Do what?"

"All their fins are pointing at us. Something's not right."

Tomas leant forward, looked over the side, and there, gnawing at the old wood of the *Iron Lady*, was a great white shark. "Your uncle said nothing about sharks," he said as he took a spear from the side and struck the creature until it swam away. He gave a sigh of relief, but then the boat was rocked from the other side.

"Oh no, oh no!" Terrance shouted.

"Do yourself a favour: get below deck and check for leaks," Jake instructed, and then the boat was hit again. "Tomas, Miles, keep them off us. We'll be there before you know it."

Miles and Tomas got to work, they took a spear each and began thrusting at the sharks. Every time they launched their spear, they pulled it back via the rope at its end. At first there were only a few sharks, but soon they were butting the boat from every angle.

"Oh no, oh no, oh no," they heard Terrance shout from inside. "There's a leak! And another! There's a baby shark in here!"

Jake continued to steer the ship; he refused to give in as the other two launched their spears at their relentless attackers.

"That's four for me," Miles said.

"Seven," Tomas replied.

"Seven? Already?" Miles lost his concentration as a shark dived the air, jaws open, ready to snack on his shoulder, but Tomas nailed it with a spear.

"Eight," he said as Miles scowled.

Jake continued to steer as best he could, but despite the favourable wind, the boat was slowing down. They were almost there, but the boat was being chewed to pieces, and then he noticed that that the deck seemed a lot closer to sea level.

Terrance screamed from within the cabin. "There's sharks down here! I can't do this; I can't do this," he yelled as he surfaced. "We're going down!" He sank down on the deck to cuddle himself.

"Tell me something I don't know," Jake replied, and then he saw that only the deck remained above sea level, and that the *Iron Lady* was sinking as they finally drew alongside the forty-foot wall of the tanker. Jake swung his grappling hook up and onto the tanker's side in haste, for in a minute the tanker would pass them by and then they would be shark bait. He pulled it taut to test its strength as his toes teased the cold water.

"What are you waiting for?" Tomas asked, and so Jake clambered up at speed using the knots in the rope.

"Get up," Tomas said to Terrance, splashing him with water. The poor fool was shaking, but after Tomas lifted him to his feet and handed him the rope he began to climb. Another shark attacked, launching itself into the air, but Tomas speared it before it took Miles down.

"Eleven," he said.

"And here's me thinking you could only count to ten," Miles replied with a smile. "Go on, Tom, get climbing."

Tomas didn't know what to say; but he admired Miles's courage with a firm nod.

"Hurry, and don't remember how I left you at the Shallows but remember this."

Tomas began to climb, then he paused and looked back. "Miles …"

"What?"

"You're not a baby anymore." When Tomas reached the top of the railing, Miles was almost up to his waist, and then he took the rope in his hands and began to climb. To his dismay, a shark dove at him, caught the rope in its mouth and snapped it clean in two. Miles fell back down onto the sunken deck, then he looked up and watched the tanker sailed on by. With no way to join the others, he jabbed the sharks to keep them at bay. "Godspeed lads!" he shouted.

"No!" Jake shouted as he tried to go back and help him, but Terrance pulled him back. "He's gone," he said.

Jake couldn't handle it, he had known Miles since he was a boy, and to see him disappear in such a way broke his heart. He needed space, and so he stumbled away from the others before falling to his knees.

Meanwhile, Terrance tried to summon some courage . He surveyed the tanker's deck, the place was dark but for the moon, and eerily quiet except for the mighty engine and the cut of the tanker against the ocean's sway. Then he heard the strangest thing: a hum, as if people were singing. He made his way onto the long platform, the cries were coming from below there. There was a crane that was used to haul supplies in and out of the storage space below, with a yellow control. He pressed the red button and then the deck opened up to reveal the last souls, huddled together down below.

"We've come to save you; now, hurry!" he shouted. The souls made their way up the staircase and out. There were so many of them, but he soon saw Rosita, the one who had betrayed Anya, and he watched Jake march toward her with a venomous look in his eyes.

"My sister, where's my sister!" he shouted.

"Jake, not now," Terrance pleaded, forcing himself between them.

Rosita fell to her knees in front of him. "I'm sorry, I let you down, I let you all down."

"We know it wasn't your doing, Rosita, it was Neptune's," Terrance insisted. "We don't have time to talk it out," he continued as he looked out to observe the Ark and the impending collision ahead.

Rosita tried to compose herself. "Sound the alarm and turn on the fog lights!" she shouted. The tanker let out its air siren and lit up the sea. Rosita, Terrance, and Jake turned to see the Ark fully illuminated: every man, woman, and child scattering before the impact.

Rosita froze for a moment as she felt the imminent weight of her consequences, but she had to do something. "Man the lifeboats!" she shouted as her people ran past, scattering and falling around her; but still she couldn't take her eyes off the raft.

"Rosita!" Jake shouted. "Look what you've done, you murderer." Jake said as he went at her again, but this time Tomas put himself between them.

Rosita couldn't move. "It's too late," she whispered as a tear rolled down her cheek, and then came the collision of two worlds. The Ark cried and the tanker roared as metal drove through wood. Everyone aboard the tanker was thrown from one side to the other, and Jake hit a metal rail before everything went black.

≈

When Jake opened his eyes, he felt a sharp shooting pain on the side of his head. He staggered to his feet and saw the last souls all around him, clambering to their feet and lowering their loved ones into lifeboats. He looked around to find Rosita, but amidst the chaos she was nowhere to be seen, and then he noticed that the tanker was sinking, too.

Jake sprang into action; he pushed through the crowds. "Rosita!" He shouted, "Rosita!" He saw Terrance limping to the ship's intercom, he picked up the mic and began to shout instructions. "Make for your rescue boats, turn on your lights and save every Arker you can. We're all that's left of this world, and any life lost is one too many!"

The words went over Jake's head as he looked over the side to see loose planks. Before he could say a word, he noticed the tanker shift onto its bow—it was going down. He jumped over supply crates, barrels, deckchairs and tables to reach anyone he knew. That was when he saw Doctor Phillips.

The doctor had lost his spectacles, and as he tried to find them Jake ran at him and gripped him by the collar. "Where's Rosita?" he asked.

Doctor Phillips clung on to him. "She said she would go down with the ship. She will be in the brig."

"Where's Wilson?"

"Wilson is in there, too."

"Can I get to him?"

"All the doors have been barred, bent or broken by that monster. We have to get on a lifeboat and get out of here, we have to go!"

Jake ignored his advice, for the old man meant more to him than anyone would ever know. He turned to see the flooding storeroom and dived into the darkness. By the time he knew where he was going, the tanker was almost fully submerged. The pressure grew with every second and all light disappeared. Soon, though, he reached the first set of doors, and he pulled at them with all his might.

Please, he begged, but they were shut tight. If he'd had an ounce of his sister's strength, he would have been there in a heartbeat, but he didn't. And he couldn't hold his breath any longer … Jake let go, he struggled for a moment, and then he found peace. He floated lifeless as Tomas grabbed him from behind, dragged him back down the corridors, out of the storeroom and then to the surface. The boat was fully submerged now, and Tomas pulled Jake up onto a piece of debris. He lay him down and pounded on his chest before Jake spluttered back to life.

Moments earlier, Wilson was still behind bars in the brig. He had been oblivious to Neptune's second visit and the tanker's destination as he wheezed with every breath due to the damage to his lung. But the world wasn't done with him yet, he knew that for sure.

Wilson was so tired that he had been half-dreaming. He was picturing warmth, green grass, and Clara— sweet Clara, who he hadn't seen in so many years. But then the two civilisations began to collide. The screeching roar of metal on wood awoke even Yan, and he shot forward from his chair. The tear in the ship was so close by that the water was already pouring in.

"Ahh! What's happening?" Yan asked as he began to cry.

"Get a hold of yourself. The tanker hit the Ark; this is it."

Yan jumped to his feet, withdrew his keys, and tried to free Wilson. The water was rising quickly; it was already above his ankles as he tried to open the cell door. When it was finally open, Yan gave a sigh of relief and approached Wilson to free him from the pipe, but he lost his balance and fell face first into the water.

Yan stumbled to his feet. "I'm okay, I'm okay," he said. "Oh no. The key! Where's the key?" he panted in frustration as he patted down all his pockets, and then he watched the keys drift through a grate in the floor. He got down on his hands and knees and tried to get his fingers through the holes. "I'm sorry, I'm so sorry," he whimpered.

"Yan," Wilson said, but the guard was in shock. "Yan," he said again. "Yan!"

Yan finally looked up at him. "I'm so sorry."

"Don't worry," Wilson replied with a smile. "It's not your fault; now, get yourself out of here whilst you still can. I've lived long enough, and I've kept someone waiting far too long."

"But Wilson."

"Just go!"

And so, Yan turned and trudged through the water. Wilson was alone, as alone as he had been in the

Ark's high crow's nest, but this time he had accepted his fate, he didn't need to punish himself any longer.

The water was cold on his feet, but he barely felt a thing. He wondered what to do with his final moments, and his only regret was what he hadn't said to Anya. He withdrew the pin from his sea hat, turned to the large white wall behind him, and began to etch a message on it as the water poured in all around him.

"Dear Anya ..."

28

WAR

The fate of the Ark was on Anya's mind as she made the long journey back towards the surface. She turned to see the trench one last time, and then she noticed that Enki was falling behind.

"You have to speed up," she said, but he was having a hard time dealing with the task ahead.

"We're going back too soon; we should have stayed in the trench."

"We don't have a choice."

"You need rest, you need your orca. If you face my brother like this, then …"

"Then what?"

"We fail."

"I'll stop him or die trying; I've no other choice, but you do. You can go back to your trench, you can hide for the rest of your life, or you can fight for Hali, and fight for your home. I'm not saying it's going to be easy; I'm not saying we will win; but will you ever be able to live with yourself if you go back?"

Enki looked towards the safety of the trench; he paused for a moment and then he turned back to Anya. "I've been running too long," he confessed, and so he swam to her. They made their way further up, but the water turned cold … Something wasn't right … "What was that?" Enki asked.

"I don't know," Anya replied. She picked up speed but then she stopped. Something or someone was coming and moving through the water at speed. From the darkness came the shapes of two sharks, and as they encircled them, Anya saw that it was Grey and Fin.

"No, no, no," Enki said, and then he remembered the day Neptune betrayed him, it all came flooding back. The confrontation with the humans; the fight with his brother; the relinquishing of his bond with Fin. The shark had been a dear friend, a fierce but loving creature, but now, as his bond soared toward him, all he felt was fear.

Enki and Anya were quick to dodge them, but then came Neptune with his trident, his eyes glowing red. "Enki, I should have known you would have something to do with this," he said.

"With what, brother?"

"You're helping her; you're turning them against me."

Enki swam towards him. "You've poisoned your own mind, no one else has done a thing. I see it now, I finally understand—your power is poison, and you're in great pain."

"You won't lay a single claw on me," Neptune said as he darted back with a vicious anger.

"You've done enough damage, brother, just let me help you."

"You would say *anything* to try and take my power."

At that moment Enki knew that he had one last trick. "Listen to me … *Ryan* … I need you to remember the days before the flood. Do you remember Miriam?"

For a moment, Neptune's eyes appeared more human, his scowl went away, but then he forced himself to look fearsome again. "Don't you dare say that name!" Neptune roared, and then he gave the signal for his sharks to advance.

Anya soared away at speed as Grey gave chase behind her. She dodged the shark at every turn, but it was closing in. When it caught up with her, she had no choice but to turn and wrestle with it. She fought with the beast head on as they smashed into the seabed, through coral and rocks. Anya caught the shark by the tail and threw it with all her might, to give herself a chance to recuperate.

Enki cut through the water, strafing left and right to escape Fin, his old bond, as its sharp teeth snapped close behind. Enki couldn't fight back, so he crashed through the window of an old rusted car and hid inside as the shark butted and dented the door.

"Can't you see, Fin, it's me?"

The shark stopped for a moment, its black eyes fixated on Enki, and then it advanced once more, chomping at the car's bonnet, battering the windshield and crumpling the front as Enki swam into the back.

Meanwhile, Anya had thrown Grey far enough away

for her to turn her attention to Neptune. "You," she said, "how could you do this, after everything?"

"I did only what I had to: humanity is a disease. And you—how can you judge me? You betrayed us all."

"I betrayed you? What happened to you, Neptune?"

"You humans, you stain the surface and cling to it like parasites. Your voices, your thoughts, they don't stop, they never stop. The surface should be silent as nature intended, and it will be silent again. The Ark and the tanker will pay the price and my sharks will finish what you started."

At that moment, Grey and Fin flew at Anya from either side; she shot out of the way and the two of them collided with each other. They gave chase and she evaded them whilst trying to fight back.

"Give in and I'll spare your Arkers the pain of my sharks … I'll let them drown and freeze instead," Neptune said.

"Never," Anya replied as she punched Grey on the nose. "As long as I'm breathing, I'll keep fighting; I'll never stop."

"Then you will die."

"It'll take more than a weak little man to kill me." Then Anya punched Grey once more, "I don't want to hurt these creatures, so let them go before I do," and with her words her eyes began to glow blue.

"A cute trick, but it won't save you. I'm only just getting started," Neptune replied. He raised his hands in the air as his eyes began to glow a darker shade. His arms began to tremble for the might of his power, and then came a ripple in the water.

"You're hurting yourself, brother," Enki warned him; but Neptune didn't listen, he only continued to shake, and then came a wall of sharks, a grey and blue barricade of creatures of all different sizes from behind him.

"Think about what you're doing, it's not too late," Enki continued.

"Oh, it's too late. Your healer, your orca, the Ark, and your tanker: they've all perished, and soon there will only be the dwellers, all under my control. Prepare for the end!"

Anya stared up at the endless wall of sharks, and then they flew toward her, a thousand razor-sharp teeth. She darted from side to side as they rained down like arrows; it was chaos, and all she could see was darkness as they came at her from every direction. But they came without coordination and accuracy, and she could evade them as they hit each other and got in each other's way. All she had to do was dodge, keep moving and their uncoordinated assault would have to end at some point.

The fight went on as Anya punched the odd shark here and there, but she saw more benefit in making them hit each other. Every so often she caught a glimpse of Enki amidst the whirl of creatures; he was doing the same, and then he caught her arm.

"We need to try something different," he said. "Here, come with me."

The pair broke free of the sharks and darted down toward the nearest trench. They flew close to the rocky seabed as all the sharks piled in close behind.

"Is this your idea?" Anya asked.

"I hadn't thought any further ahead."

"Well, I've got a better one: get behind me." Anya halted, and then she began to spin; round and round she went, building up speed as Pearl had taught her. She became a blur, and when each shark came at her she knocked it away. They kept coming, but Anya kept spinning.

Eventually Neptune brought them back into formation. He took large deep breaths as if he were tired, and it became clear to Anya that by forcing his powers to the very brink, they were breaking his mind and body.

"You're killing yourself, brother," Enki said.

"You wouldn't understand; you're weak, you always have …"

Neptune paused for a moment; he could hear something soaring through the ocean, he looked to the left and there was Oracle, and behind her were many more, at least fifty full grown killer whales, ready to strike. Oracle came to Anya's side, and the whole group fell into line behind Anya and Enki, ready for command.

Neptune laughed. "Is this all you've got?" He asked, "you have only half my numbers."

"And you have half my wits," Anya replied as her eyes continued to glow blue. Then she clambered aboard Oracle and they charged. The black and white beasts tackled the sharks head on. With their superior intelligence, strength, and accuracy they butted the sharks, bit their tails and threw them into each other. In return, the sharks used their vicious teeth to do damage where they could, but the orcas worked together and held a tight formation. They watched each other's backs and helped all those who were overwhelmed. Damage was done on both sides as they went head-to-head.

"Look around you, you're outnumbered, you can't win," Neptune said. "Surrender and I'll spare them."

Anya knew it was true, but she couldn't do it, she would never surrender. She dug deep, summoned all her courage, and readied herself to go down fighting. But then another rumble came from the deep, and Anya saw that dolphins were swimming towards them.

"Kai!" she shouted, and to her disbelief, there he was, bounding into battle as Neptune brought his sharks back into formation one more time.

"*Kai*—I wondered when you would show," Neptune said.

"Are you okay?" Anya asked, and she was right to ask, for he looked troubled and unsure of his intentions.

"Anya, I—"

"Come, Kai, we don't have time for this, join me, this is what we trained for," Neptune said as he held out his hand. His eyes turned a little redder and Kai shook his head as he tried to resist.

"No," he replied. "You don't have control of me anymore."

He and Polka swam around to Anya and Oracle's side as the dolphins moved between the orcas to even the odds.

"You'll pay for this."

"You're the one who's going to pay. You'll pay for what you did to Hali. You're a coward and a bully!"

"You've picked a losing side: the Ark, the tanker—they'll all be gone soon."

"The Ark will live as long as I do," Anya said, her eyes still glowing blue.

"Then you must die with it," Neptune replied as the sea roared and the wall of sharks clashed with dolphins and killer whales once more.

Enki looked on from the seabed in disbelief. Never in a million years had he thought it possible to tame killer whales. Hundreds of sharks, whales, and dolphins collided with each other, and many were lost on both sides, as Enki swam into the chaos. He watched Anya and Neptune go claw to claw, slashing and swiping at each other whilst riding on the back of their bonds.

"It doesn't matter what you do, or how hard you fight," Neptune said. "Every human will drown before the day is done. The tanker will hit the Ark, and there's nothing you can do to stop it."

"Look around you," Anya said as she pointed to the sharks, some of which were starting to swim away due to the strain of Neptune's bond. "You're losing, your grip on them is weakening; surrender."

Neptune lowered his brow and gritted his teeth. "Never," he said. He charged at Anya once more as Oracle and Grey fought head-to-head. Neptune tried to strike Anya with his trident, but she launched herself from Oracle's back and tackled him head on. They punched and kicked each other, throwing each other into the path of sharks and whales. Their claws interlocked as they wrestled back and forth, and at that moment, Anya felt that Neptune's grip was weakening, and that he ne was losing his strength.

The fight was dying down, Neptune was losing, and

the two leaders separated again. "Wait, Anya," he said, and his eyes appeared as they had when he had saved her from the poison, back when they had first met. In Anya's moment of weakness, one of the hammerheads flew right at her, but at the last second, she managed to dodge.

"Almost," Anya replied as Oracle drove into Neptune's side, causing him to fly towards her, and then she punched him in the gut.

"I'll never surrender," he said as he felt the pain in his stomach; then he raised his hands in the air again to muster his fleeing sharks.

"Brother," Enki said as he approached. "It's over, there's no need for more bloodshed. I forgive you; let us fix this, let us help you."

"You don't understand—you will never understand. Humanity is done, we're the next stage of human evolution, we are kings, but you—you had to bring that filth back into our lives. You had to learn from them, to try and live with them! Why can't they be quiet? They need to be quiet," he declared, his eyes a fire-fuelled red.

In return, Enki's eyes began to glow blue. "I never lost my bond, brother; I was just afraid. The sharks were never mine, or yours: they're the ocean's. Look around you, you've lost," he said.

Neptune came closer. He looked around to see that most of the sharks had broken free from his grasp and fled despite the rage he'd used to tame them. He was exhausted, his hatred had taken everything, and so he extended a hand to his brother, a hand of peace.

"Forgive me George," Neptune said as his power appeared to dwindle, his anger too. "I need help."

Enki watched his brother struggle, he remembered a time when Neptune had offered him his hand once before, when the world was flooding, and all appeared to be lost. "I love you, brother," he said. "Never forget that."

He went to take Neptune's hand, but little did he know that Fin was charging at him from behind, and that his compassion was being used as a weakness one last time. Just before the hammerheads jaws snapped shut, Enki flew to the side and in his place, the shark found Neptune.

The war was over. Enki made the sharks disperse, and then he swam to his brother's body to see that his eyes went from red, to yellow, and then back to brown. Neptune's body was human again, and George could hold his brother one last time.

"It's over now: you don't have to be in any pain anymore, you can finally rest," Enki said as he tried to hold back his tears. He made his way down to the seabed to bury him as neither Anya or Kai said a word.

Anya knew there was no victory today, and when Kai finally did approach her, she didn't know what to say until he gave her a hug.

"Im sorry, Kai, I—"

"I know."

"I didn't mean to leave—"

"I know."

"I missed you so much, you and Pearl and Hali and—"

"I know!"

As they embraced, Anya felt warm and happy as all her anxiety melted away. Her friend had come to save her after all, and she was eternally grateful. "I thought you hated me," Anya said.

"Nonsense! How could we ever do a thing like that?"

"I don't know. I had so many dark thoughts ... but with Neptune gone, it's as if a cloud has been lifted."

"I feel the same way," Kai admitted.

"God, I've missed you so much! What have you been eating anyway? How did you get so tall?" Anya asked.

"Oh, lots of fish ... and i've been lifting rocks ... You know, making sweet gains, nothing too hardcore."

"How's Pearl?"

"She misses you."

"I miss her."

At that moment, the ocean shook. The strangest roar echoed through the water and the two young fins knew that their celebration had been cut short.

"Did you hear that?" Kai asked; and then came the screams.

"We have to go," Anya replied, and then she rushed down to the seabed to speak with Enki. "We have to go!"

"I don't know if I can," he replied, unable to let go of his brother. "I can't leave his body here, I need time, time to process things."

Anya nodded. "Very well, I'm sorry it had to end this way. You did a brave thing today."

"Nothing as brave as you," Enki replied. "Now go."

Anya nodded, she thrusted herself away and clung to Oracle as Kai took hold of Polka and they raced toward the Ark. Anya couldn't help but think of Neptune's threats, his masterplan to destroy the tanker and the Ark. She didn't think it was possible, but the closer they came, the louder were the screams, and then she saw the tanker.

29

TITANIC

Moments before the tanker and the Ark collided, Isaac had been standing upon the Ark's grand stage. He could feel the tanker's hum and smell the fumes. *Come on, Jake, come on, Terrance, you can do it*, he thought. As he stared at the tanker's looming shadow, he began to realise that the Ark could be torn from him any minute. His salvation, his brother's creation, which had survived thirty years now lay in the darkness of a large metal shadow. The tanker was coming, and when Isaac finally realised there was nothing that could be done to stop it, he froze.

"Isaac what will we do?" Elder Frederick asked.

At that moment the tanker's alarms sounded, and the floodlights beamed down on them. When Isaac looked up, he saw the wall of steel and knew that collision was imminent. All he could do was shout: "Brace!"

The tanker crashed into the Ark, and the metal hull splintered the decaying wood into a million pieces. Isaac could only watch as the platform rose up and split apart. Next came a wave caused by the impact, which smashed through the structure and shook everyone aboard. The supports buckled as ropes snapped and a crow's nest came down, thundering through the Ark. Isaac watched the giant pillar split his home in two. Every nearby building shattered into pieces, and the ground beneath him split to reveal the cold dark abyss below.

The roar of the tanker, the screams, and shouts overwhelmed his thoughts as he turned to see Elder Frederick falling into the deep. Isaac only just caught him at the last moment.

"Elder, are you alright?"

"I'm fine, don't worry about me, help the others."

Isaac jumped from one fallen structure to another, riding the waves between splintered wood. "I should have raised the alarm," he said, cursing himself as he made his way across what was left of the grand stage. To his dismay, he watched split apart before his very eyes and take the floor beneath him; then he fell into darkness, the water pulled him under, and the stage was slammed back together to seal his exit shut.

Beneath the Ark it was quiet, Isaac fought to survive. Atleast he was free of the cries, the screams, and the tanker's roar as he swam for his life. Then the other mighty crow's nest came down right next to him. Isaac kept swimming through the icy waters, he was desperate to find an opening, and then he saw little legs kicking, fighting to stay afloat. Isaac came up alongside them; he forced the child out of the water and onto a piece of timber before pulling himself up.

He looked to see who it was amidst the chaos and destruction. It was a five-year-old child named Lil. She wasn't crying, for she was more confused than upset. "It's going to be okay," he said, and the words were meant as much for himself as for the child. He pulled the little girl up onto his shoulders and stumbled forward, jumping from log to plank, from broken shack to support.

The adrenaline wore off and he felt tired, so very tired. His knees were sore, his arm was split open, but he had to make it to her. "Lyn! Lyn!" he cried with Lil on his back as the child half covered his eyes and watched the ship sail away.

"The ship is sinking, the ship is sinking," Lil said.

"I know little one, don't look at it, look at my hair instead. Lyn!" Isaac shouted again, looking in every direction for his shack; but it wasn't there … and then he saw Lyn's wooden sculptures floating by.

Isaac thought the worst, he could barely breathe, and though he wished he could close his eyes and forget the past thirty years as if they were a bad dream, he could not. The child on his back kept him standing, and if it wasn't for Lil, he would have given up.

At that moment he saw the foundation of a shack floating by, it had formed a frail raft. He saw the blue barrels bobbing underneath the structure, and he remembered them from the day he had built his shack. To his relief, he saw Lyn lying in the middle of the debris, and so he made his way to her side.

"Lyn, are you okay?"

She lay perfectly still for a moment before raising

her head. "Isaac," she whispered. "I'm fine. What happened?"

"Hello," Lil said.

"Oh, hello, Lil!"

"Have you seen my mummy and daddy?"

Isaac and Lyn exchanged a look, he took her her from his shoulders and placed her down next to Lyn, and then Lyn placed an arm around her. "I'm sure they're nearby. Now you're going to wait here with me until we find them, okay sweetie?"

"Okays."

Lyn turned to Isaac. "Go and help the others. We'll be fine," she reassured him.

Having regained his courage, Isaac observed the chaos to see what was left around him. The Ark was gone; all that was left was driftwood. He saw his fellow Arkers clinging to debris and fallen structures, desperate to hang on to any thing they could.

Isaac dreaded to think of how many lives had been lost, and he turned to the tanker with anger; but when he looked properly, all his anger washed away, for it was sinking too, and he knew that humanity would be gone by the morning.

Then a number of bright lights shone from near the tanker, and it took him a moment to realise that they came from lifeboats. The last souls were shining their torches, and they were coming.

So you've come to pillage my home? Over my dead body. Isaac spotted a spear floating by, so he picked it up and made his way to the nearest lifeboat; then he jumped aboard. The last souls cowered, for he was ready to strike and to take out all his anger on Rosita.

"You will pay for what you've done, you will all pay!" he shouted.

"Uncle?" asked a familiar voice, and then Isaac saw that it was Jake. Isaac lowered his spear as Jake came forward, and then he saw the fear of the last souls reflecting in the searchlights. They looked the same as any Arker when suffering and afraid.

They pair embraced: "Jake, is that really you?"

"It's me, uncle."

"What are you doing on here?"

"We tried to stop the collision—they wanted to stop it too—but Neptune locked them in the ship. He set the course and there was no way for anyone to stop it. They had no choice, and they tried to do everything possible to stop him."

"Where's Rosita?"

"Rosita went down with her ship."

"Was there any sign of Anya?"

Jake shook his head and they embraced once more. Isaac looked around to see those on lifeboats throwing life jackets to any Arker who needed one, and inflating emergency rafts. Isaac watched them form a perimeter around the shattered Ark as they encircled the survivors and searched for all who had gone astray. But still it was still too late, and Isaac saw through their actions and beheld the truth: that despite their generosity, despite any gesture in good faith, the damage had been done.

30

SACRIFICE

Anya raced toward the Ark. Neptune's threats were only words until she saw his actions for herself. Nothing prepared her for the sight of the huge tanker resting on the seabed; it had lost all its colour and life. It was silent where it had once roared its mighty engine. When she looked up, she could see wood and debris floating upon the surface, and then she saw the legs of those kicking and scrambling for survival.

She felt helpless as she made a fist and tried to contain her anger, for after everything she had been through, Neptune had won. She couldn't move—the sight of her nightmare kept her frozen still—and only when Kai put a hand on her shoulder could she move again.

"It's okay, Anya, it's going to be okay, we can fix this —just tell us how."

"I need to help them; I must go to the surface," Anya said. She heard her own words, but it didn't feel like she had said them. She felt numb as if nothing was real.

"We can't go with you," Kai told her.

"I know."

"If there's anything I can do, let me know."

Anya nodded, then she made her way up on Oracle's back, and breached the surface. Sitting upon the killer whale, she morphed her head from scales to skin. Ahead of her was carnage: death and destruction. The whole Ark, her entire home, was gone, and though the sea was calm, the rain pelted down as the moon and the fog lights of lifeboats lit the night sky.

If Anya hadn't been on Oracle's back, she would have sunk back beneath the waves for the sight of the Ark's wreckage. Humanity had lost, and now there was no one to hold responsible. *Maybe we can rebuild*, she thought for a moment—but how could they ever rebuild after this? Without shelter, the weak would not survive the night. Neptune had got what he wanted, and Anya had lost her will to fight. She saw the lifeboats of the lost souls, those privileged few who had done Neptune's bidding, and then she heard a familiar voice.

"Anya!"

To her surprise, it was Terrance. Oracle swam towards him and found him on a lifeboat where all the sheepish faces of the last souls also awaited Anya. She wanted to shout, to curse at them, but then to her surprise, she saw that some Arkers were also aboard, wrapped in warm blankets.

"What are you doing on a lifeboat?" she asked.

"We're forming a perimeter and saving everyone we can."

"But *they* did this."

"No, Nameless, or should I say Neptune, did this. Rosita tried to fight him; they all did; we can't blame them."

"Where's Rosita?"

"She … she went down with the ship … I'm so glad you're alive. Is Neptune?"

"Neptune's gone, but he got what he wanted."

"Not quite: we're still here, and we're fighting. We'll keep fighting, all of us, but together this time."

Anya didn't know what to say. She felt lost as she looked around at all that her parents had built. Everything she had been fighting for had been destroyed, and though she considered that she may have beaten Neptune, she knew it was a Pyrrhic victory.

"Where's my family?"

"Follow me," Terrance said, and then he jumped from the lifeboat and landed on the back of a giant leather back sea turtle, which pushed the debris aside.

Everywhere Anya looked she saw Arkers clinging to makeshift floats and shivering despite their sea leathers —but at least they were alive.

"Terrance, you're smart. How do we fix this?" Anya asked, without a hope in the world.

"I-I don't know."

When Anya saw Jake's long blond surfer hair, she was relieved. "They're alive," she said to herself whilst trying to stay composed, and with one leap she went from Oracle's back to their raft.

"Anya," Jake said in disbelief.

"I can't believe it," Uncle Isaac said, and the three of them embraced. "If I had known this would happen …"

"How could we have known Uncle? And what does it matter, all that matters is that we're alive. Where's Aunty?"

"I'm here," Aunt Lyn replied, and so Anya climbed over the debris before she found Aunt Lyn sitting with her arm around Lil. To her surprise, the child was sleeping despite the chaos around her, and that made Anya smile.

"Aunty," Anya whispered and she took to Aunt Lyn's free side to embrace her and kiss her on the cheek. "I missed you so much."

"I missed you too."

"You're freezing. We need to get you somewhere warm and dry."

"Don't you start worrying about me Anya, I'll dry off. How are you?"

"I'm … I'm alive."

"Well, being alive isn't good enough. I mean't to hear how you're feeling?"

Anya thought about that for a moment. Everything dark memory flashed through her mind as she tried to keep herself from breaking down in-front of her aunt. It all seemed so surreal, she couldn't say a word, and so Aunt Lyn pulled her closer, and then Anya began to cry.

"Shh, shh it's okay. I'm here."

"I was so afraid."

"I know, it's okay. Everything's going to be okay."

Anya remained with her aunt for a while as she let everything out, but while those around her needed her help, she felt increasingly guilty.

"What happened to Lil's mother and father?"

"We don't know."

Anya nodded, there was only so long she could stay sat down, and so she staggered to her feet.

"Where are you going?" Aunt Lyn asked.

"There are people who need me. I'll be back soon." Anya wiped away her tears and smiled at her aunt, before putting on a brave face and returning to her brother and uncle. "How shall we fix this?" she asked them.

Uncle Isaac took a moment to think. "I don't know. With every passing moment, the sea takes more of the little we have left. We have no home, and neither do the last souls."

"What if we can rebuild?" Anya asked.

Uncle Isaac seemed surprised. "With the last souls there are twice as many mouths to feed. Do they even deserve a home?"

"Nameless locked everyone in the tanker's storage," Jake assured them. "They couldn't stop the ship, but none of them wanted this. I saw it for myself, with Tomas and Miles."

"Where is Tomas?" Anya asked.

"He's here somewhere."

"What about Miles?"

Jake's sighed and he was unable to look her in the eye. "He gave his life so we could board the tanker," he said with a tear in his eye.

"My turtles haven't found him," Terrance added.

"And Wilson? What about Wilson?"

"I-I tried to save him," Jake said as he made a tight fist but held back his emotions. "I tried to get through the doors, but I wasn't strong enough ..."

"Where is he?"

"He was on the ship, in the brig."

Without saying another word, Anya ran to the end of the raft and dived into the sea.

"Anya, wait!" Terrance shouted, but it was too late. She swam down into the depths, past sinking debris, all the way to the tanker, which lay upon the ocean floor. She forced her way in, tearing through doors and swimming down dark, crooked staircases and corridors.

"Wilson!" she shouted. "Come on, Wilson, come on." Anya hoped that he had escaped and made it to the surface, or that there was an air pocket of some kind.

When she reached the brig the doors were open and that gave Anya hope. "He escaped, he must have escaped, she assured herself."

Anya checked each cell and found one peculiar room which was more a bedroom than a prison. It was filled with furniture, and above the bed, she saw the bodies of two women floating, and then she noticed that it was Rosita and someone else. The other woman was blonde and beautiful, and they both looked so happy with one another.

Anya felt no anger as she realised that they had gone together. "Sleep well," she said. "Sleep well."

Anya checked a few more cells and then, to her dismay, she found him dressed in bright orange overalls, his skin as white as snow. "No," she whimpered, "no." Her heart broke when she entered and saw him cuffed to the pipe. She dived forward and snapped the cuffs as if they were nothing. She made herself glow bright blue again and again with all her strength to heal him, but it did nothing. "If I'd have been here, freeing you would've been easy." She cradled him in her arms, and then she looked past him and saw his message etched upon the wall:

Dear Anya,

I knew you would read this; I knew you would come for me, and I knew you would beat him. I'm sorry I didn't make it—but it's my own fault. Don't you dare blame yourself. If I hadn't been so stubborn, I wouldn't be down here in the first place.

I was only hard on you because I cared. The truth is that you saved my life. You gave me something to look forward to each and every day. You gave me hope and made me believe that not everything was just rain and water.

For a long time, I was lost, I was afraid. I wanted to be alone, and you changed that, you changed me. My name, my full name, was Graham Henry Wilson. In my younger days I served in the navy, I had a beautiful wife, Clara, and a dog called Winnie. Don't be sad, I can be with them now, I can rest.

Promise me you won't blame yourself; it was my time. It was my time long ago.

Chin up, kid.

Wilson

Anya swam with the old man in her arms, but it didn't feel like she was swimming at all; she was sinking, and up above her, the last people on earth would soon follow. She felt such sadness, such crippling guilt, for Neptune had won.

When Anya escaped the tanker, she journeyed down to the seabed to lay Wilson down in the sand, and there she began to dig. She dug a hole and decorated it with shells and stones, paying no heed to time or to anything else as she mourned and remembered the man who had taught her how to lead.

Her relationship with him was very different to those with her aunt and uncle. Wilson wasn't afraid to speak his mind, to say things how they were, and to push Anya beyond her capabilities. Anya thought back to every one of his harsh lessons, and she thought about everyone she had failed. This time she understood them in a different way, and she understood Wilson in a different way too. It was all part of a bigger test.

"You were the only one who wanted to teach me how the world really was, and I didn't listen. All you ever did was try to protect me. You were a grumpy old fool, and you couldn't help but push them too far, could you? I'll miss you; I miss you so much."

Anya was at her lowest and it appeared that nothing on earth could make her whole again as she stared at his grave. She closed her eyes and stayed by his side. She needed the quiet, she needed to be alone.

∼

A few hours passed before a shadow disrupted Anya's sanctity. All she wanted was to be alone, and she was about to tell the stranger to leave her, but then she saw an old friend: it was Pearl. Her eyes were a silvery white and she appeared to be glowing in the moonlight as she came forward to embrace Anya. When Anya felt her warmth, she couldn't let go.

"It's alright, it's alright," Pearl said. "I'm here."

"I've—I've missed you so much."

"I've missed you, too."

"Pearl ..."

"It's okay," she said as Anya nuzzled up against her.

"I'm sorry I left you, I'm so sorry."

"It's okay, I'm here. Nothing matters as long as I'm here."

The two were given some space until the time was right for the other water dwellers to approach. Russell, Dorian, Bow and River, Cliff and Crash. They were all there, all around her, with stingrays, octopi, walruses, and every other bond within their kingdom.

"Anya," Russell said. "He held a spell over each and every one of us, if only we had known ... if there's anything we can do to repay you, to help those above ..."

"It's alright, it isn't your fault. Where's Hali?" Anya asked, but she was met with sad expressions rather than promising words.

The water dwellers parted, and Anya saw Marina carrying Hali in her arms. She was weak, her skin was grey, and her veins could be seen through her scales. She trembled as if she were cold, and Anya knew that this was the latest stage of the kraken's venom.

"There you are," Hali whispered.

"Hali, what happened?" Anya asked.

"She cannot talk. Neptune poisoned her," Marina said.

Anya made her eyes and her hands glow blue. She tried with all her might, tried and tried again, but the glow did nothing to heal the healer.

"Come on, come on," Anya said, desperate to make it work, but it was to no avail.

"Don't fret, Anya, this is the end for me."

There was nothing Anya could do, she wished there was, but like the Ark, there was nothing. She was powerless, and Neptune had won. He had taken everything from her, her home, and her mentors. But just when everything seemed final, Enki swam down from above them. "Hali, my love," he said.

"Enki? Is that you?"

"It is," he said with a smile, and then he took her in his arms. Enki's hands and eyes began to glow, and then so did the rest of him. Slowly the heat was transferred to Hali, her veins were no longer visible, and her dark purple scales turned back to a healthy shade of green as the pair held each other. They both began to glimmer and shine, before bursting with neon brightness. Time ceased around them, they gazed into each other's eyes and then they kissed.

"It's over now," Enki said.

"I knew you were innocent; I always knew," Hali replied.

"I love you."

"And I love you too, with all my heart."

The pair held each other, as they were lost in each other's eyes. When Enki finally looked up, he saw his tribe all around him; they were surrounding the couple, and each placed a reassuring hand upon his shoulders.

"Enki, we were wrong," Dorian admitted.

"Will you forgive us?" Russell asked.

Enki was about to say yes, but then he heard a commotion upon the surface. Up above them, the last souls and the Arkers were struggling to survive.

"There will be time for forgiveness later. The humans need our help," he said, and he turned to see that all of his brethren were awaiting his next move.

"What shall we do?" Dorian asked.

"Why the hell are you looking at me? I'm not the one who gave me courage, who rides an orca and never gives in despite facing almost impossible odds." The crowd parted, and everyone turned to her. "Anya, what say you?"

In truth Anya didn't know what to say. She had been betrayed, forced to the bottom of the ocean, broken and burnt. Having faced insurmountable odds, she had won the war, but she had also lost her home, and a dear friend. She wondered what Wilson would do and took a deep breath.

"My people have lost everything," she said. "My people were pitted against each other by someone who saw them as nothing. He toyed with them, bullied them, and forced even those with good hearts to do the unthinkable. Now we've lost our home, and we cling to the surface, terrified of what's below. Today, everything changes, today we forge a new world, a world without fear; we must do better this time, we must rebuild. I ask you, all of you, to recognise that this unthinkable act and the cries you hear above you were caused by one of yours, your neighbour and your friend. I'm not saying you were responsible, but you can help fix this. I ask you to help any of my people who are drifting away, and bring them back. Guide all those who survived to the oil rig, and we will build a new home for my people. We will salvage the tanker and the Ark to build a home safe for children, one with electricity and warmth."

The dwellers bowed their heads in silence at the thought of what had occurred. "We are in your debt, Anya," said Russell.

"As am I," Enki concurred.

"And I," said many more.

The dwellers rallied to her cause and began the search for survivors. Within a few hours, every survivor was located and placed in a lifeboat or a kayak, and before nightfall the dwellers guided them to the oil rig. The work of the dwellers didn't stop there, though: they foraged day after day harvesting metal from the tanker's wreckage and retrieved the generators and any other equipment that was still fit to use. Together, the communities worked to build a new home. The rig expanded; it became a huge contraption of metal and wood that spiralled up into the sky. Its name was a testament to courage and an acknowledgement of what was lost but could never be lost again. They named their new home: Wilson's Peak.

EPILOGUE

Three years later … a new council had formed on the oil rig, but not one without its own conflict. The last souls and the Arkers had worked hard to coexist. The council was led by Isaac, Terrance, Doctor Phillips, Helga the tanker's chief engineer, and a few others. Anya was welcome, of course, but she found herself more at peace by taking a step back.

Below the surface, the dwellers thrived under the leadership of Hali and Enki. They had worked hard to help the humans and would often give them an abundance of fish in tribute. Anya frequented both worlds and she was spending most of her time assisting the water dweller's new scouting parties. The plan, aided by Terrance's turtles, was to map the sunken world in the hope of finding other civilisations.

It had been three years since the tanker and the Ark had collided, and three years since Wilson's death. The dwellers had planned a feast, and the humans would feast too, as neither community would ever allow themselves to forget that day. Even such a day of remembrance, however, would not change the minds of some, as there were those who had lost loved ones, those who had lost everything, and still felt hatred for their underwater brethren, and so they refused to feast.

As Anya soared through the water upon Oracle's back, she turned to Kai and Pearl. "We're late, it's almost past sundown," she said.

The trio soared down toward the town hall, which was becoming packed as everyone swam in to take their seats. Anya couldn't help but smile; she was almost twenty-one now, and the thought that not a single human went hungry or without a warm place to sleep kept her mind at peace.

She swam down to sit next to Enki and Hali. "Shall we begin?" she asked.

Upon these words, Enki swam to the middle of the room to face them all. "Friends and fish, brothers and sisters. It's been three long years since the crash. We will never forget the collision of worlds or the acts of my brother. We must always learn from them for history often repeats itself if we do not. We are human, deep down, and those on the surface still need our help each and every day. We must never forget."

"We must never forget," the room echoed.

"We have worked hard to build a new world, to learn from one another, and love one another. Though we have come far, we must never forget the events which led to our union."

"We must never forget."

"It's important for us to remember him, too:

Neptune, or Ryan as he was to me. We understand now, better than ever, what the strength of our bonds can do to us; that we must be careful and respect our unique gifts. For if we forget our history, it may repeat itself."

"We will never forget."

"Unlike our surface brothers, we may not have tables, or a forever flame … But we know how to eat. It's time to feast!"

Thousands of fish flew in through the roof as everyone chased their feed. Anya watched as everyone enjoyed the delicious banquet. She would never tire of watching everyone themselves with the knowledge that those above were safe and being fed too.

When the last fish was consumed, the dancing began. The heavenly choir of the water dwellers. After dancing with Pearl, Anya faded into the background to watch and to enjoy the view.

Tonight, was a strange night, and she felt a strange feeling on her leg, which reminded her of the kraken's poison. She often thought back to that day and remembered the way Neptune carried her, took care of her, took her to Hali, and their conversation at the swings when he spoke of his daughter.

Anya needed some space; she left through a side door and swam away from the town hall and out into the wastelands where there was nothing but half-buried buildings and old lamp posts. There she found the beautiful coral garden, and in its centre she found the memorial to all those who had been lost in the great crash.

There she read the wall of forty names, she felt

saddened but seeing them reminded her what she had been fighting for. She swam a little further, and then she found the name she was looking for. The stone read 'Graham Henry Wilson,' and she put a claw upon it and closed her eyes. She could almost feel his spirit when her hand began to glow.

"I wish you could see the world that I built for you old friend, but I'm sure that if you did, you would probably moan about it." Anya laughed as she held back tears. "No matter how beautiful it is, I know you're somewhere better—you have to be."

Anya smiled, and when she let go, she saw that a turtle was watching her, and the little creature signalled her to look up. Up above Anya saw a giant sea turtle on the surface. She made her way up there, and at the top she saw Terrance lying on the sea turtle's back whilst eating a piece of smoked fish. "Anya, there you are! There's something I need to talk to you about."

"Yeah, boundaries. We need to talk about boundaries. Everywhere I go there's a turtle."

"You don't understand, it's really important."

"No Terrance, *you* don't understand."

"It's my turtles: they say they've found something— something you need to see."

"Well spit it out then."

"You're not going to believe this."

"Just say it!"

"East, due East, through the mist, there are mountains. There is land!"

AFTERWORD

*Thank you for reading The Last Souls. If you enjoyed this book, then **please make sure you leave a review**! And why not check out my other series, **Titans, Cranes & Monsters' Games**.*

The story will continue in:

Anya of Ark & The Throne of Paradise

For news on the books release, be sure to sign up to my mailing list at www.kristianjoseph.co.uk, or find my Facebook group Kristian Joseph's Author Page.

Kristian Joseph

MORE BY THE AUTHOR

Titans, Cranes & Monsters Games

Part I : Sunlight

In a dark and dystopian world, the city of Sovereign is on the brink of collapse; political turmoil, protests and civil war loom as the city falls victim to a sinister plot.

Part II : The Kingdom

The Journey continues the fast-paced action adventure right where it left off. We rejoin our heroes as they deal with the consequences of their actions; some will learn, and all will lose.

Printed in Great Britain
by Amazon